magel

3/6/2017 Nooshie . . . meeting (a.)

Tapestries of the Heart

Four Women, Four Persian Generations

Nooshie Motaref

Clink
Street

London | New York

Published by Clink Street Publishing 2015

Copyright © Nooshie Motaref 2015

ISBN: 978-1-909477-57-5
Ebook: 978-1-909477-58-2

Table of Contents

Prologue

It is said that a group of Caucasians divided into two factions. One went to Europe and established today's Germany; the other group went to Asia, and settled in a land, calling it Iran, after their race, Aryan. However, when Herodotus, the Greek historian, introduced this part of the world to the West, he called it Persia and its people Persians. During the ancient time, Iranians followed Zoroaster, the prophet of Zoroastrianism. Their beliefs consisted of the two forces, divine or Ahuramazda, and evil or Ahriman. This nation was home to the oldest inhabitants who believed in one God.

Throughout the centuries, this kingdom conquered the greater part of Asia, and it was occupied by the Greeks, Arabs and Mongols.

When Iran was attacked by the Arab nomads, each attacker carried a sword in one hand and the Koran in the other. The people resisted as long as they could until they collapsed. In the end, they fell into the enemies' hands. The country was robbed of her past glory, and their religion changed from Zoroastrianism to Islam (651AD).

Centuries later, the defiant Iranians revolted against their conquerors, and claimed their independence by preserving their kingdom and accepting Mohammad as the Messenger of God. However, they followed Ali, Mohammad's son-in-law, rather than abiding to caliphs in Saudi Arabia. They established Shiism and separated their government from their religion.

When the last dynasty, Pahlavi, was replaced the Qajar Dynasty, the shah and his father Reza Pahlavi trumpeted the modernization era regardless of the Moslim instructions. In addition, these two kings failed to educate the people's minds. Each ruled with an iron fist.

Therefore, at a strategic point, the religious leaders who were pushed down or were sent to exile, such as Ruhollah Khomeini, rebelled against the government, and the shah in particular. As a result, after more than twenty-five centuries, the Islamic Republic of Iran appeared.

❏ ❏ ❏

This tapestry depicts the lives of four generations— Mitra; her mother, Iran; her grandmother, Shirin; her great-grandmother, Zahra. Each chapter illustrates how they were pulled between their religion, Islam, and the modernization dictated to them by their kings. This book is a representation of the cycle of life. The existence of these characters is interwoven with threads very different from those of kings and queens. They were fashioned into Mohammedans by a decision made for them before their grandparents were even conceived. They were told that Allah carved their destiny on their foreheads when He planted them in the middle of the stratum.

The novel blends fiction with historical events, from the assassination of the king Naser Al-Din Shah to the change of the dynasty, Qajar to Pahlavi. This is a largely true dramatization of these commoners' psychological battles that they could never win. Throughout the years, these women lived, loved, fought, and endured.

Author's note: There is a glossary at the end of the book; even though most of the idioms used are defined throughout the text.

1. Iran's Death

Adelanto, California, 1996
Mitra (age 30)

My sister, Layla, and I wiped the tears from our eyes. Before us, our mother Iran's withered body stretched on the steel table of the death room in the sheik's house. Her eyes were half open, as if she were refusing to let the world go. But she was gone. Our *Shahan Shah*—king of kings—the shah, was also dead. Our green, white, and red flag, depicting a lion holding a sword, protecting the crown, was gone. We would see the sun emerging from the fierce lion shining on us no more. Instead, they etched an absurd figure on our flag. My father's soft voice broke into my overwhelming thoughts, and the memory of his eyes behind his bifocal glasses flashed before me: "Mitra, do not think of death. Instead, concentrate on life."

My memory of him was vivid. I recalled when I was a teenager, each time he and I talked about his death, he had said, "When I die, *do not* give me any funeral— use the money to help a destitute child. *Do not* wear black clothes for forty days, as is the custom. Instead, put white clothes on. *Do not* cry. *Do not* bring a *mullah* to commiserate my death …"

1

How could I forget about his death? He died only two years ago in my birth country; today for me no father, no mother, no king, no flag, and no homeland. All the ones I kept close to my heart over these years were gone. I wondered if my father realized what an impossible task he'd put before me, to concentrate on life!

I looked around the otherwise empty room dominated by my mother's body. I thought the entire universe was dead. Until today, I had never stared death in the eye.

"Today, the Fourth of July, and my woman washer won't come to work." The sheik's broken English, spiced with Arabic, rang in my ears as he entered the room. He had to perform the eulogy according to Islam. He gestured to me and Layla, younger by five years.

"So if you two, the daughters of Iran *khanoom*, Lady Iran, want to wash her, we can bury her now. Other than that, it has to be tomorrow."

He was right. Today everybody was gone to celebrate American freedom, to congregate in parks, eat and watch fireworks while my sister and I had to give our mother's body home in a Moslim way, in this corner of the Western world.

My mother, *Maman* Iran, died yesterday morning. According to our tradition, she had to be buried yesterday before sunset. Layla and I were already sinners in the Moslims' eyes.

"When you wash your mother, Allah will open the gate of paradise to you," the sheik said, breaking the silence. "When you go to the other side, your father...and mother ..."

Layla and I burst into tears, shaking and horrified by the thoughts of getting close to a dead body. After a long pause, I breathed, "We'll do it!" I wiped my eyes yet again.

2

My voice sounded as if all my strength had been sucked out of me; then, I asked, "What do we need to do?"

The sheik rushed to the cupboard opposite the sink, took out a new, white folded canvas, and said, "Here, after washing her thoroughly, wrap her in this." Layla took it from him. He then turned to me and gave me a small bowl full of spices. "Before shrouding her, put these in the cavities. After wrapping her up, come and get me. Make sure to wash the entire body three times."

"We know!" Layla acknowledged. "For Moslims, nothing is clean unless it's washed three times."

I was stuck to the floor and felt only the warmth of my tears when Layla's voice, through the mist of her own tears, shook me. "Mitra, what are you waiting for?"

I picked up the bucket from the floor, walked to the sink, held the bucket under the faucet, and waited for the water to fill it up. The sight of my mother's yellow face took me back to the age of five.

My tall father had shaded me by standing on the asphalt on that hot summer afternoon before the two-story hospital, three blocks away from our house in the heart of Tehran. "Mitra," he said, picking me up, "look at those windows." Soon, I could see Maman through one of the windows. Her face was as yellow as turmeric, and her belly was huge. I thought she had hidden one of my balloons under her baggy blue dress. When she saw me, she forced herself to smile, but soon her plum lips closed and her brows wrinkled.

Today, standing by her body, I was finally at ease. She was in pain no more. She was free.

"Mitra," my father's voice from that day sang in my ears again. "Let's go! "Do you wish to have a baby brother or a baby sister?" he asked me.

"Baby sister!" I said my wish loud enough for God to hear it. The next day, when he came to see me at my grandfather's house, he claimed my wish had come true, and I had a baby sister—Layla.

Today, I was pleased. Layla had grown up to be my *doost*, my friend, and I was grateful that we could prepare our mother's body for burial together.

The sound of running water brought me back to the death room. The bucket was overflowing. I lifted it with difficulty. I could do nothing else except act as an obedient maid and follow God's will. Believing in kismet, destiny flowed in my blood.

While I was sponging her eyes, nose, and lips, I had to admire Maman Iran's face. Even in death, her glamorous look lingered on. My father fell in love with her beauty, and not her lineage, which can be traced to the famed Qajar Dynasty. I refused to accept that this ruling family had also perished. I looked up and stared at Layla's face. Her thick, connected eyebrows, which framed her dark almond-shaped eyes and her slim nose, were typical features of women from this royal family. She was an example of the survival of this dynasty as well. But not me! I looked very much like my father, Nima, with sharp black beady eyes, unshaped nose too big for my tiny face and high cheek bones.

I sighed and concentrated on Maman's eyes. I saw myself as a little girl, about three years old. Her wailings woke me up before dawn. Wrapped in her *chador*, something she seldom wore, in the corner of the room, she was twisting like a snake. That day, my uncle Hamid insisted on taking me to his house, and I wondered what had happened to my baby brother.

"Where is Omid?"

"Mitra, Omid, our hope, isn't here anymore."

"Not here! Where is he?"

"He's gone to Europe!"

"Eh?" I gasped, wondering how a baby whose legs were wrapped in the swaddling clothes could go so far! I could walk, but there was no way I could walk *that* far.

I tried to ponder on my task in the death room, but my mind drifted to the day Maman Iran took me to Omid's grave. With one hand, she held tight to my hand, and with her other hand, she grasped the two sides of her chador under her chin. Walking ahead of my father and the rest of the family members, Maman rushed through the graves until we reached the smallest of them all. In an instant, she forgot all about me. She let go of my hand, threw herself on the grave, and started wailing and shrieking. With her long red painted nails, she dug at the grave as if she wanted to open it up. Her screams shook the entire cemetery. "My Omid, hope of my life!" she wailed. "Your mother's dying without you. I'm here to take you home!"

Then I understood Omid, our hope, was gone to heaven.

That day, she cried and I did not. Today, I cried, and she had no reason to cry anymore. Her life circle was complete. She was united with her son Omid, her husband Nima, her brother Amir, her father, Ali khan, her mother Shirin, her grandmother, Zahra …

"She achieves the utmost freedom," my father, *Baba* Nima's soft voice said in my ears. His voice took me back to a day when he and I stood in front of Omid's grave. I felt Baba's firm hand on my head transporting his love to me. I turned and looked at his thin face full of sorrow. "As Omar Khayyam says," he whispered, "we don't know why we are here and don't know why we must leave. Willy-nilly, coming and going!"

In his life, Baba always wanted to unravel the mystery

of death. During one of my visits from America to Iran, he and I discussed life and death. He shared with me the promise he had asked his mother to give him.

"Khanoom of khanoom-ha, lady of the ladies, was still alive, but sick for a long time. I knew her end was near. I asked if she would give me one promise."

"'Promise what?' she gasped.

"'Promise me that when you're on the other side, you'll come to my dreams and tell me about the other world!'

"I don't know if …" Baba paused.

"So, Baba, did she decipher the mystery of death for you?" I asked.

Baba took off his glasses and looked afar. "She did come to my dreams not long after her death, brought your mother to me, put her hand in mine and said, 'Nima, Iran is your wife. Take her hand and go on. You will come to my world when it's your time.'"

"Baba, do you believe in fate and destiny?"

"Of course," he said with the trace of a smile.

"Daddy, you mean whatever we do, it has been decided for us, is that right?"

"Absolutely!"

"Baba joon, you're saying that it was in my fate to go to America for education, the first girl in my family whose father isn't rich and doesn't have any ties to the shah!"

"Yes!" he answered enthusiastically.

"Of course, if it wasn't because of the scholarship from the government, I wouldn't…"

Baba interrupted me. "The shah wants to show the Western world that he is emphasizing on education, sending our youngsters abroad."

I nodded. At the same time I picked up the glass of water in front of me. "Are you telling me that if I drink this water, it was meant to be my fate?"

"It's your fate if you drink it and also your fate if you don't!" His voice was as firm as steel.

Maman's cold shoulder broke my thoughts and brought me back to the death room. I started to clean her shoulder, arm, and hand. I took refuge into my childhood again.

It was some time after Omid's death. The days were long and mundane. I seldom spent any time at my house since my parents had stopped talking to each other without any reason that I was able to determine. I feared they were not even aware of my existence. There was no Omid to keep Maman Iran busy, and she continued wearing her black dress day in and day out. I could be happy staying at my grandfather's house night after night.

One day, in the afternoon, when it was still light, the door cracked open. Maman Iran and Baba Nima walked in.

"Mitra *joon*, dear Mitra come here!" Maman put down a package. She was laughing, and I was delighted. I gazed at her short-sleeved blue dress, which revealed her olive skin. I felt I was in heaven when I leaned against her shoulder and let her put a red knee-length pleated skirt on me. She completed dressing me up with a white blouse and matching red vest. I fell in love with my shiny black shoes. When she placed on my head the red hat, decorated with royal blue lace, she boasted, "Mitra joon, you're as beautiful as a *khanoom farangi*!"

Baba agreed. "Exactly! Our lady is here from Europe!" Then the three of us held hands and made a circle. Maman and I started singing and moving to the rhythm we made together.

"Washing's done!" Layla's voice interrupted my reverie. "Help me to veil her in the shroud."

The sheik responded to our call and he and his helper took the body to the graveyard. Heaps of dirt and rocks were everywhere. There were no trees, and the land was covered with red clay. Soon, two gravediggers arrived and started deepening the hole with their shovels.

"I know what you're thinking." The sheik broke through the clanging of shovels. "I'm still waiting for my bulldozer to arrive. It's tough for us to raise money. The Moslim ones around here are mostly Sunnis and don't help us Shiites!"

I wondered about this. Both groups were from the same religion with one prophet to follow and one holy book, the Koran. Why did they have such hostility toward each other?

The sheik went on, "I'm so happy! I'm the only one in this part of the world who's able to give Iran khanoom, your mother, the burial that is fit for a Shiite Moslim."

"And it was her only wish," I murmured. Drowned in my thoughts, I was amazed how our new government could make us close to our religion. I never knew Maman Iran cared so much to be buried like a Shiite.

It was impossible to understand her core beliefs. One day she was a modern woman with a career as a teacher, the next day, she was a Moslim woman praying five times a day. She left our homeland after my father's death. When she joined Layla and me in this country, she was embarrassed to be seen, even with her scarf covering her head. She even put aside her prayers when she was diagnosed with cancer. "No praying can cure me," her voice sounded in my ears.

I remembered as a teenager I had to listen to her. "Being a teacher and taking care of the household leaves me no time to pray!" she said with dismay. "And your father prefers to fill up his head with Descartes and Sartre rather than with Islam."

However, she insisted on being buried in a Moslim

way. Until today, I never realized Maman Iran's body and Islam were interwoven like a tapestry.

I found myself staring at the sheik's dark face, with his white turban and black cloak. "People call me sheik because I went to *madresseh*, school, in your holy city of Quom."

The city of Quom, with its huge golden dome, gleamed in my mind—the burial place of the Prophet Mohammad's daughter, Fatima. We went to Quom at least twice a year. My father's mother was buried there. I liked going with them. At that time, it was the only city in the entire country where women had no choice except to wear chador wherever they went—whether to the shrine, or for a walk on the streets. And I could wear my chador—white with minute prints of flowers. I was proud to pretend I was a grownup girl. However, when I became an adult, I abhorred the law that compelled women to wear chador.

One time on our way to Quom by bus, I felt my father's hands around my waist, putting me on his lap so I could see out the window. "Mitra," Baba pointed to the distance, "what do you see, way, way over there?"

"Where the blue sky meets the naked mountains?"

"Yes, dear!"

"It's a lake! Hmmm! It looks like white, foamy waves are hitting the shore all the time."

"It's a lake all right! But don't trust your eyes …"

I turned to him. "No?"

"What looks like waves are really patches of salt. This water is so heavy with salt that it barely moves." He turned to Maman and said under his breath, "This traitor, the shah, uses this lake as a graveyard. Every day, the planes drop the bodies of our young, innocent sons who dared to stand up to our corrupted regime."

I yearned to jump at the raw meat Baba threw to her

and ask him, "Why? Why, Baba?"

But Maman's tears made me swallow my words when she muttered, "Very likely that's what happened to my beloved brother, Amir, God bless his soul." I did not understand what she was talking about. I was just happy to sit on my father's lap.

The sound of *Allaho Akbar*, God is great, brought me back to the cemetery. The gravediggers were finished. Layla and I could only weep. When they took Maman's shrouded body out of the coffin and put it in the grave, I could watch no more. I turned around and walked several steps away. I heard the sheik's voice reciting, "*besme Allah alrahman alrahim. Ashhado alla ilaha illallah …*"

"With the name of Allah, there is no God, but Allah …" With this verse, all Moslims opened their prayers. I knew. I breathed easier when I heard, "*Ashhado anna alian valiollah!*"

This part of the prayer separated us Shiites from the Sunnis. We Shiites shook hands with Ali, Mohammad's son-in-law, after Mohammad's death. Unlike Sunnis, we did not follow any caliphs. We followed the prophet's bloodline. After Ali, we believed in eleven other imams who all were descendants of him.

The sheik continued his prayers in Arabic which neither Layla nor I understood.

"When do you think the grave will be ready?" Layla's voice brought me back to the cemetery. The tomb was being filled at the pace of a turtle.

At sunset, the grave was finished. While the sheik poured water on it, he said, "It's almost done. When you bring a headstone for it, then it's completed."

The headstone! According to our religion, Mohammad was against tombstones, or any type of burial chamber. He believed in "ashes to ashes and dust to dust". His grave had no headstone. I wondered if any one of us followed the prophet as he intended; not even this holy man, the sheik. Layla's voice got my attention. "Let's go, Mitra."

"Before you two leave," the sheik stopped us, "come and send a *fatehe*, a prayer, to your mother's soul."

I sat down by her grave. My mind went blank. I had no idea how to send a prayer to Maman's soul. I never really learned how to pray because we had to pray in Arabic, not in our native language, Farsi.

"God does not need us to bow down to Him five times a day." My father's words rang in my ears from the time of my childhood. "He is not our king, and we are not His slaves."

I recalled those days when at every funeral, people sent prayers to the soul; Baba had murmured, "Nonsense! A soul does not need our prayers, especially in a language that is not ours. As Gertrude Stein believed, each one of us is an island."

"Baba, what did she mean?" I asked.

"She meant that each one of us is like an island when we're born. However, that doesn't mean we must stay like that. By helping each other in this world, we are connecting these islands together, and there's an immense glory in unity."

"Did Iran khanoom pray regularly during her life?" The sheik's words came down on us like a hammer.

Layla shook her head and whispered, "Sometimes."

"You can buy her the prayers she missed," the sheik offered.

"What do you mean?" I looked at him blankly.

His eyes lit up. "If you give me a thousand dollars, I pray for her. Then, you can be sure that her soul will go to heaven!"

Without saying a word, I walked away from this man of God. I intended to get as far away from him as I could.

"What kind of Moslims are you?" he called after us.

"According to you, not very good ones!" I said over my shoulder.

We knew for a fact that we were nothing like him. *How could he buy my mother's way to heaven with a thousand dollars?*

By the time Layla and I were driving away from Adelanto toward Los Angeles, the sizzling sun had almost dipped behind the mountains. My father's voice loomed in my mind again. "Buy your way to heaven by helping mankind!"

2. Mourning

Shahriar, Persia, 1896
Zahra (8)

Once upon a time, in the land of roses and nightingales, a girl called Zahra thought she was doomed.

The red sky, the dipping sun, and the wailing river, all forewarned us—the residents of Shahriar—that the next day would be even bloodier than today. Moharram, the month of mourning, was upon us. Tomorrow—the tenth of the month, called *ashura*—was a day when we commemorated the death of one of our saints, Imam Hossein. We had to do all the preparations.

Our neighborhood girls sprinkled water over our dusty road in order to sweep it clean for the procession. The smell of water and dust reminded me of the passage from the Koran: "Allah made Adam from clay and water." I wondered whether the clay and water were from our village. Heaven had to be like this.

Thanks to the Almighty, I had nothing to do. My father, Akbar khan, was a landlord. The villagers knew him and accepted him as their master.

Proud of my father, I was ready to step inside our house. But a galloping horse brought me to a standstill.

The horse was so close that if the rider had not drawn in the reins sharply, the horse would have hit me in the face. Its loud neighing shook me. With my head down, out of the corner of my eye, I saw a mounted man.

I felt shaky and scared, thinking, *Thank Allah I was saved!*

The sound of the rider's dark boots kept me alert. He approached me.

Like a gazelle, I ran into the courtyard, shouting, "Maman! Maman!" My mother, Fatemeh, pulled her black chador over her head, covered her black scarf and her saggy black dress, and rushed through the yard to the door.

"What do you want, mister?" She sounded angry.

"Lady, where's the father of this girl?" The man's voice jolted me like our house during an earthquake. I took refuge behind Maman.

The man showed no sign of being a farmer from our village. His black trousers and his white silk shirt looked clean and new. His glittery red vest, with its paisley patterns, was regal. Unlike other Moslim men, he had no thick beard or mustache. He had to be from the royal family.

"*Agha*, mister, what's your business?" Maman raised her voice in a manner unlike her.

"Is this girl your daughter?"

"Not your concern."

"The girl's beauty is spellbinding. She's the embodiment of an angel. With those almond-shaped dark eyes, her milky skin, and her rosy cheeks, she's a perfect …"

The man's words enveloped my heart like silk. I'd never heard a man compare me to an angel. It gave me goose bumps. Of course, he could not see my hair. It was hidden under my white scarf. Some nights, when Maman combed my jet-black hair, she would praise its brightness and length.

I could resist no longer. I peeked once more. The stranger's shiny, dark ponytail and his shaven face mystified me.

Maman's angry voice filled my ears. "Mister, you're insulting me," she shouted and tried to push the door shut.

The man, swift to act, threw his arm into it and kept talking. "Khanoom, I'm Saam, one of His Majesty's eunuchs, working in the harem."

"Harem? What're you talking about, agha?"

"We're preparing to celebrate His Majesty's jubilee." He paused. "I want to bestow your daughter upon our king, Naser Al-Din Shah. Where is her father?"

I could hear my heart thumping as if it would burst out of my chest at any moment. I understood that the man wanted to separate me from my family and take me to Tehran—to the Golestan Palace. I grabbed Maman's chador harder and brought myself even closer to her. Her slim body in my small hands was trembling like a field of crops caught in a storm.

"Never!" Maman blurted in a forceful voice, as she pushed me away. "Run! Run, Zahra! Get inside!"

Maman then turned to Saam and said, "Akbar khan won't agree to send his daughter to the harem." She looked through the half-ajar door and continued. "My daughter's no animal to be kept in a harem."

I knew all about the harem. The women in our village whispered to each other: *"Have you heard?"* one might ask.

"About what?"

"About Abollah's daughter. His Majesty saw her on his hunting trip ..."

"Now she lives in the harem," another woman would finish the sentence for her.

I understood that once the gate to the harem slammed shut behind a girl, there was no way out. The women had no contact with the outside world. They were lost forever. Their families counted them among the dead.

I, however, breathed a sigh of relief. I thanked Allah for giving me Akbar khan as my father. He would protect me from the king's man, I had no doubt.

"Besides, she isn't even nine years old yet!" I heard Maman say. I gazed at the walls of our adobe house, with its huge wooden door, thanking Allah for keeping us safe from the intruder.

"Khanoom, we betroth her now and keep her in the harem until she's nine, ready for matrimony."

"Listen, mister," Maman Fatemeh shouted. "My daughter's the only child Allah blessed me with. The Almighty gave her to me after many years of *nazro-niaz*, prayers." Without wasting any more time, she pushed the door much harder. To hear her protecting me like a lioness made me feel blessed. She did not care to be bothered about her own sin, her slipping chador, revealing some wisps of her hair for the man to see.

"Khanoom! You don't understand. Tell me when your husband's in." The stranger's voice jarred me again. "Do you know what a fortune you're throwing away? Your husband is in charge of her, not you." He moved his hands as if he were angry with Maman.

"His Majesty will give her father *tala—gold!* Imagine that!" Saam blustered.

Then he took a few steps back from the door. "We put your beautiful girl on one side of the scale." He acted as if he had a scale before him, placing me on it. "And put gold on the other. Whatever it comes to, her father shall have it all, and …"

At last, Maman lost all her patience and screamed, "No need for His Majesty's money in this house, mister. You should be ashamed of yourself. Don't you know we're in the month of Moharram? Time to *mourn*! Not to celebrate!"

Without waiting for a further response from the stranger, she gathered all her strength, pushed and slammed the wooden door in the man's face, then rushed through the yard to join me inside our home. I would like to think we were the bullet that killed our enemy on the spot.

¤ ¤ ¤

A few of the king's cavaliers invaded our house, broke down its wooden door, rushed in, and snatched me from Maman's lap. They galloped outside while I screamed, "Baba! Baba!" I could feel the soldier's fingers pushing my ribcage so hard that I thought it would collapse any moment. Horrified, I opened my eyes to rescue myself from my nightmare. It was dawn. The somber smell of burning lumber and the peaceful sound of fire from my yard brought me to my senses, and the event of yesterday befell me.

I recalled the previous day's events when the angry stranger left. Maman Fatemeh rushed in, sat at the corner of our room, pulled her chador tighter over her, and started counting her holy beads faster and faster. She talked with no one, not even Aunt Zinat, who stayed with us whenever my father was gone to Tehran. Praise Allah, my witty mother never told the man that Baba was absent. Otherwise, the king's eunuch would have taken me with him right then. All night long, Maman acted like a mute person, and ate nothing. She even refused to come with us to the roof to sleep.

The women's mumbling from our courtyard made me jump. After rolling our mattresses and covering them with an old coarse *geleem*, I stepped down the wobbly wooden

17

ladder. The heavenly smell of *sholezard*, rice pudding, prevented my fear of falling.

As a tradition, every year the women whose husbands farmed my father's land came to our house to prepare this delicious dish—a blend of rice, sugar, rosewater, and saffron. From the kitchen, they brought one of our largest pots, the one I could hide in whenever I played hide-and-seek with the neighborhood girls. They never could find me there.

When I looked at the seven women in the courtyard, I wished they'd had on their usual frilled colorful skirts that jingled whenever they walked. But not today! For the entire month of Moharram, we mourn the death of our Imam Hossein—our third imam. The women put on their black clothing—baggy trousers with baggy overalls coming down to their knees. The farmers' wives wrapped their chadors around their waists, but my family members covered their heads with black scarves because there was no man in the house, so no need for chador.

"Fatemeh," Batool, Aunt Zinat's oldest daughter, asked. "Are you still scared?"

Maman sighed. "I'm afraid he'll be back again."

"It's possible," Aunt Zinat said. "If he thought our king would like Zahra, he'll be back to talk with Akbar khan."

"Very likely he will." My newly wedded cousin, a little older than me, added, "His Majesty, Naser Al-Din Shah's famous for having the largest harem ever."

"While on hunting trips or summer vacation," Aunt Zinat went on, "if our king sees a girl he likes, he'll take her with him."

"Of course," another cousin, Taherh, breast-feeding her newborn son, said. "But not by force. His Majesty and his men make sure that the girl's father gives his permission to take his daughter into his harem."

The five women assembled in the kitchen, all in their black dresses, looked like crows whispering. I wished my father would give me to someone who lived here in Shahriar, who wouldn't take me away from him and Maman Fatemeh. Then I remembered. Some time ago, a few women related to a *hajji* from our village had come to ask Maman if she wanted to marry me off, or at least betroth me to his youngest son. Now I wished I had a husband so the stranger could never separate me from my family.

"What I'm scared of," Maman said, "is that His Majesty's taken at least one or two girls from here, so …" She stopped, raising her head when she saw me standing by the kitchen.

"Zahra joon, go and cut some red roses from the garden."

"Maman, would the man come to snatch me from you?"

"As long as I live, no one dares to separate you from me."

"What about Baba? Saam knows. My father must decide!" I then swallowed.

"Zahra joon, we need the roses!" Aunt Zinat jumped in.

I started walking when I heard her say, "I just noticed, the eunuch's right. Our Zahra does look like an angel …"

I rushed outside to our lush garden at the back of our house. I wandered around the trees, picking a peach here, or some cherries there. I had to be extra careful around the rose bushes not to get pricked by their thorns, when a surge of noise from the street took my attention. "Zahra, come! Come here!" I wanted to run to my friends, but I felt no strength in my feet. Instead, I hurried to Maman and asked, "Don't you want to see the procession?"

"Zahra joon, you go, we'll join you soon."

Before I could reach our door, Maman's words nailed

me. "Don't go to the street with your naked head! Put your *hijab* on!"

I turned a deaf ear to her, rushed outside and sat under the homey shade of our old walnut tree. This tree dwelled outside of our dried mud-straw walls.

Thank Allah! Unlike the rest of the villagers, I had this cool place to escape from the heated land. I sat cross-legged on the damp ground and gazed at the snow-covered Mount Alborz. On this hot summer day, snow on this high mountain bewildered me.

Soon, Maman Fatemeh and Aunt Zinat came to the street, and each one stood beside me. Feeling protected, I clung to Maman's chador. She said, "Zahra, didn't I say to cover your hair!" I, however, dared to pretend not to hear her command. Then, there was no sound, not even a breeze. There wasn't even a whisper—as if all creatures' lips were sealed. Even the chickens and roosters were out of sight and quiet.

"Hey Zahra, look!" A girl pointed to something in the distance.

I gazed. Separated from the horizon, a patch of black cloud approached us. I thought for sure the king's men were coming to take me. I covered my mouth, and jumped up. I paid no attention to the pain caused by the rocks and gravel on my bare feet. A flock of men were marching toward us.

I gave a sigh of relief. They were local men participating in the procession, not the king's men. I sat down on the ground, reached for Maman's legs, hugged them and yearned to hear her voice.

"Maman, why do we have the procession every year?"

"We must mourn the Tragedy of Karbala."

"Where is Karbala?"

"It's in a very far land," Aunt Zinat answered.

"Why do we call it a tragedy?"

"Yazid, the caliph, ordered his men to martyr our beloved Imam Hossein, our third imam, and his entire family including women, babies and infants." She wiped her teary eyes.

In a short time, the men were close enough that I could see them.

Their appearance flustered me. Their shoeless feet, their torn black robes over their raggedy, dark pants, and their solemn looks suggested as if they were warriors returning from the front. A few older men in the first row had dried, bloody welts on their heads. Their thick, black beards and shoulder-length hair were covered with sawdust and ashes. We knew. These men came from the mosque right after their dawn prayers. Their new wounds showed that they had beaten themselves with chains, and some had even slashed their heads with daggers before starting their procession.

"Hey Maman, see," I pointed at the men's ripped-off robes. "Look at their naked, bruised backs. Why aren't they worried? We're looking at their naked bodies!"

"Allah wants the women to cover themselves," Aunt Zinat murmured. "Zahra joon, for men, it isn't a sin to show their naked bodies, but we women must cover ours, including our hair."

"Why?"

"Our mullahs tell us women's hair is a temptation for men. It's not a man's fault if he commits a devilish act toward a woman! She deserves it!"

Maman jabbed me. "Cover your hair, Zahra!"

The sound of *Allaho Akbar* blanketed Maman's order. I heard only, "Allah is great, and there is no God but Allah."

The men stopped before us. They started inflicting their exposed flesh to fervent whips of their chains.

The two flags, one in black and one in bright green, were flying high. Each flag bore the brocaded word *Allah*. At the end of each pole, the silver emblem called *"Fatima's hand"*, after our prophet's daughter, was erected in the air. Then my hand touched my own gold necklace, the same talisman, Fatima's hand, but much smaller, chained around my neck to ward off the evil eye.

My attention went to the men again. They were lashing themselves so hard that the blood rolled down their backs, and sweat covered their foreheads in thin streams.

I turned my face away from them. "Maman, how can these men injure themselves? Don't they feel pain?"

"No. They're doing it for Allah and for our Imam Hossein," Aunt Zinat answered me while she wiped her tears.

I gazed at the procession again. It appeared to me these willing and stronghearted men would join with our godly hero Imam Hossein in the battlefield if they could.

"Maman, when was Imam Hossein martyred?"

"A long time ago! At least twelve hundred years ago."

"After all these years, we …"

When the leader started reciting the story of Imam Hossein's tragedy in Karbala, even I joined the crowd and wept while we beat our heads and chests. Tears rolled down my face. I wondered. I had no pain, not even a wound, but I was crying as if I had lost my father. I looked up to Maman and Aunt Zinat. Their faces were covered in tears. I was baffled and strained.

I gazed at the green range of mountains, and caught the peak of Mount Alborz still kissing the blue skirt of sky. I thanked Allah for giving us a peaceful sky, and that what I was witnessing was not a real war.

The smell of blood mixed with the crowd's sweat called me back to the procession. My woozy stomach and teary eyes made me wish our twelfth imam, the last imam, Mehdi, our Savior, would appear and rescue me.

We took refuge in our belief that Allah concealed our last leader, Imam Mehdi, from everyone's eyes when he was twelve years old. We believed he would return one day. When black clouds would spread over the sky and no more vegetation could grow on earth, Imam Mehdi, a brave man, would become visible to all of us. As the messenger of Allah, and as our leader, he would be here to cleanse the earth from the devil.

"He's our last *omid*, hope! Imam Mehdi is our savior and one day he'll show himself to us," I murmured. "Maman, how can Imam Mehdi purify the world?"

"By killing the evil ones."

"Who?"

"The friends of *shaitan*, the devil!"

I could see it in my mind. The dead bodies stacked up like a mountain, their devilish blood covering Mehdi's horse stirrup, and the streams of blood that would rake the entire land. I was horrified and closed my eyes when I heard Aunt Zinat's voice: "At last, when no sinful person remains alive, Allah will wash off the black clouds from the sky and replace them with the sun. By all means, Mehdi *will* arrive one day."

"Killing ... isn't it a sin?" I asked.

"No! Allah sends Mehdi to cleanse the earth from shaitan." Maman gazed into my eyes and whispered, "Mehdi has to kill the wretched people to save the innocent ones." She paused, took a breath, and went on, "Imam Mehdi does a righteous act! A divine man must kill many sinful people to purify the world." She wiped her tears. I shook my head and brought myself back to the procession. But I felt relieved. We had a Savior. He would arrive one day to rescue us all. Then our king could not separate some daughters from their families anymore.

When the men finished the eulogy of our Imam Hossein, they sat down on the ground. Maman and Aunt Zinat hurried inside the house.

In a short while, Maman, as the landlord's wife, carried a large clay bowl of water. She was the first woman to come out. Soon after, the other women brought more bowls of water filled to the rims with chunks of ice. To my amazement, the leader passed the bowl to the man next to him, without drinking anything. The next man did the same, and on and on.

"Aunt Zinat," I shook her chador. "Why didn't the first man drink?"

"In Karbala, right before the last massacre, when Imam Hossein received the bowl of water, he passed it to the warrior next to him without even wetting his lips." She paused, wiped her tears and continued, "This saint refused to drink unless everyone in his camp had a chance to drink before him." Because of her tears, she stopped, and swallowed. "The water then was passed on through the line until it reached the youngest lad at the end. Right before anyone could have a sip, the caliph's men ambushed and martyred our holy man, Imam Hossein, with his entire family, including women and children." With the last word, her wailing became louder.

"Is this the reason we give water to animals before killing them?"

Her tears prevented her from speaking—she only nodded.

Maman's voice filled my ears. "We want to show we're not vicious as Yazid." She wailed as if our martyr's body were before her.

I could no longer look at Maman's teary eyes. I turned my head and gazed at the glazed sky-blue bowl. It was stained from the men's dusty fingers as they passed it from one to another. The red rose petals floating on the bowl and the smell of rose water reeled me in. They comforted my steaming heart, putting my mind at ease with their heavenly aroma. They reminded me of the sweet yellow sholezard.

I ran into the kitchen where three ladies were each ladling the yellow blend into several crockery bowls, while some other talented women with cinnamon powder drew the word *Allah* or *Hossein* on the surface of each full bowl. My cousin placed one of the bowls in front of me. The first spoonful put me at ease. The procession, the stranger, the king and his harem all became a distant memory.

¤ ¤ ¤

Day after day, I kept a mysterious knot hidden inside me, and I wondered if the king's man would return. Every knock at our door reminded me of Saam. In every prayer, I beseeched Allah not to send the stranger back to our house. Every night, I refused to close my eyes to give life to my nightmares.

I kept praying to Allah for Baba's return from Tehran. I remembered a few springs ago when I was six. One early morning, I opened my eyes and saw Baba, with his hefty body, leaping toward me as he snatched a scorpion from my toes and crushed it under his feet. Like a wind, he swiped away this despicable creature. I went on living, unlike some other unfortunate children who did not have fathers as brave as mine.

I'll never forget the evening when we were praying, our front door banged open and broke our prayers. I recognized Baba's footsteps. He had cut his trip short, returning even before the second full moon.

This time, he failed to hold me in his strong arms. I yearned to run to him, but something about his look nailed me down. His usual delightful face was pale. His black straight hair looked gray and dusty. From his teary eyes and wrinkled cloak, I understood that he had gone through a hard time. Maman, Aunt Zinat, and I said nothing. Baba sat at the head of the room. A white cushion was always reserved for him. He turned to us and whispered, "You won't believe what I saw today!"

"What happened?" Maman asked in her soft voice.

"I'm afraid His Majesty, our king, is dead!"

"Akbar khan, what are you saying?" Aunt Zinat burst into tears, and Maman hit her head and cheeks.

"It's exactly what I'm saying," Baba said, hitting his forehead. "I don't know what we, as a nation, have done to cause Allah's wrath." He held his head. One of the maids brought him tea, put it before him, and sat down by the door.

"Tell us, tell us!" Aunt Zinat exclaimed, rushing to Baba and sitting beside him.

"Today, at noon," he said wiping his eyes, "as usual, I went to the shrine of Shah Abdol Azim to pray." Baba paused, scratched his beard, and my heart thumped faster and faster.

"Actually, His Majesty, Naser Al-Din Shah had ordered that this ancient mosque be renovated," Maman whispered.

"Yes, and Allah bless his soul!" Baba raised his hands toward the sky. "After my noon prayer, I sat down on the veranda with some other friends and talked about how Allah has been good to us this year. We've had suitable weather and our crops plentiful. There were some people inside the shrine and some outside—many of them clergymen and mullahs. Suddenly, we heard some people shouting, 'His Majesty's here, His Majesty's here!'

"A mullah next to me murmured spitefully, 'and no one has thrown us out of here to reserve the House of Allah exclusively for His Majesty!'

"Soon a few guards came in and ordered everyone to stand up on the both sides of the courtyard, so His Majesty could go through.

"We all swiftly stood up. I was on the veranda, a few steps away from the door to the shrine. Expecting to see an old man, I was quite jolted. Our king, erect and stern, entered the courtyard while some crowds accompanied him. His cone-shaped black hat with the emblem of imperial majesty—the lion holding a sword, and the sun emerging at its back—set him apart from the others. His Majesty was clothed in a long, fitted black jacket that reached to his knees over dark gray trousers. Its buttons were gold and trumpeted his royalty! His cleaned shaved face with his long, thick mustache revealed his identity right away.

"I even heard when one of the guards whispered in his ear, 'Your Highness, there's only one clergyman praying in the shrine, and he refuses to leave.'

"We know how benevolent our king, Naser Al-Din Shah is. He did not mind to pray side by side with a commoner! He responded, 'Don't bother the holy man's prayers. Let him be!'

"As soon as His Majesty walked into the shrine, the sound of a pistol shook us all. I saw His Majesty on the floor, drowning in his own blood."

"Allaho Akbar!" Aunt Zinat murmured and started

hitting her head.

"Baba, did the clergyman kill His Majesty?" I questioned.

"I'm afraid so!"

"Did you see the clergyman?" Maman asked.

"No! Right away, the guards closed the door to the shrine and we heard another shot."

"Allah! Help us!" Maman raised her hands to the sky.

"Now Allah will punish us all!" Aunt Zinat shouted.

"As far as I could tell, one of the guards fired his weapon and killed the clergyman on the spot." Baba gazed into space and continued, "A few moments later, they announced that His Majesty was injured and we all had to leave the shrine."

Baba sighed. He poured some tea into his saucer, as it was our way of drinking tea, put a sugar cube in his mouth and took a sip.

"So, our king's injured," Aunt Zinat lamented.

"No!" Baba shook his head. "That's what they want people to believe. I saw His Majesty's body laying there with the bullet that had ripped through his chest."

"What devil would do such a thing? What's this world coming to?" Aunt Zinat kept wiping her tears with her chador.

Maman said, "The world must be coming to an end!"

"That's right!" Aunt Zinat turned to her. "It's unheard of! A holy man murdered our *shadow of Allah*, Allaho Akbar!"

"As far as I can remember, this is the first time a king of ours has been assassinated," Baba said.

"By a holy man, a mullah! How dreadful!" Maman reached to hold my hand.

I wondered how a holy man could be a murderer. I could see the news of the king's death had devastated Maman, Baba, and Aunt Zinat. But I couldn't explain a

28

soothing feeling that had draped my heart.

Maman, Aunt Zinat, and the maid began to cry, beating their chests harder. "Baba, why do we cry for the death of strangers?" I enquired.

"For the love we have for them. By crying, we show we have passion for them. Don't forget, he was our king. To us, he was the *shadow of Allah*. When we harm our king, Allah turns his back to us. Only Allah knows what will happen to our crops and livelihood in the years to come."

To love our saints, and to cry for their deaths every year, I understood. But to love a man who separated some daughters from their families, I did not.

"Baba, now, we won't have a king anymore, right?" I wanted to put an end to my nightmares.

"Not true! We can't survive without our king." He paused, had a sip of his tea and continued, "Our crown prince, His Majesty's eldest son, will be our new king." Baba finished his tea. "They haven't told us the king's dead. The crown prince resides in Azerbaijan. They're waiting for him to get to Tehran. Then they'll break the news." He then got up to leave the room. "I need to get ready for my prayer."

"It's difficult for me to believe that a clergyman, a man of Allah murdered our compassionate Majesty," Aunt Zinat reiterated with teary eyes while I crawled onto Maman's lap.

"We continue praying for His Majesty's recovery," Aunt Zinat said as if she did not believe my father.

I whispered in Maman's ear, "Do you think now the new king's men will come to get me?"

Maman caressed my waist-long hair and murmured, "Never! Not even the new king dares to take you away from me."

I felt safe in her arms, praising her for rescuing me

from the wolf's mouth. At that moment, I could breathe much easier.

After several days, the news from Tehran reached us that the king was indeed dead. With the entire country, I put on my black clothes, covered myself in black chador, and mourned our monarch's death for forty days.

I knew then that Allah's will was not for His Majesty to celebrate his jubilee. He reigned two years short of fifty.

Alas, my fate was not to be a princess.

3. Hope

Tehran, Persia, 1910
Shirin (8)

In my chubby hands, I cupped tight some breadcrumbs, making sure not to lose a morsel. Maman Zahra had saved them for *abgoosht*. The word meant the juice of cooked meat. But Maman bought bones from our butcher, added water to them, and boiled them with dried peas and beans. Then, in a bowl, we mixed these breadcrumbs with the juice. More often, it was our lunch or dinner.

"Abgoosht is more delicious with bones than meat," she said whenever my younger sister, Pari, or I questioned her about not having any meat.

This afternoon, I tiptoed to the round pool in the backyard, which was a perfect place for my few birds to fly into our yard. Soon, they hovered over me as if they knew I was their doost, friend. I whispered, "Pigeon joon, dear sparrow, come, come to me."

This early afternoon, I had to be quiet so as not to awaken my grandmother, Fatemeh. I loved her very much, so I called her *Aziz*. She and Pari shunned the sizzling sun, taking a nap in our room. Maman Zahra was sitting cross-legged on the veranda, shaded by a hunched tree with a

31

wrinkled trunk. She was busy feeding my brother, Hassan. Maman had grown up in Shahriar. About her village, she said, "During the summer, its days are always cool because of its lush trees and rivers. At night, its shinning stars twinkle in the sky." Here in Tehran, we endured the torturous hot days, and some nights the breezes from Mount Alborz could not even make a dent in its heat.

I also knew my father, Baba Mehdi khan, had decided to move Maman and my grandmother to Tehran. However, for some reason, one day, Allah sprinkled sorrow over our house. When Baba Mehdi left in the morning, he never came back. Then, Allah brushed everything in black. Wherever I went, I saw darkness, even in our courtyard. There were no birds singing. Instead, snow piled up on our two naked trees and two rosebushes.

I recalled after a few weeks of my father's absence, one night, Grandma Aziz and I were at the mosque when the mullah blurted out the news: "Last month, our king, the servant of Russia, ordered the Russian troops, not our soldiers, to attack our *majlis*, parliament. Their barrage of cannon fire destroyed this new building, the house of the people. Some of the innocent demonstrators were also killed. Their blood is on His Majesty's hands."

"Our youths sacrificed their lives for us to have majlis," the lady next to Aziz muttered.

"My son-in-law was one of the youths," Aziz said while wiping her teary eyes.

"His Majesty thinks we're his herd," the mullah's angry voice hit my head like a hammer. "So, he wants to tame us at any cost." He sounded furious. I could not see him through the dingy white cloth that separated him from women. I wanted to get up and snatch the curtain down, but I had no strength, and my hands were small. The men with all their strength and huge hands ignored the curtain and let it veil the women. Therefore, I sat and turned a blind eye to my surroundings. The mullah's angry voice jarred me again. "The king does not respect his father's signature to allow us to have our majlis." He paused. "The king knows he's losing control over us …"

"Shirin joon, someone's knocking," Maman said, and brought me back to my birds and the hot summer afternoon. The one nightingale among the sparrows flew away. I pleaded, "Wait! Wait!" I felt an ache and wished to have wings too, so that I could soar into the blue sky and visit faraway lands with my friends. I was, however, stuck in my house like a prisoner, as if my feet were tied. I wondered why Allah had given me no wings.

"Shirin joon, will you get that?" Maman said, a little louder this time.

I crept toward the door so the birds still on the ground would not leave me. I opened the door to a lady. I remembered her gleaming face from my father's funeral. She was one of Maman's friends from her village, Shahriar.

"*Salam*, Fereshteh khanoom!"

"*Salam'-n-allaykom*, Shirin joon! Is your Maman home?"

I moved away and pushed myself against the wall to make room for this angel to walk into our portico. Fereshteh's shiny black chador looked like two wings when she opened her arms to embrace me. I gazed at her black shoes. I wondered whether my *kismet*, fate, would be to one day dress like her.

"Who's there?" Maman asked from the other side of the veranda.

"Zahra joon, it's me, Fereshteh."

When I looked up, Maman stopped feeding Hassan, tucked her breast into her black blouse, put him in his hammock, and rushed barefoot toward us. She tossed her two thick braids to her back; very fast, she rolled her hands over her hair. "Welcome! Come in!" Maman's grin made me happy. Since my father's death, she seldom laughed or even cracked a smile. In those days, Maman Zahra, engulfed in tears, kept pushing me and Pari to her bulging belly, repeating, "My orphan children, my …"

"Please, don't open the guest room for me," Fereshteh's voice rang out. She wanted to be where Hassan was. I was happy. I could sit with them and hear all the gossip. I did not wait to hear Maman's insistence, or for Fereshteh to change her mind. I rushed ahead to our room where Pari and Aziz were sleeping. Energetic as a butterfly, I brought out two cushions and placed them on the floor side by side. I protected Fereshteh's expensive chador from our rough washed-off geleem. As soon as Fereshteh sat down, I jumped on the other cushion where I could catch her heavenly rosewater aroma. I also stared into her clean, smooth face, free from any stray hair, and her two arched eyebrows, darkened with charcoal, signaling she was a married woman. She had no makeup for the month of Moharram, the month of mourning.

"Zahra joon, you have a quaint house, the two big trees—that one is a weeping willow," she pointed, "but what is this one?" She turned to the tree over the veranda.

"Maman and Aziz," I could not keep the words in my mouth, "call it the good-for-nothing tree! I think my father planted it. Is that right, Maman?"

"No, this tree was here when Mehdi khan, Allah bless his soul, bought the house." Maman stared at me. "You were perhaps three or four when we moved here. Because it is barren, we called it the good-for-nothing tree."

I looked at Fereshteh and wondered why she had no children with her.

She was careless about her chador when it slipped

34

down to her shoulders, for there was no man in our house. My eyes then fixed on her transparent, black, scarf displaying her reddish hair. Its shade of henna was rather exciting and unlike Maman's hair, which was dark as a winter night. Fereshteh was dressed in black, like every woman during the month of Moharram, to show her solidarity with men during the mourning of the Tragedy of Karbala. Yet Maman wore black every day and that put a cloud of sadness over my heart.

Only once, when she gave birth to Hassan, did she wear white. Aziz ripped off the black dress from her and pushed a white one on her. After a few days, she put her black clothes back on and said, "I'm a widow, mourning my husband Mehdi khan's death for the rest of my life."

"Zahra joon!" Freshteh smiled. "Why didn't you come to our house for *rozekhani?*"

As a custom, the rich women invited a few mullahs to their houses to commemorate Imam Hossein's death. By reciting the Tragedy of Karbala, the women could weep and cleanse their souls. In addition, they also fed the men who participated in the procession.

"On the ninth and tenth days of Moharram?"

Fereshteh nodded.

"Don't know … maybe, Hassan …?"

I understood Maman could not show her face among those wealthy women. After all this time living in Tehran, she still dressed like Kobra, our servant from Shahriar. This girl—a villager—appeared to be a little older than me, for her chest was already developed. Her parents had ten children and could barely feed them. Therefore, Aunt Zinat sent her to us to help Maman and to share our bread. To me, Kobra looked funny, with her baggy black pants under a pleated *shalite*, a ridiculously short skirt, with a cheap blouse. Thank Allah, Maman's skirt had no fake coins sewed on it; there was no embarrassing jingle from her skirt.

I was mesmerized by Fereshteh's appearance and gazed at her again. I admired her for being an elegant woman. Under her chador, she wore a long, loose, tailored dress made out of linen, showing her body's curves. I asked Allah why Maman could not dress like her, why He took her husband away from her so soon.

I recalled, a few full moons after Baba's death, Maman started to weave a colorful tapestry to display before our neighbors, covering us being poor. To my amazement, she *never* talked about us skipping a meal here and there, and eating abgoosht instead. Our wealthy neighbors and relatives from Shahriar knew that Zahra khanoom's children were happy and well-fed. They could see our rosy cheeks but not our empty stomachs.

From the kitchen came Kobra's footsteps, along with her jingly skirt. Whenever we had a guest, she brewed fresh, strong tea. In the mist of the whistling bronze *samovar*, Fereshteh began, "Zahra joon! I'm here today because …"

Maman diverted her gaze from my brother. With a tired look, she stared into Fereshteh's face.

"My very dear friend, Mehri khanoom, is a distant family to our princess, Tajal-Saltaneh …"

"One of Naser Al-Din Shah's daughters!" Maman interrupted her.

Fereshteh nodded, and I added, "He reigned longer than any other king, for almost fifty years."

"Bravo, Shirin joon," Fereshteh said, smiling.

"Aziz told me how benevolent he was," I noted.

"Naser Al-Din Shah opened the gates of our country to the occidental world and was the first king who traveled to

Europe," Fereshteh explained. "We're lucky to have had him as our king."

"But the clergyman who assassinated him was opposed to the king and to his way of life," Maman interjected. "His Majesty refused to follow Allah's laws, and ..." Maman sounded as if she approved of what the clergyman did.

"Well, the man was ignorant. He was a devil in the dress of a clergyman." Fereshteh swallowed. Maman and I stayed silent. "I've heard that if His Majesty were alive, he would've allowed us to have a parliament like the Westerners."

"There's a rumor!" Maman gushed. "His daughter can speak the language of infidels!"

Freshteh nodded and said, "Zahra joon, you mean French!" She smiled. "Tajal-Saltaneh accompanied her father several times to Paris."

I thought, *If only the clergyman had not killed our king, then we would have our majlis without any demonstrations. No Russian soldiers would have come to our land to kill my father.* I knew it was our fate and Allah's will.

"Fereshteh joon, maybe you're right," Maman's words without any strength disappeared in the air.

"Naser Al-Din Shah was an extraordinary king." Fereshteh's excitement grabbed my heart. "Allah bless his soul. His Majesty built the glorious palace, *Kaahk-e-Golestan.*"

"For himself and his wives," Maman's whisper passed Fereshteh's ears.

"How many wives did he have?" I asked.

"Let's talk about the Golestan Palace."

"Palace of flowers! Right?"

"*Marhaba*, bravo, Shirin joon," Fereshteh said.

She then stirred up the pot of my imagination and

raised the fire beneath it as she dipped me into this luminous palace. She bathed me with images of its glory.

"Naser Al-Din Shah brought the Golestan Palace to life by setting it at the heart of Tehran." Her words came to me as if she'd opened the gates of the palace to us.

I devoured every word she said. It was as if she were holding my hand and leading me from one room to another, showing me everything. "The king receives the dignitaries in this room, the Hall of *noor*." Fereshteh then stared at me, and I could swear that I saw the hall of lights in her eyes while Kobra's colorful shalite caught the corner of my eye.

Carrying a tray, she climbed the stairs and approached our guest. She put before Fereshteh a porcelain bowl with slender cucumbers, peaches, nectarines, and grapes, enough to feed us for several days. Maman Zahra did not pay for them. Aunt Zinat sent them from Shahriar. In a short time, Kobra came back with the tea and offered it to our guest. Fereshteh picked up the porcelain saucer with its dainty tea glass erected on it and set it on the geleem.

The saucer and its glass, with their matching gilded trim, pulled me in while I screamed in my head, *Our secret has been revealed.* Today, Fereshteh knew we had no silver or gold tea set. She understood we had no *aberu*, dignity. Our dignity was lost, and Maman's haughty tapestry, which was meant to hide our poverty, was pulled down.

Next, Kobra put down the sugar bowl before our guest. The sugar cubes were the results of Aziz's toiling. Every morning, she hammered and shaped a sugar cone into these identical cubes. I yearned for them to become gold coins, so we would be as rich as our king. Then today, Maman and I would not be embarrassed.

I ignored the shame of our poverty and wanted to hear

more about the Golestan Palace. "Fereshteh khanoom, what does this hall look like?"

"The high ceiling of this gigantic room, with its numerous arches, an outstanding replica of our ancient architecture, lures in everybody. Shirin joon, the mirrored artwork on the walls and ceiling with all its eminence, is a duplicate of the shrine of Imam Reza, our eighth imam."

"Does this room have any rugs? I've heard our shrines don't have any." Maman narrowed her eyes, and her brows wrinkled.

"Of course there are rugs!" Fereshteh winked at me and continued. "A regal red silk carpet covers the marble floor of the Hall of noor."

The red carpet in the Golestan Palace reminded me of our silk kashi in our guest room. This room still looked the same as it did before Baba's death. Its satin cushions to sit on and its few shiny *poshti* to lean against could transport me right into Aladdin's Palace. I never dreamt that the Golestan Palace was even more majestic than Aladdin's.

"Such an unbelievably expensive palace!" Maman's heated voice brought me back to the harsh geleem under my legs. "Fereshteh khanoom, how did our king have so much money to build this palace?!"

"And from the occidental world," Fereshteh turned a deaf ear to Maman and continued, "the huge prismatic chandeliers, shiny colorful tapestries, and the stylish chairs can transport us right into a country such as France or Russia."

"Chairs? What are those?" I had no idea.

"Well dear, in the West," Maman interjected, "people attach four legs to a small wooden platform and sit on it. They don't sit on the floor like we do." I was amazed Maman Zahra knew about chairs.

"Also," Fereshteh indicated with outstretched arms, "they use a big wooden platform, and build four legs to it, and call it table."

"Don't they eat their meals like us on the floor on a *sofreh*, a piece of cloth?"

Maman shook her head.

"Do you know where His Majesty sits?" Fereshteh asked me.

"I know he has a throne!"

"The Peacock Throne is set at the head of the hall, the sparkling jewels completely covering its body would, without a doubt, attract everybody's notice in the entire hall."

I imagined climbing its three small steps and sitting on it. But I then startled, and asked Allah for my forgiveness. I knew well this seat was reserved only for our king, and no woman could ever replace him. I covered my mouth.

Then Fereshteh talked about the gleaming globe, clothed in gems.

"Oceans are in turquoises ..."

"*Abi*, blue!"

"Shirin joon, and emeralds are for jungles."

"What gems are used for our homeland?"

"Rubies, my child! Our land shines like pomegranate seeds in the world."

She exclaimed, "This precious globe's laid on a gold stand, kept under a locked glass encasement."

I fancied everyone in the world was our king's prisoners, locked in a glass box.

Fereshteh put a sugar cube in her mouth, and mumbled, "Shirin joon, let me tell you about the rest." At this time, I could no longer ignore the jingling of her gold jewelry, which reminded me of Maman's empty hands.

There were days when Maman's hands had also jingled

like Fereshteh's. Not long after Baba's death, one day, she came back from the bazaar, her gold bracelet gone, and the next time her bangles disappeared. Just the other day, she came back without her wedding ring and band. Instead, she had bought a sack of rice, and a sheepskin full of cooking oil. She even sold some of the rugs from her dowry.

"This palace is surrounded by the lush, spacious garden filled with birds, especially nightingales, as if it were all created by Allah ..."

"This sounds like what Maman told me about her village, Shahriar!"

"Far from it!" Maman said.

"Where's the harem?" I asked.

"The harem is in the middle of the court, like a gem in a ring ..."

"Where's the *birooni*?"

"The quarter for men is at the outskirts of the same courtyard." Fereshteh looked into Maman's eyes. "Such a pity! If your parents had agreed to marry you off to Naser Al-Din Shah that day, we could come for a visit and see the Golestan Palace with our own eyes."

Maman diverted her gaze without a word.

I stared at her, realizing that if my mother had lived in the harem, she'd have silk dresses and jewelry much finer than Fereshteh's, and she wouldn't have to wear those old, dingy black clothes.

"Dear Allah!" I covered my mouth, as I gasped, "I could've been a princess."

"Well dear, I don't think so!" Maman muttered.

"Why not?"

"Because the king was killed in the mosque shortly after his eunuch came to our house."

"What did your father, Akbar khan, have to say?"

Fereshteh asked.

"I don't think my mother ever told him anything about it." Maman sounded tired. "She treated the episode as a nightmare that never happened."

Regardless of what Maman said, I still imagined myself as a princess running around in the garden full of colorful flowers and old trees, with the birds singing for me. I rushed to enter the birooni, but a guard stopped me. *"No girls allowed here."*

"When your mother was about your age, everyone was talking about her ravishing beauty."

"Obviously, it wasn't my destiny to end up in the palace. I'm thankful for whatever Allah wants for me," Maman Zahra sighed.

"Fereshteh khanoom, what else does the king have that we don't?" I said in wonderment.

"His Majesty even has electricity," Fereshteh said, adding to my awe.

"Are you telling me that the king, unlike his people, has no oil lamps?"

"Shirin joon, the king always lives ahead of his people," Maman Zahra commented through her teeth.

"Allah chooses our king and sends him to us. The king's destiny is to be our master," Fereshteh responded. "Allah is first, then our king." She raised her hands to the sky. She beseeched Him to keep our country and our king away from any evil eye. Fereshteh also appealed to Allah to bless Naser Al-Din Shah's soul, and concluded, "Long Live our Majesty, Ahmad Shah!"

"Amen!" For once, our voices came together.

"Everyone's life is in Allah's hands." Maman Zahra stated.

"So true, Zahra joon. Allah is great. He'll soon send

His grace toward you. Have no doubt." She turned to Maman. "Soon my afternoon prayer will lapse! I'm in search of some girls for Mehri khanoom to teach them how to read and write."

"Boys go to *mactab*, school, to learn, but not us!" I said, praying she might be considering me.

"Shirin joon, how old are you?" Fereshteh asked.

"I don't know exactly, for sure, seven or eight!" I felt embarrassed because I had no idea of my exact age. None of us knew.

"Perfect …"

"Girls learn how to read our holy book in Arabic, Allah's words, and that is enough," Maman said.

"Maman, we can only talk in Farsi."

"Fereshteh joon, tell me, what's the use of knowing how to read and write? A girl has to marry one day, anyhow," Maman asserted.

"Maman!" At this time, I took hold of the conversation and ran with it. "Fereshteh khanoom's right. It'd be a miracle if one day I could read and write."

"What's so good about that?" Maman said flatly.

After a pause, I picked up my enthusiasm, "Well then, I read and write your letters saving you lots of money. No need to go to Mullah Mashdi's stall!"

"She's right, you know." I read admiration for me in Fereshteh's eyes.

At last, Maman melted under her fiery words and agreed to think about sending me to Mehri khanoom's house the following week for some lessons.

¤ ¤ ¤

At night, the heat of the day gave way to the pleasant

breezes from Mount Alborz. I snuggled with Aziz Fatemeh on her mattress, spread out in the courtyard under the sky with its twinkling stars. "Aziz," I said, "Isn't Fereshteh khanoom really an angel, just like her name?"

"How so?"

"She brought me the best news. Soon, like boys, I'll learn to read and write!"

"A Moslim girl must follow her religious duties, obey her husband, and take care of her children—nothing else."

"Aziz!" Ignoring her words, I said, "This afternoon, when I heard the knock, as always I thought it was my father. I'm thrilled that it was really an angel who brought me a token of good news."

"My dear child," Aziz kissed my forehead and said in a soft voice, "maybe she was the real angel sent by your father from heaven. Let's get some sleep!"

My eyes fixed on the dark ocean of sky. For once, after a very long time, I felt my heart fill with joy. That night, the stars seemed closer to me. I reached to grab them, and I believed I did!

4. Sin

Tehran, Persia, 1918
Shirin (16)

Thursday afternoons belonged to *mordeha*, dead people.

I had to cut my lesson short with Fereshteh and go home early to look after my brother Hassan and sister Pari. According to our belief, on Thursday nights, Allah let the spirits of our dead relatives come down to earth. Maman Zahra and Aziz went to the cemetery. She had to show Baba she was still faithful to him.

Today on my way home, for the first time I stopped thinking about my veil. That our house was a hovel compared to Fereshteh's did not bother me. Maman's covering us with her invisible tapestry pretending we were rich burdened me no longer. I breathed in the delicious cool air of this fall afternoon and breathed out all my sorrows. The day was beautiful.

I remembered three springs ago when my teacher, Mehri khanoom, complained to Maman, "The older girls aren't allowed to sit beside the younger ones." She stared into my face when she continued, "We don't know what the older ones teach those innocent ones." Before Maman could open her mouth, Mehri khanoom went on with her pompous demeanor, "Zahra khanoom, why don't you marry off Shirin?"

Unlike the majority of my classmates, who were married at nine or ten, I had no suitor, so no marriage for me.

"No pretty girl, no husband," I kept hearing, in addition to, *"No dowry, no suitor!"* I wished our king had never brought the Russian soldiers to bomb our majlis and murder my father and the other protestors. Then, today he would have been alive, and for sure, I would have my dowry. But, *Thank Allah!* Fereshteh, like her name, was an angel to me. Ever since I was forbidden to go to mactab, she took me under her wing. Every day, she delivered to me fresh poems from the vast realm of our poetry. Whenever she read a new poem, from her smile, I knew it was as if she soared to heaven and took me with her. She was very proud of me when I could recite word for word from Khayyam's *Rubaiyat*, Firdowsi's Shahname, Sa'di's *Golestan*, and Rumi's *Masnavi*. I felt no particular closeness to any of them, but I was gratified that I was able to read. Fereshteh miraculously brought light to my eyes, as if I had been blind before. I was the only girl in my household, or even in our neighborhood, who could read and write. Maman was even pleased. She stopped going to Mashti's stall for her letters and I saved her many *shahi*, coins.

This morning Fereshteh introduced me to Hafiz. "The heart must cry," Fereshteh had read. "Even when the smallest drop of love is taken away ..." At that moment, I felt happiness filling my heart. The baggy black pants I wore under my long gray chador felt rough no more. To my amazement, the heavy weight of my chador had disappeared. I was at peace with the world. I knew Hafiz was in charge. I even believed he breathed into me a new soul. His poetry fired up a brazier in my chest. I touched my forehead, then my cheeks, looking for some fever. I knew I had chosen him as my master. How could I not? He had brought me heavenly joy.

"Shirin joon," Fereshteh's question of this morning echoed in my ears, "you really like Hafiz, don't you?"

"Hafiz knows what goes on in my heart," I confessed. "Such a shame that we have to cut our lesson short for today," I sighed.

When she read the tremendous disappointment in my face, she trusted me with her precious book, the collection of Hafiz's poetry, *Divan*.

This afternoon, I was pressing the book closer to my blossoming bosom. I stared at it as if Hafiz were with me. Its brick-red cover with its glittery calligraphy looked heavenly. I heard Hafiz whisper to me, "A blooming flower … growing … in a black forest …"

Then, I felt no pain in my feet from the old shoes I wore over the rocky path to our house. In no time, I found myself before our door. I pushed it open with my shoulder and hurried to our room, passing the guest room. It was empty and locked. Maman Zahra had had to sell off everything inside it. My Aladdin palace was full of air. Crossing the yard, up the stairs to the veranda, I turned left. The room was empty and the house was quiet. I felt a tickle. *More time for Hafiz*, I thought. No one was there, not even my sister Pari.

Pari and Hassan had to be at a neighbor's house. Unlike me, Pari had many friends. Only two springs younger than me, she was so different. Malleable Pari followed Maman and Aziz's footsteps. Without any push from them, she wore her scarf and chador over her black long hair. Like a sheep, she said her prayers five times a day, every day. So they gave her permission to go and see her friends. No one questioned her as long as she covered her head and took the Koran lessons from Aziz.

Maman kept saying, "She's my favorite daughter." And Aziz often repeated, "Shirin, unlike your name, you're not a sweet soul. Why can't you be more like Pari?"

In the room, I imagined that by then Maman and Aziz were in the cemetery where Maman could no longer resist the mullah's heckling. "*Khanoom jan*, want a wash?"

At last, she would take out a shahi from her knotted handkerchief, safeguarded in her bosom, and plead with him to pour a bucket of water over Baba's tombstone. But she could spare no more shahi for the mullah to send some prayers for Baba, Akbar khan's soul. Maman and Aziz had to do the prayers themselves.

"Khanoom," the mullah kept insisting. "Your prayers won't be answered like mine. I'm a man, closer to Allah."

I wondered, was this possible? Could Allah, the Almighty, the source of justice, really favor men over women?

Maman Zahra's image flashed again in my mind. With her back to the mullah, she would put her right hand on the stone, asking Allah to bless Baba's soul and murmuring fatehe.

I sat down, and spread out *Divan* and my notebooks on the floor and thanked Allah for leaving me alone with Hafiz. Laying down on my belly, I felt exuberant. My body on our rough-hued Kermani rug was awakened. I kicked my legs in the air when I opened my newly-bound notebook. It was one of my creations. I made this one with paper Maman Zahra had bought from the Mashdi's stall some time ago. By enfolding the long sheets, then slapping them with two cardboards at the front and back, I connected them with some packing threads. I set aside this notebook for Hafiz.

I opened *Divan* the way Fereshteh demonstrated for me this morning. I closed my eyes, made a wish, and opened the book to wherever my finger landed. My eyes gazed and I recited,

> *"The dream of you, like a morning breeze,*
> *Awaken me*
>
> …
>
> *Lying down beside you"*

"Shirin joon!" Fereshteh's voice from this morning interrupted me, "Even though his poems are all about love, wine, and beautiful women, Hafiz was quite a religious man. Amazingly, he could recite the entire Koran, from memory!"

With Hafiz melting sugar in my belly, I looked through his *Divan* again and began to recite.

> *"My beloved, your loveliness*
> *As a garden of roses*
>
> …
>
> *Come, come, and fill up my cup with your love"*

By Allah, I never knew a man of cloth could be so interested in flesh too. *Thank Allah*, as if Hafiz was right beside me and did not care that I was not pretty and had no rich father. I was spellbound; I had an urge to impress Hafiz. I closed my eyes, drew in all my passion, and with an even louder voice I continued,

> *"Wandering in desert alone,*
> *Hafiz's dreaming of*
> *Sitting by a river, under a weeping willow,*

49

Waiting for you,
My beloved, to pour wine
Into my chalice"

Satisfied, I closed my eyes. I felt my soul was united with Hafiz. I tasted happiness in my mouth as if I were under the willow, filling his cup!

Then, feeling intoxicated, I heard the door bang open.

Aziz ran toward me. Without any hesitation, she snatched the book from me and started shaking and pressing it to my face. I could not believe my eyes. My adoring Aziz had transformed into a *jinni* as if fumes of anger were gushing out of her nostrils. She erupted. "You're reading *love poetry* with dirty words! Shame on you!" Aziz was bombarding me with her words when I grabbed the book from her before she could tear it completely.

Dumbfounded, I protected my face with my hands against her strikes. She was pounding me with her hands, the same way she hammered the sugar cones into the sugar cubes. She grabbed my hair and screamed, "*Khake-allam-be-saret*, all the ashes of the world on your head."

There was no end to her strikes—each fell upon my body harder and harder. My tears rolled down. I was bewildered.

At last, I wiggled and twisted myself away from her. With *Divan* safe in my bosom, I leaped to the door and hurried out into the courtyard. Even under our willow tree, I could still hear her: "Allah, rescue me from all these sins! Where can we go? Death is the answer for a girl reading dirty words. Allah, come and take me away from this shameful girl."

I never knew that loving a holy man like Hafiz could be so very wrong!

□ □ □

Some footsteps awakened me. The *muezzin*, with his heavenly voice from the mosque, reminded us of the dusk prayers. Maman Zahra with Pari and Hassan walked into the yard. They saw me on the bare ground.

"Shirin joon! Why are you …?"

"Zahra, all the ashes of the world on *your* head!" Aziz jumped out of her room, stood on the veranda, and screamed, "You have no aberu anymore. Do you know what your daughter has done?"

I wished I could extinguish Aziz's fire. I was drowning in the sea of my disbelief.

"What is it?" Staring at my torn-up clothes, Maman asked, "What happened to your—"

"You idiot woman!" Aziz wailed while beating her chest with her fist. "Shirin has disgraced us all!"

I prayed and wished that Maman could dampen Aziz's fury.

"What has she done?" Maman asked. Without waiting for an explanation, she dropped her black chador. With her yellow face, she looked like an old woman. Maman crept to the stairs connecting the veranda to the courtyard and she sat there as if to keep herself from fainting. After a short pause, she raised her hands toward the sky moaning, "Allah, help us!"

"Yes! Allah better help us!" Aziz wagged her finger at me as if I had committed an unforgivable crime. "This afternoon, your daughter committed the most sinful act."

"What did she do?" Maman's voice blended into the sound of my thumping heart.

"I heard her reciting some lovers' poems."

"Oh, my Allah!" Maman hit herself on the head and

broke down on the ground, bursting into tears. "We have no dignity. We have a dirty daughter."

I didn't understand why reading Hafiz's poems and dreaming of his love was such a sin.

"See, this is what you get," Aziz said with exasperation. "How many times have I told you not to send her to Fereshteh khanoom?" She was too stormy to wait for an answer. "A dirty daughter—no way to clean her."

I was even more baffled when Maman accompanied Aziz: "Such a scandal! My daughter's ruined. Today she reads love poems—what will she do tomorrow? What a disgrace!"

These two women acted as if I had done an unimaginative deed with Hafiz—so unbelievable! I wanted to scream at them that reading Hafiz makes me feel good, but it was as if my tongue was cut off.

"You *must* put a stop to this!" Aziz wailed and stormed back inside her room.

I watched as Maman cried until the darkness covered the sky. I could only pray to Allah for His forgiveness.

Today at dawn, when I woke up for my morning prayers in Shahriar—Maman's and Aziz's birthplace—I marked my notebook out of habit to remind me of how many days I was stuck in this village. The marks had covered the entire notebook except for the last page. *Thank Allah*; I could hide my notebook under my chador when Grandma Aziz was busy packing. I wished I had *Divan* with me too. But I was scared. I did not want to see Aziz transform into a jinni again. The nightmare of our final night in Tehran returned to me.

That night, my last night in Tehran; the same night I read Hafiz. When Maman could cry no more, she called Pari and Hassan to dinner. They ate flat bread, goat cheese, and pieces of watermelon. From the veranda, I could see them by the light of lantern. Maman cracked open the watermelon with the kitchen knife and gave Hassan and Pari each a piece. I waited for her to call me in for my piece, but she didn't. I knew she must have been truly angry with me.

When everybody went to bed late that night, I tiptoed to our room. I could no longer stand the wet ground and cool air. I chose to put some distance between my bruised, swollen body and the rest of the family. I refused to sleep on the same mattress beside Aziz. I took my chador, spread it by the door, placed my beaten-up body motionless on one side, and shrouded myself with the other side.

"Zahra, you've got to do something," Aziz's whispers sharpened my ears.

"I don't know what."

"It's not good for a girl to read all these dirty words. They're Satan's commands. Shirin must read the Koran— Allah's words—not the words of a sinner!"

"She has no friends," Maman said in a shaky voice. "Almost all of the girls her age are married …"

"They even have some children too." Aziz moaned.

Maman then talked about our neighborhood matchmaker. "I've talked with Bagoum khanoom, over and over."

I knew it. Even Bagoum khanoom with all her wisdom refused to untie my ill-fated knot. I'd heard her tell Maman several times, "They're all prettier than her, all at a ripe age—nine or ten—and with dowries."

I felt the same stubborn knot rise in my throat, just as it did when I heard Bagoum tell my mother, in her vulgar voice, "Well, obviously Allah was in a rush to create Shirin!"

When it came to my looks, even my own mother forgot her kind heart. Maman referred to me as her doll, with two black dots for eyes on a plump face.

"I'm so sorry that my daughter with her hefty body has put an enormous burden on your shoulders," Maman apologized to Bagoum khanoom.

"Allah threw two eyes on a dough face with two puffy cheeks," Bagoum khanoom said. "The Almighty then slammed a short wide nose in the middle of her face, dropped a thick, dark kinky rag on her head for hair, and sent her here to us. Zahra khanoom, do you want *me* to find her a *husband*? And then, what am I answering when the suitors' mothers drill me about her dowry?"

To interrupt my thoughts and settle the conflict in my heart, I raised my hands toward the sky, beseeching to Allah. He understood my stormy heart. He was my master and I had no choice but to obey His will.

Regardless of whatever Maman thought of me, I admired her. Like a hen, she was protecting her children under her wings in a flimsy nest. This hen resisted the pressure of Aziz's thumb pressing on her to remarry. Bagoum had assured Aziz and my mother over and over. With Maman's milky skin, her beautiful face like a full moon, and her slim figure, even after giving three births, Bagoum would have no trouble finding a new husband for her.

Men wanted to marry beautiful girls! No wonder the king's eunuch, Saam, wanted her for our king, Naser Al-Din Shah. I dreaded, however, the day when Maman would remarry, and a stepfather would be the one to feed and clothe us. Then, for sure, he would believe he owned us. No wonder Maman kept weaving her invisible tapestry and hiding our misfortune behind it. She did not want us to feel obligated toward anyone. We, the three orphans, could never have another father. I wondered whether our king understood that when my father was killed alongside the other demonstrators, we—Maman, Aziz, Pari, Hassan, and I—were dead with him too.

"We can send Shirin to Shahriar," Aziz's angry voice came to me again from the last night in Tehran. "We can send her to your aunt Zinat to find a husband for her. In Shahriar, people still remember your father, Akbar khan, the landowner."

When Maman broke the news to Aziz that, unlike me, Pari had some suitors, Aziz sizzled. "No, no! Oh! My Allah! You *can't possibly* marry off the younger sister before the older one. What would people say?"

No explanation was given to Pari or me when, the next day, right after the dawn prayers, Aziz wanted us to pack our knapsacks and leave for *dahat*, the village, with her.

Thank Allah, Maman had sent Pari with me.

◻ ◻ ◻

Life in Shahriar was unbearable. I was far from my beloved Hafiz. My heart was a dark house with no light. I saw myself like one of Aunt Zinat's cows, whose invisible leash chained her down to this dahat. I hated the smell of manure mixed in with dirt and dust. I detested my closeness to nature and my distance from Hafiz. At night, when everyone went to sleep, I wept for Hafiz. I became Laily, the fictitious beloved who was cut off from her lover, Majnoon. Their separation killed them both.

Today, after I finished my chores, when the sun strutted to the middle of the sky, I felt my chest growing smaller and smaller. It had no room for my heart anymore. I reached out to Pari. I wanted to open my heart to her, so I went to her and whispered, "Let's sneak to the barn, I want to have a word with you."

"What now?" She rolled her eyes and followed me to the barn. It felt like her stomping was crushing my chest.

The cool, quiet barn sheltered us. Before we even had a chance to lie down on a stack of hay, the door screeched open halfway. The sunlight poured into the barn and brought a male silhouette into sight. We narrowed our eyes, tilted our heads, but to no avail. Neither one of us could tell who he was. His huge, staring black eyes scared me the most. He closed the door behind him and toddled toward Pari and me. My thumping heart raced so fast I thought it would jump out of my chest, when a storm of thoughts hit me. Allah, this boy should not have snuck up on us like this—to be alone with two girls. What if a grownup opened the door and saw us with him! In my heart, I asked for Allah's help. I grabbed my knees to prevent them from shaking like willow trees caught in an angry storm. I hid my fear and like a lioness, I roared, "Hey, you! Why did you close the door?"

The boy dared turn a deaf ear to me. Instead, in Shahriari twang, he said, "I'm Mohammad."

When I saw his face under the beam of light coming through the ceiling, I disliked his clownish smile.

"Shush! I'm aware of why you've come here!" Before either of us could reply, he continued, "You came here to marry. Which one of you wants me to send my mother to your uncle's house for *khastegari*?"

From his short sprouted beard, I gathered he had to be fifteen or sixteen, the right age for taking a wife. But I could not believe how harebrained he was. I couldn't believe this peasant boy would even think of marrying a city girl like one of us. I turned my back to him to avoid his face. Yet his odor of dirt and sweat filled the room. His shoeless feet, black baggy pants, torn, droopy shirt, long nose, and his dusty hair and face loomed in my mind. His stench practically shouted that he was a peasant. At last, Pari broke the silence. "You're that plowboy! You work for our uncle Mohsen!"

"Yes! A wonderful husband for either of you," he boasted.

I refused to stand still and listen to this farm boy's insults any longer. I couldn't abide hearing a boy as ill-bred as he was contemplating a marriage with either of us. *What a daring wish!* However, a Moslim man was allowed to marry up to four women at the same time, but he was forbidden from marrying two sisters at once. He also had to divorce one before marrying the other. I had absolutely no interest in this bovine boy, but for some reason, in my confusion and in my desire to punish him, I ran right at him. He was much taller than he had initially appeared. I backed up a few steps. He and Pari were now engaged in a conversation. Their words sounded like two bumbling bees.

I ran to the other side of the barn where I had left the wooden stool after milking the cows earlier that day. I picked it up, rushed back, nailed it down right before him and, like a ball of fire, jumped on it. I put all my strength into my hand when I slapped him, and said, "Here! This is what a peasant deserves to have!"

As I climbed down, I could see the marks of my chubby fingers on the boy's face. No one said a word. I felt the air in the barn getting thicker, almost unbearable to breathe. As if I were in the bottom of a well, I struggled, beseeching Allah for some air. At last, with my head down I leaped to the door, opened it, and as I threw out myself into the fresh air, I heard Mohammad groaning, "Unlike your name, you're not sweet at all, *Shirin* khanoom!"

That night, no sleep came to my eyes. I was frightened.

I had acted like a man and had hit a boy! I had no idea what I would do if he or his mother came to complain. I had lost all my chances of finding a suitor in this village.

The same night, when everyone fell asleep, I climbed down from the roof on our shaky ladder and tiptoed to Aunt Zinat's room in search of my notebook. Then I made my way to the courtyard and sat under the moonlight where I wrote to Maman all that I had wanted to reveal to Pari earlier. I remained there for the rest of the night listening to the crickets.

At dawn, when everyone woke up to the muezzin's voice from the top of the minarets of the nearby mosque, my plea to Maman was tucked into my bosom. I stood up toward Mecca. Instead of saying my prayers, I repeated what I had written to Maman the night before.

"This life in Shahriar is choking me, and I'm almost on my last breath. Come and rescue me, or soon you'll end up with no Shirin at all. I have no idea how long I can live here." I knew that if my mother refused to take me back to Tehran, I could end my life and become one with my Hafiz. Suddenly, however, the thought of killing myself startled me. I had dared to let the notion of committing suicide enter my head! *Allah, forgive me!*

Later on that morning, rather than milking the cows, I asked Aunt Zinat if I could help her instead. We had to prepare some sacks of flour and grains to send to Tehran for Aziz and Maman. At one moment, when no one looked, I shoved my note into one of the sacks and sealed it.

It seemed an eternity until the letter from Tehran arrived. Maman demanded that we return at once. Aunt Zinat asked me with bewildered eyes if I knew why my mother had changed her mind. My lips were sealed. I shrugged before leaving the room.

Pari made my return to Tehran take much longer. She

kept repeating how much she enjoyed life here, how much she didn't want to go back home. I had to wait even longer until Maman and Aziz granted Pari permission to stay in the village.

The day I left Shahriar with Uncle Mohsen, I considered myself one of the happiest maidens in the entire world.

5. Wedding

Tehran, Persia, 1922
Shirin (20)

On my way to my tutor Fereshteh's house, I praised her for opening my eyes to all the Persian poets, especially my beloved Hafiz. As I walked through the ancient gates of the bazaar, I remembered Scheherazade and her story. She must have been Allah's favorite. According to Aziz, the sultan had cut off many girls' heads. It was not Scheherazade's fate to be like them. She entertained the sultan with her stories for one thousand nights. *Such a lucky girl*, at the end, the sultan even married her. I wondered whether a girl could be blessed as much as she!

Today, Maman permitted me to go to Fereshteh's all by myself—very odd! I had been under house arrest since I came back from Shahriar two springs ago.

"Shirin joon, why don't you go to Fereshteh khanoom's house today?" Maman had said.

"Maman, are you coming with me?"

She shook her head.

Thrilled at being released from my cell, I jumped to grab my old, faded chador.

"Take my black one," Maman instructed. "Fereshteh khanoom doesn't need to know we're poor."

As I stepped out she called after me, "Stay there until Hassan comes to fetch you."

Soon, the glorious bazaar with its smell of spices and its few beams of light from the roof lured me in. I approached the second corner and closed my eyes as if the gold jewelry had blinded me. These hanging ornaments had covered the walls of stall after stall. I gazed at two women hovering around one of the stalls, bargaining over the price of a necklace. The shopkeeper picked it up, "Khanoom, you'll never find any necklace as genuine as this one!"

I had to raise my face to the sky to prevent the necklace's sparks from hurting my eyes. I knew. Tala, gold, was a forbidden fruit for me and my family, like the apple for Adam. I picked up my pace, determined not to be tempted by its wooing.

As an obedient Moslim maiden covered in chador, I continued my walk with my head down, staring at my feet, being certain not to make an eye contact with any man.

After a long curve, I left the bazaar behind and entered a street called Bagh-e-shah, the king's garden. This street belonged to the wealthy people. The sycamore trees on each side guarded the pricy houses, and at this time of the year, the sound of their coppery yellow leaves crunching under my feet was delightful. The street was quiet, and the houses looked as remote as their residents.

On this street, I looked for evidence of any changes since our new king had come to power. Some of us believed that with the help of some of our soldiers, Reza khan, a military man, overthrew the last king of the Qajar Dynasty and had established the Pahlavi Dynasty. Some others, however, believed that our majlis voted that he be our king.

I wondered which group was right. *Thank Allah*, we did not hear any girls lost their fathers in this major change.

This new king was supposed to be the best for our country. But so far, I could not pinpoint any improvement. The bazaar was the same; Bagh-e-shah was the same, and all the roads were muddy because of the earlier rain. I still had to struggle with my chador. I wished to be as tall as Maman so the chador would stop at my ankles and never touch the grubby roads. At last, I pulled both sides up to my waist, gathered them together, and held them under my right arm.

Then, I noticed. I saw more young girls wearing only scarves to cover their heads and fewer women behind their *pichehs*, veils. Perhaps this new king would make a better life for all of us after all.

At the end of the street, the familiar poplar, walnut, and fig trees raised their heads out of Fereshteh's yard and wooed me into her house. Her husband was a wealthy hajji. Almost half of the stalls in the bazaar belonged to him. Fereshteh must have been lucky to have married such a rich man.

I remembered—when Fereshteh could bear no child for her husband, he wedded Zobaydeh. The new bride was Fereshteh's *havoo*, her co-wife. Zobaydeh gave birth to several boys and girls and they all lived together in this house. Hajji was pleased. His name and wealth were preserved. "Zobaydeh's been a good havoo for me," Fereshteh repeated. "Thank Allah. She respects and treats me politely."

I wondered if I had a havoo, *I* would be happy! It was up to Allah. If He wanted me to have one or more, I'd have to live with them. It was not so bad that I wasn't pretty. After all, Allah was great.

I stopped before the massive wooden door, grasped the

heavy iron knocker, and rapped. A boy-servant opened it.

"Is Fereshteh khanoom home? I'm Shirin!"

He led me through the courtyard, passing the quarter for men, and through their beautiful garden. I sank into the past, when Fereshteh used to give me private lessons.

As soon as the weather warmed up, we used to come to the balcony overlooking this majestic garden. Very often, we sat on a blanket, looking down to the garden where the cherry orchard, the rose garden, and lush, green weeping willows were our visual feast. "Oh," we sighed together as we breathed in those sweet cherry and plum blossoms while we recited poetry. Every single poem reminded me of this garden, as if each poet had lived here.

I even imagined all of the poets gathered under the weeping willows, dancing and laughing while their beautiful female cupbearer glided to fill their chalices. I imagined the poets living in an everlasting bliss.

In an instant, I shook away these old thoughts. In reality, each poet lived in a different century and they had never known each other.

Today, on this cloudy fall afternoon, I gazed at the bare trees. They were stuck in the muddy yard. No flowers, no birds, not even a nightingale. The garden was naked, and all its beauty had melted away.

The servant stopped before a hallway and led me to the quarter for women and children. I walked the short dark corridor and knocked at Fereshteh's room.

"Come in," she said.

As I entered, I saw her seated on a cushion with her back against a poshti. The smoke of tobacco from her hooka filled the room. The old rich women, just like their men, smoked water pipes, *ghalyan* at least twice a day—mornings and afternoons.

Fereshteh's delightful voice called, "My dear Shirin, it's

wonderful to see you, my child! Come, come, and sit by
me!" Joyful Fereshteh pointed at the cushion next to her.
I rushed to her and we hugged and kissed. Fereshteh's
appearance gave me quite a shock. I saw the footprints
of the years on her face. Her peachy skin was replaced
by wrinkles that reminded me of the cracked roads in
Shahriar. Her hair, parted in front, carried tremendous
white strands. The years had replaced her well-shaped
figure with a much heavier body. Her coarse voice carried
many years in it. All the same, Fereshteh was still the angel
who had cultivated me.

We talked about the past, about my life in Shahriar—
from milking the cows and feeding the chickens, to
cleaning up around the house.

"I can't tell you how much I despised my life there!"

"Of course dear, you're a city girl." The ghalyan's
bubble trumpeted joy in my ears.

I didn't tell her that I hated the village so much that I
had a thought of killing myself to escape it.

"Fereshteh khanoom, Pari's a married woman now!"

"Did you go to the wedding?"

I shook my head. "Even Aziz wasn't there."

"Your grandma must have been upset." She took a puff.
"A younger sister marries before the older one!"

At this time, one of her maids, Jamileh, walked in with
a tiny tray. Her jangling skirt reminded me of our helper
from long ago. Jamileh put down the dainty glass of tea,
a sugar bowl, and a dish of grapes before me. She didn't
serve me tea in their gold tea set. Apparently, my mother's
tapestry pretending we were rich had really come down.
They were aware that my family and I were destitute.

Jamileh jingled to the other side of the room and
kindled the hurricane lamps, one after another. She was
extra careful with two tulip glass candlesticks sitting at

each side of an oval mirror. As a custom, her husband had bought them for Fereshteh at the time of their wedding.

When my curiosity boiled over, I asked, "Fereshteh khanoom, can I borrow Jamileh?!" Fereshteh's eyes met mine when I continued, "To come with me to my house! We won't be too long! Please!"

"Why?"

"It's been strange. Maman allowed me to come here alone and not to go home until Hassan comes to fetch me."

"That *is* strange!" She took another puff from her ghalyan.

Fereshteh's quietness gave me more courage. "Please! It's getting dark, and I'm not supposed to be alone on the streets."

"Jamileh!" Fereshteh called.

◻ ◻ ◻

Jamileh and I took off like two arrows released from the bows. As soon as we arrived, a ray of light from our family room attracted me. As we climbed the stairs, I took off my shoes and instructed Jamileh to do the same. We tiptoed to the veranda. The door to the room was closed. I yearned to open it when I heard a strange male voice among more familiar voices. Curiosity conquered me. I stuck my ear to the door. No use! Hopeless, I looked around and stared at the so-called good-for-nothing tree. After a short pause, I dropped my chador, grabbed the trunk and climbed the tree.

"Khanoom, what …" Jamileh, also being from my family's village, whispered in her Shahriari twang, staring at me with wide eyes. She couldn't believe a girl was climbing a tree.

"Shush, Jamileh!"

In no time, like a snake, I moved up the bough toward the room. I refused to pay attention to my burning hands and legs—the tree had scraped them. At last, I sat on one of the higher branches and hugged the trunk as if I were a tiger eyeing my prey. *Praise Allah*, I was on top of the world. The window was open, and the room was well-lit by several lanterns and oil lamps. I could see and hear everything.

The stranger had occupied the cushion at the top of the room. *Very odd*, I thought. This seat was always reserved for my grandmother, Aziz, as the oldest family member. Tonight, she was sitting to his left. On his right side, I caught sight of Uncle Mohsen, and next to him, I saw Cousin Taghi. Maman sat directly in front of the stranger. All of them looked as if this man was their master. By the door, there was yet another strange man kneeling down while holding the nobleman's cane and black hat, which looked very similar to a coronet.

Allah, what are these well dressed men doing in our home? I wondered.

My eyes caught the man's shimmery, fine frock coat, which covered most of his slim figure. His bone colored shirt looked new and fresh. His salt and pepper hair added to his dignity—very becoming. His olive skin with some distinctive wrinkles on his forehead gave him a mature look. He seemed to be the oldest one in the room. I wondered, *what's a noble man doing in our house?*

"Zahra khanoom!" The stranger's voice like a knife cut through me and his bold eyes fixed on Maman. "I have a close relation to our benevolent king, Naser Al-Din Shah!"

"Allah bless his soul!" everyone murmured.

I screamed inside my head, *Oh Allah*, he was in fact royalty. A prince in our hovel, *unbelievable!*

I crawled closer to the window and poured all my strength into my ears, and eyes. "If it weren't because of this starved soldier, Reza khan," the man stared into Maman's face and continued with a softer voice, yet with anger beneath it, "calling himself, 'the king of Persia', I could have done much better now."

"What about your children?" Uncle Mohsen asked.

My uncle wanted to grasp the stranger's attention away from Maman. A Moslim man had to refrain from staring into a woman's face, even though she was covered by her chador. The stranger was an uncanny man! He had to be Maman's suitor!

"It was very unfortunate that," the man turned to Uncle Mohsen, "my beloved wife died some time ago. Both of my children live with their maternal grandmother."

"Will they live with you after the wedding?" Maman asked like a maid.

"My daughter, Sima, is about the same age as your older daughter." With this line, he reached inside his coat, took out some paper money, and put it in the middle of the circle. It looked not much.

It was customary that the groom had to pay for the wedding expenses, not to give cash. Perhaps, because of Maman being a widow, he paid cash instead.

"This is all I can afford." The stranger's voice broke my thoughts. "You decide what to do with it," the nobleman said in a forceful voice. "As you are aware, I don't expect any dowry, and I will take good care of you and your son." With these words, the gentleman got up and so did everyone else. His servant rushed to him and handed him his hat and cane. When he put his hat on, he raised his head and looked up in my direction. I felt his sharp eyes pierce my heart. *Allah*, I wondered if he had seen me.

"You already know everything about me," the man said and turned to Uncle Mohsen.

"Yes, Bagoum khanoom admires you a lot!" Uncle

Mohsen lowered his head, as if he was bowing to this royal man.

"There is no reason to delay the wedding. A week from today ..."

I never heard the end. I jumped down, picked up my chador from the ground, and Jamileh and I ran like two foxes being chased by a shepherd. While putting my thin shoes on, I covered myself one more time so that no neighbors could recognize me. We dashed all the way to Fereshteh's house.

"Thank Allah!" I gasped for breath and said, "At last, Maman has been bent under constant pressures from Aziz and Bagoum khanoom. By this time next week, she'll be a married woman."

¤ ¤ ¤

The next day at dawn, the sunless sky and thick clouds gave me chills as I washed the breakfast dishes by the pond, occupied by the thought of my future stepfather. I wondered if he would be kind to Hassan and me.

"Shirin joon, how are you?" Bagoum khanoom, as had been her habit the last few weeks, walked into our yard. After spending a long time with Maman and Aziz behind closed doors, she came to the veranda. "Shirin joon, leave the dishes alone and come inside."

I entered the room. Aziz's warm voice and her face, free of any signs of anger, put me at ease. She pointed at the cushion next to her. "Here, dear! Sit down by me."

"A noble man came to your house last night!" Bagoum khanoom started.

"To marry Maman," I grinned.

"How do you know that?" Maman turned to me.

"No!" Bagoum khanoom's eyes made me swallow the knot in my throat. "Ali khan is *your* suitor!"

"*Mine!*"

"Yes! Your family is very pleased." Bagoum khanoom, with her peasant twang, said, "He's a marvelous man. Your wedding is a week from today."

I shivered as if my mind had shut down. For me, the world sank into darkness. I could no longer think straight—it was as if I had turned into a stone. I wished the earth would open up and swallow me. In the past, over and over, I prayed to Allah to send me a husband, but not an old man like Ali who looked even older than Uncle Mohsen and needed a cane to walk.

"His face shows he's a genuine aristocrat!" Aziz's chatter pulled me and Maman's and the matchmaker's attention followed.

"Everyone can tell his glory by a glance." Bagoum khanoom shoved her henna-hair under her rainbow scarf. "He's pleased that Shirin joon can read and write!"

"He can have any girl he wishes," Maman murmured.

"He could even have you as *sigheh*!" Bagoum khanoom blared in my ears.

I knew. Sigheh was a marriage with a time limit, and usually men would not sigheh with a virgin girl.

"Thank Allah!" Maman said. "Ali khan wants to have you as his lawful wife."

According to Islam, a man was allowed to sigheh as many women as he wanted. To our eyes, a woman who had agreed to be sigheh was not a lady. Above all, any children that resulted from this kind of marriage were illegitimate.

"Ali khan could've married several girls if he wanted to," Bagoum khanoom interrupted my confused thoughts. "He didn't even marry right away after his wife's death.

He looked into his children's upbringing!"

Their chatter about Ali khan flew to my ears like lost birds from all over the room. I was under attack and in distress. Each woman wanted to upgrade Ali khan more than the other. At last, I lost my patience when I could no longer swallow my words. "But …"

I then took a deep breath. When the room filled with thick silence, I dared to contradict the older women and said, "He's too old!" The words came out of my mouth as if I were in pain.

"Nonsense!" Aziz thundered.

"Listen dear," Maman exploded, "*You're* old. You should've been married at age nine like most of the girls, not this late, at twenty, more than twice that!"

"It's so unfortunate," Bagoum khanoom started again, "Ali khan lost most of his wealth!"

"Allah knows!" Maman conceded, "This house is in desperate need of a master, no doubt!"

I lingered on Maman's words. I wanted to ask, "Maman, what're you saying?" But, I swallowed my words. I yearned to speak out; instead I kept my mouth shut to prevent my stormy stomach from jumping out of my throat.

"Lucky you!" Bagoum khanoom's words hammered my head again. "You don't have to live with his parents, or have a few havoo to live with, unlike every other girl in this land!"

"He and his servant will be moving in with us after the wedding!" Maman announced.

I wondered whether Maman knew her invisible tapestry was all washed off. *We will have no dignity before our friends and neighbors. "Zahra khanoom's son-in-law moved into her house, so ridiculous!"* I could hear them whispering.

"When is the wedding?" I forced myself to ask.

"Next Friday and …" Maman began.

"We must hurry before you get even older," Aziz interrupted her.

"Ali khan's been talking with us, through Bagoum khanoom, for a long time." Maman stared into my face.

I recalled. Every day, she came to our house and the three of them talked behind the closed door for a long time. Whenever I walked in, they stopped talking and Aziz counted her holy beads faster and faster repeating "Allaho Akbar!" I kept myself busy with Hafiz. He was the only man who could make me feel happy and put me at the urge of finding a perfect lover. Besides, as a girl, I was the last person to know about my matrimony, thanks to our tradition.

I had no idea why no one from Ali's side—his mother or his sisters—came to our house. Customarily, our marriages were arranged. By traveling through the different neighborhoods, Bagoum khanoom, with her owl eyes, could locate a suitable bride for a son whose mother had instructed her. Then, she arranged for his mother, older sisters, and aunts to go to the girl's house for wooing her family into marrying their son. When the female guests were sitting in the room, the future bride would bring them tea without covering her head.

In an instant, a family's guestroom could transform itself into a market where buyers had come to purchase a cow. As the girl offered them tea one by one, she was close enough so that each relative could see whether or not this cow was worth buying. She had to be pretty or have a rich father. In some cases, the women even looked into the girl's mouth to see if she had a healthy set of teeth.

Upon their return, for days, the women contemplated whether or not the girl was worthy of further pursuit, and if she was worthy of Allah's blessing to have many healthy children. If they all agreed that she was a valuable commodity for their son, they would send the future groom's father, older brothers, and uncles to negotiate the money, which was called *mehrieh*. At the time of the ceremony, the groom gave his words on agreed-upon sum to the bride's family in case of a future divorce. Another task of one of the groom's male relatives was to find out how much the bride's dowry was worth. At last, when the bargaining was over, they were ready to set a date for the ceremony.

"Every girl has to get married sooner or later," Aziz's words crashed over my head, "and in your case, sooner is preferable!" She clutched her beads repeating, "Allaho Akbar."

"Besides," Maman said, "Uncle Mohsen already agreed to give you away to Ali khan."

Her words tormented me. I wished to burst out crying and to beat my chest with my fist until I collapsed. Instead, I did nothing. I opened my mouth, but no words came out. I believed something had blocked my throat. I had no voice. I understood. A girl without a father was like a body without a spine. I brought my head down and wondered if my life would have been different had my father been alive.

The sad part was that the girl's or even the boy's approval was never solicited in this transaction. The man closest to the girl is in charge of choosing the best suitor for her—in my case, that was Uncle Mohsen.

"Without further delay, let's start the preparation for *aghd*, the ceremony," Aziz announced, turning to me. "You'll have my blessing."

I was their lamb. They would sacrifice me with or without my will. I knew.

¤ ¤ ¤

The following few days, our house changed its face. Maman, with the help of Bagoum khanoom, opened the doors to the other four locked-up rooms. They rented rugs, cushions, and poshti, back cushions. The helpers from Shahriar cleaned the house as if they were getting ready for our new year, Nowruz. Uncle Mohsen arranged for the delivery of arrays of colorful fruits and vegetables. If I had been born into a wealthy family, my uncle would have brought a sheep to kill, not just a few legs of lamb and some chickens.

The seven hens detained in a long wicker cage took my attention. They were placed in the courtyard beside the kitchen. They had no idea about their fate. These tied-up creatures could only poke their heads in and out of the holes, trying to free themselves. The scene was unbearable for me to watch. I had to resist my urge to open the cage and free them.

Two days before the wedding, most of our relatives from Shahriar came, including Pari. She, as a young married woman, was in charge of cracking open the mystery box of the first night's nuptials for me.

"Shirin joon, do you know who my husband is?" Pari giggled.

"He's one of Uncle Mohsen's farmers—we heard."

"His name's Mohammad!"

"So?"

"He's the same boy who came to the barn the day you and I were there. After you left, he and I saw each other secretly. It was because of him that I didn't want to return to Tehran!"

"I sensed there must have been something holding you to that village. Why didn't he come with you?"

"Well, he said his cheek's still burning!"

73

We both laughed as if we were two doves, surging to the sky.

In one way, I was happy that my fate was not to marry a peasant. On the other hand, I did not feel happiness in my heart when I thought of Ali as my husband.

"See, Shirin joon, you're a very lucky girl," Pari pointed out. "Ali khan doesn't have any family members to sniff around you, and he'll be moving here."

"You're calling me lucky? How many times have *you* heard of a groom moving in with the bride's family?"

"Yes!" Pari's smile, like the sun, dipped into the clouds when she said, "It's not easy to live with in-laws." After a pause, she continued, "Mohammad's mother controls his income and I'm not trusted with any money. Even when I'm hungry, I have to wait until the meal's served."

"Pari joon, how can you tolerate it?"

"Every day, I do my duties—I sweep the floor, wash the dishes, and take the dirty clothes to the river to wash."

"Allah bless you!"

"I do all that for the nights when Mohammad comes and lay down beside me. I feel good having him next to me."

"Like reading Hafiz's poetry?"

"Who is he?"

I had forgotten Pari's eyes were never open to Hafiz's poetry. So I asked, "Are you happy?"

"Shirin joon! Happy or not, it's Allah's will. My wedding night was a nightmare …"

"Is this about the bloody handkerchief?" I asked and Pari nodded.

"After all the guests went home, Mohammad and I were left alone in the room. As the tradition permits, his mother and three of his oldest sisters stayed behind the closed door.

They had to see the proof of my purity with their own eyes." Pari then lowered her head and covered her face with her scarf so I could see her red face no more. "They had to see the 'bloody handkerchief'," she confessed.

"Was it painful?" I whispered.

"I would have been happier if Mohammad had killed me. I laid there like a corpse, waiting for him to take over me."

"I've heard an obedient wife must let her husband do whatever he desires."

"Yes, of course! But hearing the murmurings and mutterings of these women, like bees in the beehives, was even more unbearable and ..."

Our conversation stayed unfinished when Bagoum khanoom brought Effat khanoom to the room to make me look like a married woman.

I sat with my legs crossed before her and stared out the glass window that faced our courtyard. The tradition of removing the girl's facial hair before her matrimony was to set her apart from the unmarried girls. This would make it easy for a matchmaker, like Bagoum khanoom, to distinguish her on the street, or in the neighborhood bath house.

I saw this process done to many girls. It was similar to men's shaving, except instead of a blade, a thread as thin as a wisp of hair was used.

Effat khanoom twisted a piece of thread around her fingers. "With the name of Allah!" She reached to my face and put the thread on my chaste skin and started from my forehead. She put one side of the thread into her mouth and circled the other side around her fingers. She moved her head and hands at the same time pulling out several hair strands from my face as if she were in the garden weeding. At last, when I could bear no more pain, tears rolled to my cheeks. Effat khanoom turned a blind eye.

I then decided to focus on the events in our courtyard. A male helper took a hen out of the cage by its wings and stuck its head into a bowl of water. Like a master, he laid her down on the ground, positioned his feet on her legs, held her head up with one hand, and with a butcher knife cut it off. The blood erupted and covered the ground. He stayed motionless for a few moments, and then he went for the second one. The hen, with her head somewhat still attached to her neck, flapped and flapped until she could flap no more. A maid came out of the kitchen, picked the hen up, and plunged her into the boiling water. By holding the chicken's legs, she brought the hen up while a victorious smile covered her face. The hen's naked body was revealed to the whole world. As part of her duty, she pulled out the hen's feathers one by one. I thought the hen was lucky. She was dead and could feel no pain.

"My bride, Shirin joon!" Effat khanoom finally said with a smile. "The pain gets less and less over the years. You won't even feel anything at all after a few years. You'll get used to it, don't worry."

She shaped my eyebrows into two perfect arcs tending my eyes. I despised the whole custom, but I did not fight. I had to keep up with it for the rest of my life.

ㅁ ㅁ ㅁ

On the wedding day, right after the morning prayers, Bagoum khanoom and Pari accompanied me to the nearest public bath. "*Hammam*—For Women Only," the sign read. I took pride that I was the only woman among us who could read. We walked into a foggy, spacious room. A few women congregated around the steaming bathing-pool in the middle. Some were washing their long black hair while others were dipping their soapy bodies into the murky water. Yet a few were busy drying their children— many girls and a few young boys.

A *dallak*, a washer, approached us. "Ladies, need a wash?"

"Oh, yes!" Bagoum khanoom replied grinning. "Today, I have a bride with me!" She pointed me out to the washer.

"Why isn't the bride happy?"

I wondered. A dallak who just met me could see my sorrow right away. How could Maman and Aziz fail to see it!

"Let me tell you about the groom," Bagoum khanoom circled in. "He's a nobleman from the Qajar Dynasty!"

"Is that right? These days it's no good to be from that dynasty!" the dallak muttered while she put henna on my fingers and toenails, before she began to polish my entire body with her linsey-woolsey, as if she were Mashdi in the bazaar, in charge of whitening our sooty pots and pans.

"Where are his relatives?" the washer asked.

"Well, his parents passed away a long time ago!" Bagoum khanoom lowered her voice. "Ali khan has cut off all ties with his relatives, even with his siblings. One of his brothers is our king's *hakim* …"

"Bagoum khanoom," I had to correct her, "you mean a 'doctor'!" I rolled my eyes. She still used the old words.

"In reality, he hates them all. He calls them traitors and vultures." Bagoum khanoom's words jarred me.

"Really!" the dallak said, busy washing me.

"Yes! As their oldest brother, Ali khan disowned them all. Now he wants to have a family of his own, far from the *vultures!*"

The dallak took me behind a curtain. "Lie down on your back here." She pointed to a platform and brought a gooey paste with a foul smell. She applied it to my legs, under arms, and pubic hair. When I frowned, she said, "Listen, if you want to keep your husband, you must have a body as smooth as a baby's skin. Men don't put up with hairy women! I'll be back." She left me there alone.

I kept biting my lips. *Why can't a man, my husband, accept me the way I am?* I closed my eyes and imagined that Allah had planted me in a wealthy family. The previous dynasty, Qajar was still in power. My suitor, Ali khan, was a young nobleman. He had asked my father for my hand in marriage. On the day of my wedding, my family took over the entire bathhouse. Many young women from both families brought me here to accomplish this cleansing ritual. The sound of *mobarakbad*, congratulations, filled the house, bouncing off the fresh clear water in the pool. I could easily see the blue tiles covering the bottom of the bathing-pool. When it was lunchtime, several male servants each would carry on his head a *tabagh*, huge tray, full of food to feed not only the family members, but also everyone who was there that day. The aroma of rose water and the color of saffron would make every woman pray to Allah for the bride to give birth to many boys. Then it would be impossible for a dallak to see any sorrow in the bride's face.

At last, the washer returned to wash me with soap and a soft cloth.

After I finished getting dressed, Pari shook my shoulder. "Time to go!"

I understood. I had to follow everyone like a sheep!

¤ ¤ ¤

At last, the time to sacrifice the lamb arrived. As I was slipping my white dress on, I felt close to the sheep at the time of her immolation. At least that tongue-tied creature could protest with a few bleating sounds as she was pulled to the altar, but not me. I did not have even that much voice.

"My dear Shirin." Maman walked in. "Thank Allah! Our long wait is over. Allah answered our prayers and you're getting married!" She then concealed me with the new white chador from head to toe. "Come out of your marriage only when this chador covers you as your shroud."

Shy of wearing makeup for the first time, I gazed at the floor. "Look at me!"

Maman raised my chin, "Your made-up eyes with charcoal are very becoming. You're presentable."

"No bushy eyebrows or pockmarks—they're all trimmed and filled," I said through my teeth.

At this time, she left me with Pari and some other young women to guide me to the other room for the ceremony. The divorcees, like Bagoum khanoom, or widows like Maman and Aziz, were not allowed to be in the same room with me during aghd, the wedding ceremony. According to our beliefs, these women could transfer their unfortunate luck to the bride.

"Shirin joon, you're as beautiful as a hoori …" Pari said.

An angel! Such a false comparison, I knew.

"Your unbraided, wavy black hair is a perfect frame for your face."

"Effat's skilled hands prettied me up."

Pari led me toward my new life while I was listening to the jingles coming from her ridiculously short pink dress, which she wore over black, baggy pants. *Black*, such an unfit color for a wedding! Her white scarf covering her head and shoulders looked like the typical dress code for a peasant's wife. She was blind to the way we dressed in Tehran.

I wondered. It had to be the hand of fate, or will of

Allah, that she married before me. She could not possibly have waited until I got married. My destiny was not to be married at the age of nine to a fifteen-year-old lad, which was the Moslim way, so we could grow up together and know each other passionately.

Soon, I found myself walking through the door, connecting this room to the one where the ceremony was about to take place. The naked wooden door at the end of this room separated me from the room where the men were sitting. This door was shut. Still another closed door isolated the men from the room where the women and children were congregated. These four rooms, from one side of our veranda to the other, all tunneled together into a maze and I was lost in it.

The sight of the sacred *sofreh*, a white cloth, spread on the floor dismayed me. At one glance I saw. Everything was rented including the rug, cushions, and some poshti, even the two candlesticks and the mirror which is a *must* in any matrimony. They could bring light and happiness to the newly-wedded couples. Every groom had to buy them for his bride. But no man would spend his money on an old maid. For me, tomorrow, this set of light would be returned—not a good omen!

"Shirin joon, go and sit on the *soozani*!" Pari whispered into my ear.

When I saw the enchanting red brocaded fabric with its paisley pattern wafting at me, I screamed silently, *Allah, I've found an oasis in this Sahara.*

A time when I was a little girl flashed before my eyes. I always used to hover by Maman when she aired out her old possessions, safeguarded in her metal chest. Among her bundles, I clung to this soozani like a bee to a red rose.

"This is the toiling of your great-grandmother ..."

"Maman, how did she do that?" My eyes were fixed upon this piece of beauty while I pressed it to my flat chest.

"It's woven with silk and silver threads." Hastily, she grabbed the soozani from me. "Shirin joon, I'll protect this for you until you wed. This travels through the chain of time. When it comes to you, keep it safe until your oldest daughter gets married. Then it's hers to pass it on to her daughter and on and on …"

Today, it was my turn to sit upon the soozani unfolded on the floor waiting for me. Anxious to place myself upon this paradise, I grasped my white satin dress and chador, pulled them up to my knees and rushed toward it. Then, to my amazement, I was even able to ignore my churning stomach.

At last, I sat on this piece of heaven, with my legs crossed. When I gazed into the mirror before me, I thought I saw the image of Maman, as a young bride. Behind her, Grandma Aziz's face was shining—they were both smiling at me as if they were welcoming me to their world. I understood. Today, I added a new link to the chain of womanhood. They could not treat me like a little girl anymore, ordering me not to read Hafiz's poetry. From this day forward, I would only obey my husband. He was my master. Hopefully, he wouldn't mind me reading Hafiz.

"Shirin joon, read this." Pari handed me our family Koran. This holy book belonged to my father. A peacock feather lay between two pages marking the specific page for me to read in silence. Instead, I turned to the last page where all of our birthdays, including Baba's and his father's, were recorded. I read, *'Mehdi khan, Son of Abdul Karim, Born 1175 Hegira—Died 1195 Hegira, Allah bless his soul.'* He died so young. If only he had stayed home that day instead of marching before our majlis, then, today he would be alive and could protect me from this old man.

I wondered. *Why don't we read Divan-e-Hafiz instead of the Koran which we can't understand?*

The soothing smell of the colorful herb seeds pasted into two triangular tabagh called my attention to the altar. My wedding sofreh was sacred; I diverted my attention from the storm inside of me to the two tulip-glass candlesticks burning on each side of the mirror. I thought they winked at me through their prismatic glass, as though trying to blow away the dark clouds from my heart. I took a deep breath.

At the sound of the women's gleeful cheers from the courtyard, my heartbeat escalated.

"The groom is here!" Pari murmured in my ear.

I wished my prayers to Allah had come true, and that this groom would never show. But then I could never have any children, or a life of my own. I had to bow to Allah's will.

I recalled climbing the tree a week ago—an unusual way for a girl to first see her suitor. On the top of the good-for-nothing tree, Ali's eagle eyes stuck in my mind. I wished he didn't look as old as Uncle Mohsen. At least, thank Allah, he dressed as a city man and didn't look like my sister's peasant husband. How could Pari stand her husband's smell? I still had the farm smell in my nose.

Serving as my sanctuary, the Koran's glittery calligraphy reeled me in. I started reading, *'besme Allh alrahman alrahim ...'* my eyes stopped moving. I wished again that instead of this holy book that I could not understand, I had Hafiz's *Divan* on my lap to soothe my soul. I hammered my head with piles of words until I concluded: Allah wanted me to marry this man. In this life, my fate was to be united with this old man and there was no way for me to object to this marriage; even though I could say no when the mullah asks me. *No way, no how I could have done that.*

The screech of the wooden door shook me out of my thoughts.

"Is the bride ready?" I heard the mullah's spiced Arabic voice.

Pari and the other women clapped. "Yes! Yes!"

Of course, the bride had no other choice except to play along with this immolation.

"Not until the third time—don't say anything." Bagoum khanoom had reminded me of this tradition earlier that day. I had to keep my mouth shut until the mullah asked me three times—then I could answer. Of course, nothing but, "Yes."

I knew that if the groom were rich, each time that the bride kept quiet and delayed her answer, his mother would slip a piece of jewelry or a gold coin into her hand—sure enough, there was nothing for me today.

I could not compare myself to the rich brides. As a Moslim woman cemented in Islam, I had to be obedient to Allah's will. I collected my stormy thoughts and concentrated.

After he recited some verses from the Koran, the mullah called, "Shirin khanoom, I'm Ali khan's delegate ..." he paused. I sighed to avoid the sound of my thundering heart.

"Ali khan agrees to pay a weight equivalent to two peas in gold as your mehrieh when he takes you as his wife!"

I was aware that Ali khan did not have to pay this gold to my family right then and there. In the future, if he decided to divorce me or if he died, then, perhaps I could collect my two gold peas. But it was different when the king Naser Al-Din Shah wanted to marry. As we had heard, he gave gold to the father of any beautiful girl based on her weight. This way, the king obtained her father's consent and took her to his harem without force.

"Do *you*, Shirin khanoom, want to …"

I turned a deaf ear to the mullah. I wished that I had enough strength in my legs to run out of this room, or even out of this world so I could chase Hafiz in paradise. My heart belonged to Hafiz. My heart forbade me from marrying this old man. However, the *soozani* chained my legs tight to the ground, and I had no power to break away. I imagined I was an ant caught in the web of a spider.

"Do *you*, Shirin khanoom?" the mullah repeated. "This is the second time I'm asking …"

Wishing this! Wishing that. My thoughts annoyed me. Once more, I decided to take refuge in the Koran in my lap. I called on Allah. I put myself in his hands. His will for me was to marry this man, and I could not question that. I was a morsel in His …

"Shirin khanoom," the mullah's loud voice stirred me again. "This is the third time I'm asking. *Do you* …"

Today everyone was happy for me, but I felt my body collapsing, and my soul …

A sudden joyful burst from the women returned me to the ceremony. Their gleeful scream jarred me, "*balleh, balleh!* Yes! Yes!" They clapped and each hugged and kissed me, saying, "*Mobarakbad! Mobarakbad!* Congratulations!" over and over again.

Apparently I had answered yes! *When did I do that?*

After a few moments, Ali khan came into the room. I was anxious to see my husband and had hoped that he wasn't as old as I saw him the other night. Pari and the other women made room for Ali, the nobleman, to get close to his wife.

"*Dorood bar shoma!*" His Persian way of saying hello

rang in my ears when he glanced at me. Before I could even raise my head, he dashed out.

In no time, the celebration started in two separate rooms—one for men, and one for women and children. Several samovars in the corner of the courtyard were bubbling, and soon fresh-brewed, strong tea was served with homemade sweetmeat. On the women's side, some young girls and children danced flirtatiously to the beat of a tambourine and *donbak*, a drum, while others clapped and sang.

If my wedding ceremony and its celebration hadn't been cramped together like this, it would have been a cheery event. Even better, if I had been nine years old, after the aghd and a short celebration in my father's house, the groom and his family would have gone home. Once in a while, the groom would have come to see me. Of course, I would never be left alone with him, even though I was lawfully his wife. This interlude would give me time to grow up and develop the body of a woman ready to have a husband. But there would be no break for me! I was fully developed, with the breasts and hips of a grown woman.

At night, the enchanting smell of food filled the rooms. Placed on the white sofreh before us, the roasted leg of lamb, chickens simmered in turmeric and cinnamon, and basmati rice decorated with saffron, heaped in oval plates, looked delicious.

"Shirin joon, what would you like?"

When I kept quiet, Pari put some *polo*, rice, on a plate, with some chicken and lamb and gave it to me. It felt like there was a huge knot in my throat preventing me from swallowing anything. I had grown up believing we all were equal in Allah's eyes. But then, in this land, no one had ever heard of a groom who moved into his bride's house. Ali would live with us in our house from this night forward. I supposed that after my father's death, we were in need of having a master. So, Allah sent us one.

My mind wandered again. According to tradition, when it was time for the groom to bring his wife home, he and some of his male relatives and friends would go to the bride's house to fetch her. The festivity could come to life by immolating a lamb on the threshold, right before the bride stepped into her new house. Then, throughout the night, a group of *motreb*, professional dancers and singers, all men—some performed in women's clothing— entertained the audience with the sound of bagpipes, drums and tambourines. Some folks referred to it as *shab-e-motreb-zani*, the consummation of the marriage.

◻ ◻ ◻

At last, after all the guests had gone home and I was left alone in the room, I took off my chador. From behind the curtain, I brought out my coarse black and white striped mattress, satin comforter, a sheet, and two matching pillows. They were my dowry. I set up my virgin bed to share it from then on with Ali—a man to whom I had not yet spoken. *Such a peculiar tradition!* My shaking hands went to unbutton my dress; instead, I jumped under the white comforter and pulled it over my face. I was unable to accept that a strange man, being my husband since this afternoon, saw me nude. Sweat covered my forehead and dampened my palms. My dress stuck to my body. Like a nightingale, fluttering in my cage, I was fearful of the cat.

I heard the door open and close—the floor creaked with every step Ali took. I bit my nails and waited. He put the kerosene lamp on the shelf, walked toward me, and sat by me on the mattress.

"Why are you hiding?" He extended his hand and

touched me over the quilt. He pulled his hand away quickly as if he'd touched a heap of blazing charcoal.

"What's wrong?" he asked.

I kept quiet. He pulled the cover back from my face.

"You're trembling!"

I always thought having a husband, like reading Hafiz, would make me feel good. But similar to an antelope, I was fearful of my hunter. He was separating me from my beloved Hafiz when I felt his sharp eyes pore over my body. Like a rock, I remained motionless, wishing he would disappear.

"If you feel that terrified, I don't have to sleep beside you!" He purred in my ear.

He stood up, took a pillow and the sheet, went to the other side of the room, and lay down for the rest of the night.

Since that night, there was a special corner in my heart for him. I was relieved that indeed my husband was a nobleman. He had rejected all the traditions of the shab-e-motreb-zani. He had refused to conquer me right then and there.

◻ ◻ ◻

In the following spring, six months after my wedding, we were invited to Sima, Ali's daughter's aghd. On that day, Tehran looked delightful. Ali, Ebrahim, his servant and I walked through the alley, with a gutter for a spine, connecting us to one of the city's asphalt roads. Based on our tradition, I could wear my white dress to Sima's wedding. It's less than a year from mine.

The dress barely fit me anymore. I was holding on to my chador hiding my bumpy stomach. This dress was made for covering body of a pure girl, not a woman who had experience doing the most embarrassing act with her husband. I had mixed emotions. On surface, I was at ease. Finally, I was a married woman whom our relatives from Shahriar, neighbors and even Maman Zahra and Aziz started respecting. God's willing; soon I would be a mother. By having a husband, my children and I wouldn't be hungry, like we were before. But, when I turned to my heart, I could feel no joy. It was extremely difficult for me to accept any satisfaction in being a married woman. I remembered. After the first night, Ali's kindness more or less stopped. There was no kissing or touching between us. Any night that he desired me, he pulled my cotton trousers and underwear down and before I even had any sensation of wanting him, he was inside of me. He would get slimy in me. Then, without even looking at me, he turned his back to me. In no time, his snores would fill the room. He was even oblivious to the bloody handkerchief which was the result of my pain and torment. I heard that some rich husbands gave even gold coins to their wives. I was baffled. I felt that he had cut me in two parts. On one side, I could see myself like a doll, detached from my mind and heart being there for him whenever he coveted me. However, when I considered my soul, I saw that it was separated from my body floating free in search of Hafiz, my beloved poet.

Oh Allah! Forgive me: questioning my husband was not allowed; especially in his love making—something so personal and sacred. I knew. I had to do my duties as a wife and be ready to please him. I was very embarrassed to admit that some nights, I covered my face with my chador, pretending he was Hafiz, and then I enjoyed having him inside of me. But these times were too short and too far in between.

"Khanoom," Ali called to me. When I raised my head,

I noticed a *doroshkeh*, a carriage, stopped before us. Until that day, I had never ridden in one before. I glided in and sat next to Ali when Ebrahim took a seat beside the driver.

By thinking of Hafiz, I felt so exuberant that the torn red cloth of the seat appeared the same to me as one of the finest ruby velvets exported from France. The aged black carriage made a fashionable presentation with its golden handles and trim. The bony old horse appeared to me as a white Arabian stallion. I turned a blind eye to his callous skin, caused by his master's constant whipping. *Thank Allah, since a couple of months ago, because of me being nauseated, my master has left me alone.* The horse's gallop made the carriage float through the clouds, as if it was taking me to paradise.

The sun was playing hide and seek with me among the trees. The smelly driver's clothes, with their several ill-sorted patches, became, in my mind, a brand-new khaki jacket with matching brown pants. His hat completed his uniform and covered his soldier-like haircut. His black, shiny knee-high boots were anchored in my mind. His hawk eyes fixed on the road, showing his determination to deliver me to felicity. After Hafiz, I believed this new leader, our king—Reza Pahlavi could govern all of us. I had seen his pictures in the newspapers.

With confidence, I basked in cherry, plum, and peach trees with their breathtaking white and pink blossoms. I could heed the melody of hope from every flock of acacias in their new violet dresses. The sweet smell of jasmine made me believe that I was in heaven.

I was, however, shaken by the sudden sound of a horn, trumpeting in the air. When I turned, a shiny automobile determined to overtake our doroshkeh, pushing us to the side of the road.

"Of course, we know who *this* belongs to," Ali snorted.

I kept quiet. I refused to destroy my dreams.

We arrived at Sima's grandmother's house on an island north of Tehran, far from the city's heart and away from the bazaar. As soon as we entered the courtyard, Ali's brother took him to the room where the ceremony was about to begin. A lady offered the last stylish chair by the door to me. Ebrahim kneeled at my left side.

The white, pink, and blue hyacinths placed around the room trumpeted the celebration. The tables, grouped together in a horseshoe shape, crept through several rooms. The silver dishes heaped with homemade cookies, candies, and *noghl* were ready for the celebration that would follow the aghd. The colorful rugs went from wall to wall in each room. I never imagined a family could possess so much. I was baffled by the difference in wealth between Ali and his brother.

However, my eyes feasted on the colossal oranges, apples, and pears. My family and I were deprived of out-of-season fruit. I yearned to press my teeth into one of the apples, yet I felt no strength to get up and choose one. Our tradition cemented my feet. I had to wait to be served. A maid nevertheless brought me my favorite cool, sweet drink—*sharbat*. To my amazement, she was better dressed than my sister Pari for my wedding—there were no embarrassing jingles coming from this skirt. She looked like a blossom in her colorful, long dress with her white scarf covering part of her black braided hair. She had to be from one of our tribes. A dainty glittery headband covered part of her forehead.

Today, for the first time, I witnessed the mingling of men and women in Western clothing. None of the women wore chador except me. They stared at me with their shrewd eyes. I felt lower than the rest of the guests for wearing it. Every woman in her ornate dress and made-up hair and face looked like a khanoom farangi, just arrived from Europe.

Soon, I learned that the groom, who had been educated in Paris, was Sima's paternal cousin. His father, Ali's brother, was the court doctor. I remembered the day of my wedding in the public bathhouse. Bagoum khanoom had told the washer about this brother to show how important Ali was. I had never seen a clan so interwoven together like this. These people were hooked together like a bracelet, and I was its eyesore clasp.

When my curiosity boiled over, I turned to the young lady in a dashing rainbow dress sitting next to me and asked, "Do you know if there's anyone here who's not a relative of the family?"

Before the lady could respond, another, much older woman, Sima's grandmother, answered in a loud spiteful voice.

"We, the royal family from the Qajar Dynasty," she said, throwing a stern look toward me, "*do not* want to intermarry with either peasants or members of the vulgar classes. We abhor the mixture of blood in our children."

The whole room went quiet. I wiped my forehead, wishing the earth would open up and swallow me. I raised my head to prevent my tears from rolling to my face. On the wall, I saw a gold-framed portrait. It was a rectangular silk Kashi rug, depicting a miniature picture of a king on his hunting trip, ready to shoot his prey with the bow and arrow. I yearned to exchange my seat with the king's prey, for there was only one arrow aimed at this tiger. But for me, there was an entire room of arrows.

In Islam, it was a sin to draw or create any faces. We were allowed to create only patterns and sometimes images of flowers. According to our beliefs, the Almighty was the creator—not us. I was amazed how rich people could have Allah's permission to do whatever they desired without being held accountable for their sins.

"Khanoom *jan* means," the younger lady clarified as if I didn't understand their language, "we want our children, generation after generation, to have our royal blood." The woman hammered her words into my ears. "We must keep the nobility in our family. We want to stay *pure*!"

I used all my strength to stay calm in this stormy situation and whispered, "Like oil and water that never mix."

"Precisely!" Sima's grandmother thundered again. "We're like oil, always rising to the top, and if ..." She paused to cough and take a breath. "And if one of us goes against our custom, we will cut him off like a dry branch of a tree."

I felt the sky collapse over my head. I looked around. To my surprise, Ali was approaching me. Like an animal of prey in the mouth of a fox, I looked into his eyes, pleading for help. I knew he understood my pain when he, like a savior, murmured in my ear, "Let's go!" He took hold of my arm and we left.

Thank Allah, Ali khan was a true nobleman!

"I wish I were dead," he said on our way home, "so I wouldn't have to face these vultures."

"As the father of the bride, you had to be there."

"Let me tell you," he stared at me, "as their oldest brother, I cut them off, not the other way!"

¤ ¤ ¤

The red sky and the *azan* were calling us to our dusk prayers. When we entered the courtyard, we saw Maman and Aziz performing their ritual ablution by the pond. I went to the kitchen to prepare Ali's water pipe. Since my wedding, I had begun to skip my prayers. Ali never prayed and he didn't seem to care whether I did or not.

As soon as I put his bubbly ghalyan before him, Ebrahim and Yusof, Ali's son, entered the room. Without a word, I went and sat down in the corner facing them. Yusof looked like his father—sturdy, with wide shoulders, and he had to lower his head to avoid hitting the door beam. He kissed his father's hand and kneeled beside him on the floor.

"Father, you left so soon. I wanted to talk with you."

"About?" Ali took a puff from his ghalyan and turned to Yusof.

"I come to say good-bye! I'm moving to Shiraz, the city in the south."

"I know where that is, but why are you going?" Ali took another puff.

"I joined the army."

At this moment, Ali's face turned as red as the charcoals on the top of his water pipe and the words flew out of his mouth like bullets, all aimed at Yusof.

"Army? You're going to work for this Hungry Soldier? The one who destroyed your ancestors, the one who calls himself the king of Persia, sitting upon the Peacock Throne? *How could you?*"

"Well, I must ..." murmured Yusof. His expression was like a frightened deer searching for a shelter. I craved to rescue him when Ali roared again.

"*My* son, the descendant of Naser Al-Din Shah, has made friends with my foe! Do you believe it?" His eyes radiated as if they were on fire and the foam of anger covered his mouth.

I knew it was impossible for him to understand that his son had to work and live like everyone else. Ali Khan told me once that as far as he could remember, he never had to work. Each time he needed money, he would go to the Golestan Palace, and the man in charge of the treasury gave him a bag full of gold coins. I wanted to defend Yusof, but dared not to say a word out loud. I kept my silence.

"His Majesty," Yusof said calmly, "Reza Pahlavi did nothing to your ancestors! Our parliament chose him to be our king, and our leader!"

"Not so true!" Ali groaned. "This Hungry Soldier planned a coup d'état and marched to Tehran with his few followers, claiming to be the king."

I thought. *We commoners heard that when Reza khan, the brave soldier, made this coup d'état, the last king from the Qajar Dynasty escaped to Russia, and Reza Pahlavi became our king.* Again, I swallowed my words for I knew women should not enter the realm of men.

"Agha joon, let me tell you, the government provides us with housing, living expenses, and an excellent training. They've brought high-ranking officers from the West to train us."

"Of course." I could resist no further. I covered my mouth. I felt the heavy weight of four bright eyes on me. I read in their eyes, *"How dare you meddle in men's conversation?"*

Like a disobedient child, I ignored both of them, and continued, "His Majesty, a soldier himself, wants to make a soldier out of every youth in this country."

"You're right, Shirin khanoom." Yusof's words made me soar to the sky and I could not stop.

"Our king's determined to build a modern country and give us back the glory of the Persian Empire," I said.

"You're all naïve. You believe in whatever is written in the newspaper. The people's interest is the last thing on this king's mind," Ali clamored in his steel voice. "This soldier is only building up an army. He's wasting our oil money to buy bunch of *toop-o-toffang.*"

"Father, he's buying canons and guns to modernize our army."

Ali paused, giving Yusof the courage to go on. "To tell you the truth, His Majesty is the best thing that could happen to this nation."

"There's no way he could have overthrown the Qajar Dynasty without any Western supports, especially British! He's a traitor, and God knows what he's promised them in return. "

At one time, the Russian soldiers came to our land to help our king. They bombed our majlis and caused my father's death. These days, the British decided Reza Pahlavi should be our king. *Allah, help us.* I swallowed my words to avoid adding more fuel to their argument.

"Agha joon, this king's already done a lot for us! We're in the process of building modern schools to replace our old mactabs! He's building a modern university for us!"

"For girls too!" I announced in a rather loud voice. *I had to open my big mouth again!* Once more, I tried to be quiet.

"That's right!" Ali nodded. "The Darolfonoon high school built by my ancestor Naser Al-Din Shah, is apparently no longer adequate, and this no-good soldier wants to build yet another one."

"Agha joon, let's not forget. Darolfonoon and the idea of creating a parliament for the people came from Naser Al-Din Shah's Prime Minister, Amir Kabir. Please do not give Naser Al-Din Shah the credit for everything."

If that was true, then, Fereshteh, my beloved tutor, had misled my mother and me when she told us that the Golestan Palace was a creation of His Majesty—Naser Al-Din Shah.

Would it be possible, we, the regular folks, would ever know the truth? I held back my question.

"Then who built the Golestan Palace?" I asked.

As if my words had melted in the air, neither of the men responded.

"Agha joon, let's also not forget that instead of rewarding Amir Kabir for his good work, Naser Al-Din Shah ordered that he be murdered by cutting his jugular vein while he was taking a bath."

"A painless death though!" Ali countered.

Listening to this was difficult for me. I wondered whether I should believe Ali or his son, Yusof. I remembered. According to Fereshteh, Naser Al-Din Shah was a benevolent king. He was slain in the mosque and, therefore, he was a saint. Allah had chosen him to be our king. *Would Allah choose a murderer to be our king?*

"Let's not forget that this soldier is nothing but a dictator!" Ali made a fist and raised it in front of Yusof. "Your king is ruling with his fist before the nation's face! Except my fist contains flesh and blood, and if I hit you, you'll be wounded. His is an iron fist. When it hits, it'll kill you!"

Ali's stern face, with its red eyes, petrified me. This scene reminded me of the battle between our legendary hero Rostam, and his son, Sohrab. According to *Shahnameh*, the epic story of our kings, the father defeated his son, Sohrab, and slew him. In that book, they fought like two enemies. They acted like two foes as though they were made from the same fabric. I wondered why they couldn't unite with each other. I was about to leave the room to avoid witnessing this war between a son and his father, but Yusof's words nailed me to my seat.

"Agha joon, are you denying that our king's rebuilding our country from the bottom up?"

"From top to bottom!" Ali muttered. After a pause, and another puff at his ghalyan, he said, "As much as I hate to admit it, I have to give him some credit …"

What? Ali khan gave our king some credit? I breathed a sigh of relief.

Yusof's big, round face opened up with a smile like a boy who at last caught the ball in a long tiresome game when Ali continued, "He's the only king who's risen above these *wretched* mullahs." He shook his head as a sign of disbelief. "For many centuries these hungry creatures sucked the nation's blood under the name of religion and took advantage of the ignorant poor people."

"So His Majesty needs us to stand behind him as a force to pull out the root of these despicable mullahs!" Yusof remarked, and with that, it was as if he had poured a bucket of water over the burning fire of his father's anger. So, at least, Ali pretended, smiling through his teeth.

He invited Yusof to stay for dinner, though he was unable to. The next day before sunrise, he had to leave for Shiraz to start his new life as a soldier.

6. The Secret World

Tehran, Persia, 1924
Shirin (22)

On a cool spring morning, the sounds of chopping and sawing woke me. I rushed out barefoot without my chador. Ali's servant, with some other workers, was after the good-for-nothing tree with a vengeance, and was cutting it down, limb by limb.

"Ebrahim, stop, stop!" I screamed.

"My master ordered us to pull out this tree from its root," he replied under his long, thick mustache.

"But ..." I swallowed my words. My father Mehdi khan's face and his curly hair appeared in my mind. I remembered that day he pointed and said to me, "See, Shirin joon, this tree will grow with you. Then, after your mother and I die, your children and their children can be reminded of us by this tree."

Allah, help me! My husband was cutting off my tree from its root!

Ali's firm footsteps thundered in my ears. From the other side of the courtyard, he hurried up the stairs to the veranda and with his strong hands shoved me into the room.

"I want to build a room so that I can be away from you women," he roared. I heard no more. He was deaf to my stormy heart and blind to my teary eyes.

Maman and Aziz never approved of Ali's way of life. Several times, Aziz grilled me. "How come he doesn't pray every day like the rest of us? Not to mention going to the mosque on Fridays …"

"Ali khan isn't a proper Moslim, is he?" Maman murmured in my ear.

"Why don't you ask him yourself?" I groaned.

At last, one day, Maman asked Ali the reason he turned a deaf ear to the divine sound of the muezzin, which invited everyone to pray. His calm response amazed me: "We don't have to bow down to God five times a day to prove that we're Moslims."

Then, he turned to me with a winner's smile. My eyes fixed on his clean, close-shaven visage, with its perfect rim of mustache and understood. His bare face was obvious proof. He was not a religious man.

"Ali khan, aren't you a Moslim?" I asked.

"I'm first a Persian, then a Sufi, and both of these before I am a Moslim," he answered.

"Did you say Sufi? Who is he?" I wiped my forehead with my white handkerchief and its rose-water aroma soothed my soul. It was usually difficult for me to understand him.

"He's a mystic man believing in *oneness* and *unity* with God." His stern face made me aware that he was not thrilled about explaining all this to three ignorant women.

Maman quietly pulled her chador over her scarf when she asked, "Ali khan, what does that mean?"

"A Sufi refuses to follow a structured religion the way a Moslim does."

"Does a Sufi believe in Allah?" Aziz asked and counted her holy beads even faster.

"Of course!" He closed the door behind him after saying, "But he isn't a follower of Islam, only God!"

I concluded that Hafiz must have been a Sufi lamenting, in his *divan*, that he could not wait to unite with Allah. The love he talked in his poetry was for Allah.

Clearly, Ali knew a lot. He was a nobleman, a descendant from the previous dynasty. When he went to school, he pored over our nations' poetry and philosophy; he was not like us, the ignorant folks who had only the Koran to read and nothing else.

Standing among my three family members, I felt as if I were a fragile bridge stretched between my husband and those two bullheaded women. I believed that he had lighted our home with his presence. He was a wise man who knew everything.

Today, I felt the ache in my heart still yearning for this storm to blow over. Perhaps by sacrificing my father's tree, the good-for-nothing tree, our lives would be smoother. As long as I lived, I kept the tree close to my heart. The tears rolling down my cheeks were tribute to that.

¤ ¤ ¤

Since the two new rooms began, under the control of Ali and his servant, the mysterious cloth shrouding him grew into a thicker blanket. I wondered if I could bring down his veil of secrecy. He used the rooms to entertain and live a life separated from us. Tonight, sitting under the branches of the weeping willow tree, I went over my thoughts about him again. I had no idea what he did to earn a living. Once in a while, he went to his wooden chest, took out an heirloom, and left the house. I dared not question him. Upon his return, Ebrahim carried a sack of rice and a leg of lamb. As a Moslim woman, I adhered to the religious maxim, *"Allah gives life and He provides for it too."*

Tonight, the darkness of the night concealed me from Ali and his lighted room. I felt sheltered under the willow tree, with the full moon and the gleaming stars. The cool breeze from Mount Alborz kept me awake. At last, I decided to put a stop to the nagging voice in my heart. I felt as if I were a fish out of water floundering to quench my thirsty soul.

Since my marriage, I had grown accustomed to these gatherings. They went on through the night until right before the dawn prayers. As a Moslim woman, I could not join in, not that he cared. I relished, however, the freedom of serving his guests tea without my chador and soon, without even a scarf.

At first, I felt shy and guilty. I knew I was doing something against our Prophet's command. So I asked Allah for forgiveness profusely. I also prayed to Him to keep Maman and Aziz in the dark about my sin—they would be angry and mortified if they found out I was serving strange men with a naked head. Whenever I thought about the possibility of their discovering this, perspiration beaded my forehead.

Soon, from Ali's room, I heard soul-awakening music along with a deep, male voice singing to the whispers of *ney*, the flute:

Heed the story of the reed,
Of its separation from its root ...

I held on to the feeling of joy that I had married well. Because of Ali, I could listen to the heavenly words of Rumi set to the soothing sounds of the flute.

I learned that, according to Rumi, the reed cried

generation after generation to lament its separation from its creator. The ney, with its thin melody, always soothed my soul and washed away my sorrows. Its angelic music could transport me to heaven.

The sound of the ney reminded me of my good-for-nothing tree. Its shiny green leaves loomed in my mind and I tasted tears in my mouth.

The sound of clinking wine glasses and the aroma of hashish drew my attention to his room, lighted with candles. I wondered how these men could commit acts forbidden to Islam. Then I witnessed it. They passed the water pipe to each other. After they finished smoking, the strange looking men, according to Maman and Aziz, or dervishes, according to Ali, were ready to dance to the rhythm of the drum. To me, they were men of Allah. Whenever I read or heard Rumi's or Hafiz's poetry, they transported me to heaven.

Tonight, I was in the dark, and the men were in the light. The dervishes stood up barefoot and made a circle. I gazed at their white shirts with their loose, flared sleeves that looked like wings, which hung over their white tight trousers. Their maroon hats planted tight on their heads reeled me in. When the dervishes began to whirl to the sound of the drum, one beat at a time, I became all eyes. To me, the beat sounded like a drop of water separating from its spring and falling to the ground, one after another. Then the drops picked up speed until they sounded like a waterfall—steady and rhythmic. The dervishes followed the rhythm. They spiraled toward the sky like flames of a single fire. They spun and spun as if they were eagles leaving their nests, hurrying to free themselves. They swiveled toward the sky even higher than the minarets. I could believe that if they even reached and touched the sky, they would become one with the stars.

They're returning to Allah while their bodies remain on earth.

When I traced their path to the sky, I could see some patches of white clouds enveloping some of the stars. *Did they really soar to heaven?*

I understood those dervishes found their way to their roots with their dance. I yearned to learn how to soar to my root and creator. I rushed to go inside their paradise. To my dismay, I realized the separating veil, a sheer cloth, seemed heavier than a brick wall, preventing my passage. I banged and hammered at the air, at the impasse between me and the secret world, but to no avail! Allah's curtain was a mirage of steel that stood between us. It remained there forever.

7. Childbirth

Tehran, Persia, 1925
Shirin (23)

All night long, I found no sleep. With my pregnant belly, like a rock, I lay on my mattress without wanting to disturb my husband. I understood that Allah had made all of us from the same clay—whether Irani or foreigner, it was of no matter. We women had to bleed every month, considered not to be clean. For those few days in a month, we had to remain separated from the men, live like lepers, and be excused from praying. In addition, we had to give birth through pain. I wondered whether Allah was just.

The smell of fresh tea from the kitchen told me Maman Zahra was up. I crawled to my chador, pulled it over my baggy gray dress, and waddled out of Ali's room. The winds, with some dark clouds, were typical weather for fall. As I stumbled upstairs to the veranda, a few drops of rain on my dried lips brought me a taste of hope. A sharp pain forced me stop halfway going up. I relied on Allah to protect both of us.

In the room, sitting by the samovar, Maman was ready to eat before sunrise, for the month of Ramadan was upon us. My brother, Hassan was gone to Shahriar, as usual. Since my marriage, he spent most of his time in the village.

Maman placed a piece of goat cheese on her flatbread, put it in her mouth, and took a sip of her sweetened tea.

"Some tea, dear?"

"No!"

"It looks like today is the day!" Maman stared at my belly.

"Perhaps!"

"Do you think we ought to fetch Sakineh khanoom?"

"Don't know!"

Once more, she stared at my eyes as a *hakim* would do. She confirmed that it was time to send someone after our neighborhood midwife. She then finished her tea and said, "Shirin joon, with Allah's will, you and your baby will be safe. Rely only on the Almighty. He's the only one in control."

"Allaho Akbar!" Aziz was facing Mecca, praying.

I knew Allah was great, but my stormy thoughts did not leave me alone. I had already lost my first baby before it reached full-term. Even though this was my second pregnancy, I was ignorant about the whole process. I was afraid that by bringing my baby to life, I might be journeying to the valley of death.

"*La ilaha illa allah,*" Aziz continued when she sat down. She bowed forward and put her forehead to the holy clay seal. One of her friends had brought it for her when she returned from Mecca.

I glimpsed at Aziz's frail body, wondering how she could have stood up to the eunuch, Saam, from the Naser Al-Din Shah's court almost thirty years ago. My grandmother had to be brave, blocking the eunuch from taking my mother Zahra to the harem. If I had a daughter, I would not let anyone separate her from me.

When Aziz came and sat cross-legged on the floor by the sofreh, she drank her tea and swallowed her bread without chewing. In the recent days, she had lost most of her teeth. Her black scarf covered most of her white hair. Maman and Aziz always wore their chadors because of my husband, Ali. This baffled me, for he was their son-in-law, and, in the eye of Islam, he was considered to be as close to them as their son.

Throughout the day, waves of pain hit me one after another, with erratic pauses in between. Late that afternoon, when Sakineh khanoom thought it was time, she arrived. She rolled her right hand over my tummy and her eyes sparkled like a wise man. She ordered, "Get the room ready!"

The neighborhood women had prepared a room. While the women led me to this makeshift birthing chamber, I prayed to Allah to give me a boy. Not that Ali khan would love me more. Very likely, he would sit in his room, smoke his ghalyan, and, in a stiff voice, devoid of feeling, proclaim, "It is not important whether the infant is a boy or a girl. As long as it's healthy, that's what counts."

However, if I were from a rich family and had given birth to a boy, my husband would sacrifice a sheep to protect his son and his wife from the evil eye.

I wished to have a boy so Maman and Aziz could walk in the neighborhood saying, "I'm so proud of Shirin joon, she gave us a son!" But, in my heart, I prayed to Allah for …

The stiff plaster floor under my bare feet cut me off from my thoughts. My eyes fixed on the washed off geleem in the middle of the room when I lay down on the thin mattress. Everything was so different from the day I sat by the sacred sofreh in front of the mirror and was married to Ali. I still wondered if I had really agreed to marry him.

I turned my head and stared at the four sun-dried bricks. These building bricks were laid at the corner of our kitchen since my belly became larger. During the childbirth process, they could become handy.

Today these bricks were stacked on top of each other, two by two, and set a short distance apart from one another. Enthralled by the sight of the warm ashes in the gap between the two bricks, I exhaled and inhaled, feeling like a locomotive on an uphill track.

The raindrops began to beat the window when I saw Maman rush to the kitchen to cook her special dish for the mother-to-be. She swore that by eating her special food, made out of flour, rosewater and saffron, right after giving birth, any mother would regain her strength in no time.

Not long after, Aziz entered the room. She sat on the floor, completing the circle of neighborhood women around me, and began to pray. She clutched to her holy beads praying and calling out, "Allaho Akbar! Allah, today, this woman comes to you in her utmost agony. Show her your mercy! Relieve this faithful mother from her pain."

Other women murmured prayers, too, calling on Mohammad's daughter, Fatima. They prayed to her, the reverent woman, who gave birth to two sons, Imam Hassan, and Imam Hossein, our second and third imams. They appealed to this holy woman to rescue me from this rocky road and to give me a healthy son. They continued begging Fatima, the holy woman. They implored her to show me the safe path of bringing a son into this world. They asked her to allow my baby to arrive in safety.

Regardless of their passionate prayers, the waves of pain continued to bash me. Like a stream flowing in the gutter, sweat ran down my back. Soon, I felt I was drowning in one of Shahriar's clamorous rivers, buried under its huge waves. The excruciating pains jabbed me as if I were that cow on the farm not willing to plough. With every attempt to seek my freedom, the waves smashed my fragile body harder and harder. I had to open my eyes to escape my nightmare. I wished that I had Aziz's holy beads to cling to. With an empty hand, I prayed. I begged Allah to redeem me and forgive my sins. I promised Him from then on, I would be a good Moslim woman—that I would cover my head before strange men, that I would no longer read Hafiz, and, above all, that I would stop questioning the destiny He chose for me. I also concentrated on the women's prayers. To my amazement, the pain went away, for only a short time, but what a blissful relief.

However, new waves of pain rippled through my body again when Sakineh khanoom ordered the women to help me over to the bricks. I had to squat, to put my feet on the bricks, one foot on each side.

"Push! Push!" Sakineh khanoom commanded.

I yearned to scream, but I knew well that this was forbidden. In Islam, a woman could not raise her voice to the level that neighborhood men could hear it. It didn't matter if she was in a dangerous or even life-threatening situation—there were no exceptions. Therefore, I veiled my screams. Like an obedient servant, I listened, crouched over the ashes, and pushed my hands against my knees as hard as I could—all without a sound. As my labor progressed, I felt weaker and weaker. At last, I gave up all resistance. In the back of my mind, however, I still heard the women's intensified prayers. The blurry look of the room gave me assurance. I realized I still had a grip on this world.

In a moment, the image of the good-for-nothing tree, with its sturdy trunk and its shimmering leaves flashed before my eyes. I remembered the day the men were slaughtering that beautiful tree, limb by limb, without realizing how close the tree was to my heart. The only token from my father's life had been destroyed. In the midst of my disappointment, my father's face and his curly hair came to my mind. He said, "It doesn't matter! Thank Allah, you're alive!" His smile appeared to me as if he were in the room. "Don't forget, my dear Shirin, as long as you're alive, I'm alive as well as our tree. Be strong, you are accomplishing one of most difficult tasks in the world. Right now, you're close to Allah because you're giving life to a soul." I felt tears of joy rolling down my cheeks. I sensed that I was between this world and the other. At that moment, I learned to cling to my secret world. I knew I could soar to the sky, like dervishes, that I could even see my father in heaven.

"Are you going to give me a boy? It feels strong like a boy," Sakineh khanoom's enthusiastic voice filled the room. But, in no time, her voice turned somber.

"I guess not!"

The moment Sakineh khanoom lifted the baby from the bloody ashes, my daughter began to cry. Sakineh khanoom cleaned her up and wrapped a blanket around her. As she did this, the other women assisted me to bed. Sakineh khanoom put the squalling baby into my arms, saying, "So fussy and loud. But pretty."

Filled with pride, I looked at her thinking, *Iran joon, don't you know that girls are not allowed to scream?*

8. Iran's Liberation

Tehran, Persia, 1936
Iran (12)

No school for us today! The heavy snow of the night before has blanketed our entire yard. A few months ago, Maman Shirin's grandmother, Aziz, had passed on while visiting her relatives in Shahriar. So, my mother and grandmother Zahra are in mourning by wearing black clothing.

"Iran joon," Maman Shirin jabbed me while sitting beside me, feeding my baby sister. "Hurry up! Go and tidy up your father's room while he's out." Baba did not come home last night. He sometimes spent time with his friends, dervishes. They danced, sang, and drank wine until dawn.

I put on my overgarment and covered my head with Maman's rough, large shawl. Amir, my younger brother, was busy shoveling the snow from the roof. Thanks to him, the wool socks in my slippers would not get wet, for he had made a clean road from the veranda to Baba's room and to our kitchen.

Baba's room smelled heavy and damp. The odor of tobacco from his ghalyan still lingered in the air. I opened the two tall glass windows to let in the bitter, freezing air. The *korsi* in the middle of the room needed my attention the most. I took out the cold brazier hidden under its wooden stool. In the kitchen, I pushed aside the warm ashes with an iron spatula. There was barely any fire left. From the basement, I fetched four charcoal balls. They were the result of our hard work—my brother Amir, my sister Pouran, and me. We had put them together from ground charcoals with water; then we left them in the yard under the sizzling summer sun. I set the new charcoal balls on top of the almost-melted balls from yesterday, and I spread the ashes from the sides to the middle. After putting the brazier under the hollow platform, I took each mattress—four in total—and shook them outside, one by one, then spread them by each side. I then folded each side of the quilt hanging from the stool. To finish it off, I spread the blanket over the korsi. It was now ready for Baba. He could sit on his seat at the top of the room and pull the quilt over his lap, feeling warm and cozy.

When I went to pile up his newspapers and notebooks, I could not miss the large picture of our king on the first page. It was printed a few days ago, but it was the first time I had seen it.

The picture showed our king coming out of his palace accompanied by our queen and his daughters. The women wore no veils. The queen dressed in a fur coat and hat. We knew. His Majesty had two other wives, but he claimed the crown prince's mother was our queen. My eyes fixed on the princesses. They looked only a little older than me. Their outfits were much like our soldiers' uniforms—except instead of trousers, they wore straight skirts, which went down to their knees. The translucent stockings displayed part of their legs. They had to be nylon. Unlike us, they did not have to cover their legs with rough, thick socks. Their shiny shoes confirmed they were blessed with abundant wealth. The white shirts and cravats looked masculine and their hats, with their edges standing up, revealed part of their short hair and slim faces. For sure, they were not dressed anything like us. We wore baggy dresses with trousers underneath. No thick chadors covered these princesses from the eyes of men.

I read the headline: *"His Majesty Takes yet Another Step toward Modernization of our Land. He Orders Women Not to Wear Veils Any More."*

Bravo, Majesty! He did for all the women what my father did for me a few years ago. I felt proud to have such an open-minded father. He was my idol.

I recalled. On the first day of school, when I finished putting on my black, baggy cotton uniform, and Maman went to fasten my white scarf with a safety pin under my chin, Baba rushed toward me, pulled the scarf from my head, and growled, "Khanoom, do not do this!"

"But she must!" Maman Shirin responded, and I was pleased that Baba was against covering my head. I considered myself as equal to Amir and other boys and they didn't cover their heads. I never understood why I had to do it.

"Soon," his firm voice rang in my ears, "there will come a day when our women do not have to cover their heads, so my daughters can get used to it now."

However Ebrahim, Baba's servant, had to accompany me. He had to protect me from some of the women and boys who threw rocks at me, screaming, "Shame on you! Aren't you a Moslim? Cover your head!" After his death, God bless his soul, Maman or Baba had to come with me for my safety.

Today, *thank God*, our king, Reza Shah, would shelter all women. Not long after that picture was taken, it was illegal to cover our heads in the streets. It showed. Our king was brave to turn a blind eye and ear to this Moslim rule. We were free. No woman was allowed to cover her head with the chador, or even a scarf. This was the time when Mamani Zahra's misery began.

This defiant woman rebelled against our new law. Each time she returned home, I listened to her lamentation. "Today two *ajan* saw me ..."

"Mamani, you mean policemen!" She still used the old vocabulary as if we were not moving toward the gate of westernization.

"One of them leaped toward me like a tiger." Mamani Zahra ignored my words and continued, "One of these ignorant men grabbed my arm ..."

"Why, Mamani?"

"Doesn't he know he's a strange man and isn't allowed even to look at me?" She swallowed her anger. "This unenlightened man, not afraid of Allah's wrath, dares to clutch to my arms, so the other ajan could pull off my chador." Mamani Zahra pulled back her chador over her head. "He doesn't even stop there. After that, with his *baatum*, he hits me several times as if I'm his mule, straying away from my path!" She showed me the bruises on her legs after pulling down her black socks. She even rolled her sleeves up to demonstrate her battered arms. The black and blue marks on her frail body stayed fresh, for each time she went into the street covering her head, the policemen gave her more wounds. Sometimes, she even came home with a bloody nose or lips.

"Mamani, why don't you leave your chador at home?" I suggested one day.

"Iran joon, years after years, generation after generation, we're told to cover ourselves from head to toe. A strange man is not allowed to see anything except our faces. Now, one day, our king comes out of the palace with his wife and daughters dressed like farangi ladies, expecting all of us to be like them. Not me! Without my chador, I'm naked. We must follow our Prophet's order. And what's wrong with that?"

"Zahra khanoom," Baba came out of his room, "How do you know the Prophet ordered you to cover your head?"

"Ali khan, it's in our Koran!"

"Nonsense! Who told you that?"

"My leader, Mullah Karim ..."

If it wasn't in the Koran, and if it wasn't our Prophet's order, our religious leaders must have been lying to us. But, my heart was on fire for my grandmother Zahra. I wished I could rescue her from all the beatings. But what can a twelve-year-old do against policemen with batons?

ꗊ ꗊ ꗊ

After a few weeks, early one afternoon, Baba Ali came home. For the first time, he was out of his brown cloak and in Western outfit—he wore a gray suit and blue cravat. He looked very chic. However, his eyes carried no spark—it was very unlike him. He approached me and put his hand on my head. His eyes looked like a wounded lion rattling in his cage, roaring in silence. I used to imagine him as my rock of Gibraltar. That day I understood my rock was shaken.

"We're moving to Shiraz!" Baba announced in his somber face.

"Where Uncle Yusof lives," I said, and he nodded.

After a moment, he stepped away from me, "For the sake of my children, I sold my soul to this devil, the Hungry Soldier, so at least they won't starve to death."

"What?" Maman asked as if she did not trust her ears.

Like a volcano, Baba erupted, "For my children's sake, I had to kill my soul and shake hands with this Western puppet, this Hungry Soldier. Clearly we're his slaves, and he's our master."

I comprehended Maman's astonishment. In the past, I had to listen over and over to her weeping about how Baba had no job like other men and not much left from his heirlooms either. "If he would only go to his brother—His Majesty's doctor—and ask for a position somewhere, we wouldn't be so poor."

"Maman, why does Baba need to go to his brother?"

"Iran joon, in these days, if any man wants a decent job to be able to feed his family, he has to get close to His Majesty's ears. For your father, it's very easy. His brother is already very close to our king!"

This evening, Baba informed us in his solemn voice that he had obtained a very important job—to be the head of the Communication Bureau of Shiraz. He wanted to travel ahead of us to find a house. After that, Yusof would send us the military trucks to move us there.

I was baffled. *Why was Baba sad?! Why couldn't he be happy like Maman?*

◘ ◘ ◘

The following summer the sound of banging on our door, late one night, awakened all of us.

"Open the door! Open it right away!" men were shouting.

Maman Shirin quickly pulled her gray overgarment and covered her daily dress. She had to be scared, with no man to defend her. The men's pounding sounded strong enough to break down our door at any moment. I was shaking like a lamb without her watchdog.

Amir, my younger brother, without any shoes, grabbed the lantern from Maman, and ran to the door. Upon the screeching of the key in the lock, three policemen forced the door open and hustled into our portico.

"Tell them not to come in. I don't have my chador on!" Mamani's voice trembled from the courtyard where my other brothers and sisters began to moan and groan.

"Stop, stop!" Maman Shirin ordered the men. She sounded like a master in charge. "My mother doesn't have her chador on!"

"Chador?" The uniformed man ahead of the two others said *chador* as if this word was foreign to him. "Khanoom, haven't you heard our new law forbids any woman to cover her head?"

In that moment, I forgot all about my grandmother's misery. I was overcome with joy at our new law. Ever since, no man dared to throw rocks at me for not having covered my head.

"She's in her house. Can't she do whatever she wants in her house?" Maman growled louder than the officer.

"Khanoom, we're looking for Hassan Daryani! Is he your son?" The man's stern voice frightened my three smaller siblings. Their weeping concealed Mamani Zahra's wail of, "Allaho Akbar." My sister, Pouran, and I took the children to our bosoms and tried to calm them down.

"Where is he? We need to search the house. Get out of our way!"

"Not here, mister!" Maman said, like an old wise man. In a calm voice, she continued, "We don't even know where he is! Go …"

Before Maman could even finish her sentence, the leader tapped his baton on his palm and led the way while the other two, carrying rifles, followed him. They marched over our mattresses spread across the floor. No one could miss their boot prints on our sheets. They were no longer white. I wished my father, Ali khan, were here tonight. He would never have allowed these policemen to barge in on his family like this in search of Uncle Hassan.

I wondered why they were looking for my uncle in our house. He did not live with us. We never knew where he was. Sometimes, a friend from Shahriar would bring news that Uncle Hassan had sent his regards, and he was doing well.

"Khanoom, why are you packed?" The officer's voice startled me.

"My husband, Ali khan, has been appointed as the head of the Communication Bureau in Shiraz, and we're going to move there. We're waiting for the trucks to arrive." Maman stared into the leader's face while twirling her thumbs.

"What is your husband's last name?"

"Amirian!"

"Is Ali khan the brother of His Majesty's doctor?"

"Yes," Maman nodded. "He's his oldest brother!"

"Khanoom, we're very sorry for the disturbance! I promise this will never happen again."

Unbelievable! As soon as they heard my father was close to His Majesty's ears, they transformed into angels.

"Officer, why are you looking for my brother Hassan?" Maman asked.

"He's a fugitive." The leader sounded calm and kind. "Your brother failed to register for the draft, and as you know, according to His Majesty, every single man must register with the police. Please give my regards to Ali khan-e Amirian."

The three men left without further questioning.

I thanked the Almighty for rescuing us from these cruel men.

☐☐☐

117

The next morning before dawn, I thought I heard Uncle Hassan's voice whispering something to Maman and Zahra. Or perhaps I dreamed it.

However, I remembered the men failed to look in the basement under the kitchen, where we kept our sacks of rice, beans, and a sheepskin of cooking oil. But last night, Maman and Zahra had piled all of our bundles and belongings on its door and covered it very well, so that a stranger would never know such a basement existed.

9. Persepolis

Shiraz, Persia, 1939
Iran (15)

At night, when my father noticed my excitement about going to Persepolis (I was washing my school uniform and ironing it), he said, "This Hungry Soldier wants to squeeze the past glory of the Persian Empire out of today's Iranians in a hurry!"

"Baba, what do you mean?"

"Those days were glorious for us. But, the so-called king is spending our poor nation's money to dig out this palace of despair."

"What's wrong with that?" I loved the way I could discuss things with my father and ask him questions. Not every girl was this lucky.

"Our people are starving, and we pay a hefty salary to some Western archeologists to dig this ruin out ..."

"Baba, we want to display our past glory ..."

"Right," he answered through his teeth. "This king tries to hide the nation's poverty behind the 'glory of the past'!"

"Is Persepolis as majestic as they say?"

"It doesn't look majestic now! But, can you imagine how it looked during its highest glory?"

I shook my head and pressed my lips.

"My child," Baba puffed on his ghalyan. "The religion that believes only God is the creator can destroy our imagination just like killing a baby in its mother's womb!"

"I don't understand!"

"Iran, look at the rug on the floor. Do you ever remember seeing any images or pictures of people? In Islam, we're only allowed to create patterns."

"That's right! In our mosques, only some verses of the Koran are written on the walls."

That night, while spreading out my mattress, I tried very hard to imagine Persepolis, but to no avail.

◻ ◻ ◻

As the first student off the bus, I jumped into Persepolis. The desert wind caressing my face tied me to my royal ancestors of the Persian Empire. We, the students from the only all-girls high school in the city of Shiraz, brought it to life.

"This palace," our teacher announced, "is the survivor of our heritage. It was excavated by Americans hired by His Majesty, Reza Shah."

I looked up at the colossal columns touching the turquoise sky, and I felt lost. I never imagined this palace would be as majestic as a ruin.

"See, girls!" Our teacher showed us a tablet with some characters etched on it. "This decree is what's left of Cyrus the Great, who ruled in 600 BC. This edict, *Human Rights Decree*, was the law of our homeland. His ruling was based on this dictate from over two thousand years ago!" Our teacher, in her black uniform, with her long hair pulled back, appeared to be very hot. She wiped her forehead.

"Does it say anything about women's rights?" I asked.

"We can't read it to find out—it's in the ancient language they used in those days."

I turned a deaf ear to her when I saw the figures carved on the walls depicting men and women. They were taking some of their harvest, or sheep, to the king. I understood. During those days, women were allowed to go to the palace to offer some token of their labors to their king. The men and women were dressed very much alike. To my surprise, the women wore no veils.

I raised my hand to ask for permission to speak again.

"What is it, Iran?" our principal responded as if slightly annoyed by my questions.

"In those days, didn't they have a religion other than Islam?"

"Yes, they did!"

"Weren't the people Zoroastrians, not Moslims?!"

She nodded, and one of the other girls asked, "How do you know?"

I pointed and said, "If you look at the pictures engraved on the walls, the women have no veils …"

"Look at these unusual stairs!" our principal's loud voice muffled my words. I imagined, by climbing them, I was shoulder to shoulder with Cyrus and Darius the Great, our kings of the Persian Empire.

"Who can tell us the reason these stairs are so extraordinarily long and wide?"

Persepolis dipped into its darkness. No one breathed. I raised my hand. When our principal ignored me, I lifted up my head to the turquoise sky, knowing its beautiful blue color always brought me happiness. As if I could reach the sky, I touched my necklace—a speck of holy turquoise sitting in its gold frame.

My grandmother, Zahra, had bought it for me during her pilgrimage to our holy city of Mashhad—the burial place for our eighth imam—Imam Reza. She put it around my neck and said, "Iran joon, wear this. I've circled it around the Imam Reza's shrine. It wards off the evil eye."

But in Shiraz, as soon as Baba saw it, he grumbled, "What is this you're wearing?"

"It's my talisman from Mashhad."

"Take it off. You are not a donkey and have no need to wear a talisman."

I'd taken to hiding this piece of sky under my clothes so no one can see it, especially my father.

Today, I yearned to see myself in the glorious past, when I could have walked freely, shoulder-to-shoulder with my brother or husband, to bring the king a token of my toil. I yearned to see myself without the talisman, the collar of a donkey or cow ...

"How come no one knows the answer to this?" The principal's irritated voice jarred me.

"What was the question?" a girl asked.

I smiled. "I know—but you didn't call on me!"

"Iran, you girls must only talk when we give you permission!"

"Yes, Madam Principal!" all the girls uttered like sheep.

"The reason is obvious!" I said confidently. "These stairs are unbelievably tall and wide for the soldiers to ride their horses up to the entrance of the palace."

"Bravo, Iran!" our principal said through her teeth.

Like a blind person, I touched the horses engraved along the wall and marveled at them. They felt sturdy and masculine. I wished I could ride one of them. I imagined myself riding so high and fast, almost reaching the clouds—a magnificent feeling.

"Who knows what happened to this glorious palace at its end?"

When I looked around again, I was the only girl among all fifteen of us who raised her hand.

"Go ahead!" The principal looked at me like an angry bear.

Without any fear, I said, "When the Greeks attacked and conquered Persia, one night, their leader, Alexander the Great, drank lots of wine—so, he was drunk and …"

"Then, he ordered his soldiers to set fire to Persepolis!" our teacher finished my sentence.

"They say he was jealous because Persians had Persepolis, but Greeks had …"

"Why are you the only one who knows anything?" a girl enveloped in her black uniform interrupted me.

"Because my father, Ali khan, is from a royal family, and he knows everything!"

"Is he from the Pahlavi Dynasty?" the girl next to me asked, her eyes going wide.

"No! They came from Tehran," another girl said, rolling her eyes. "She thinks she's so important!" Her huge body made me uneasy around her. When I first moved to Shiraz, she had tried to be my friend. Only God knew I could afford no friends. I had five sisters and three brothers in addition to Pouran and Amir. As the oldest child, I had to look after them. Maman was sick all the time, either from being pregnant or from giving birth. Today, for example, when I left in the morning, Maman wanted me to come home as soon as I returned from Persepolis. She kept to herself most of the time. Thank God, Mamani Zahra had come with us to Shiraz to take care of us.

"God bless His Majesty, Reza Pahlavi, the shadow of God." Our principal's voice brought me back to Persepolis. "We can come to this majestic palace and be proud of our heritage."

As soon as I headed for the stairs, our teacher shouted, "Iran, you can't climb those stairs. Come back here!" She sounded as if I was a sheep separating from my herd.

"I just want to touch the statutes of the lion with its two wings sitting on the top!"

"Iran, we're forbidden to climb to the top!"

"I want to see why this lion has wings. Lions don't have wings!"

The principal said through her teeth, "Iran, I order you!"

"Everybody back to the bus!" The bus driver's shout stopped me from climbing up there, and perhaps his shouting had also saved me from being beaten by the principal for my defiance.

When we left Persepolis, this glorious palace sank in its darkness again. Heaps of thoughts about Maman Shirin filled my head. I wondered if she was pregnant again!

◻ ◻ ◻

I arrived home, without a word to anyone; I hurried into Maman Shirin's room. Her face was as yellow as mustard. She wiped the last speck of vomiting from her mouth with a white handkerchief.

"Iran joon," Maman said in a weak voice, "I want you to do something for me this afternoon."

"What?"

She reached under her pillow and took out one tuman bill.

My eyes flashed at seeing a brand new bill. I had not seen one except when my father carried a few of them, and every four or five weeks he gave grandma Zahra one to buy food for us.

"Go to Marta's …"

"Marta? I've never heard such a name!"

She nodded and said, "A *koliy* …"

"A gypsy?" I whispered, wondering how Maman knew her.

"Give this money to her. She lives out of town …"

"We heard some gypsies put up their tents …"

Maman nodded. "She has some medicine for me."

Before I left, she pleaded, "Iran joon, swear to Allah that you won't talk about your journey to anyone. Keep this secret in your blossoming chest forever."

I wondered why I felt as if my heart had been thrown into a fire. A shower of questions rushed into my head. Instead, I said, "Don't worry, dear. I'm a tough girl. I will carry this secret with me for the rest of my life."

I wandered through the streets of Shiraz. While I was following the desert sun's path, I made some calculations. My baby brother, Jahan, was about six months old. Maman had to be pregnant again. If so, Marta's medicine must be preventing her from throwing up. But I was unable to calm my churning stomach.

I quickly tired of all the questions in my head and looked ahead to the road of nothingness as I left civilization. Soon, the asphalt road ended, and not very long after the dirt road began, I saw several black tents spread out in the desert, an eyesore. Marta had to live in one of these tents. When I entered the first tent, it shocked me. The floor was bare—there were no rugs to cover the dirt and rocks of the ground. A woman breast-feeding her baby sat on a sheep skin—a goat next to her was chewing some weeds. Flies and mosquitoes buzzed inside the tent. A few dirty little girls and boys with torn, faded clothes ran to me. "Khanoom, have anything for us?" I felt their hungry eyes pierce my body. I brushed my hair from my face and asked the mother, "Are you Marta khanoom?"

"Go down three more tents."

I did as instructed and entered a practically identical tent.

"Marta khanoom." I stared into her blue eyes, and extended the bill to her. "The money's for you. My mother wants some of your medicine."

The sight of Marta with her jet-black hair as long as her violet, patchy dress that fell to her ankles, made me tremble. Her legs were covered with soiled white pants. Her feet were dark, as though she hadn't washed them for a long time. I'd never seen a person with black skin before. Her toenails and finger nails were unusually long. She could not belong to any groups—she was not a city woman, nor was she dressed like a farmer's wife, or a woman from one of our tribes. She was a living, breathing gypsy standing before me.

"Divide this root into three parts," Marta said without moving her lips. I was transfixed by the rhythm of her breath, the way it made her breasts heave up and down. "Pour hot water over each part, and feed it to your mother for three days."

"Will she be healthy again?"

Marta remained quiet while preparing the medicine. When she fitted a handful of the radicle in a box, I grabbed it from her, shoved the money into her hand, and dashed out.

I heard the azan for the dusk prayer when I opened the door to our roomy house. Knowing Mamani Zahra, was busy praying, I snuck into the kitchen, divided the root, poured hot water over it, and gave Maman the first part. The following two days, I obeyed Marta's instructions.

The days went by. Maman looked paler than the day before. No one seemed to care, not even my father. He very seldom went to her room. Most of the time, though, when I brought him his dinner, he asked me about her. Only Mamani Zahra prayed more often, beseeching Allah and giving food to beggars to appeal to Him to improve Maman's health. But at the same time she said, "Iran joon, we have to obey Allah's will. She's sinned, and we hope Allah forgives her." She counted her holy beads faster and faster. "Whatever your mother's destiny is, it will happen, and we're unable to change it! She's in Allah's hands."

At last, Baba came home with a doctor. They went to her room, and after not very long, I heard the doctor proclaim, "Khanoom's bled too much. She lost the baby. It's too late to do anything for her."

At last, one night, while I was holding her hand, her heart stopped beating. No one was there to listen to my crying. Not even a neighbor or a relative came to weep with me.

The next day, as we returned from the cemetery, no one talked to us, and everyone turned away from us. I wondered about the reason all of our friends and even our neighbors turned away. Without a word, Baba went to his room. Soon, the smell of his water pipe filled our house. Like our father, my younger brother, Amir, did not cry either. Mamani Zahra sat down by her prayer mat and murmured, "Allah, I know you're testing me. I'm still bowing to your glory." She then wailed and cried as if she wanted her heart to stop. Soon, however, she dried her face with her chador, turned to us, and said, "Praise Allah, I have you all." She picked up Jahan and pressed him to her chest. My sister Pouran and I showed no tears to the other children. We sat down and took all of them to our bosoms. For Maman's funeral, we ate *halvah*, the sweet dish cooked with flour, rosewater, saffron, and sugar pretending nothing important had happened.

I did my best to calm the storm within me. I wondered whether the roots I fetched had anything to do with my mother's death. If I had refused to go to Marta, would Maman be alive today? Days and nights came and went while I drowned in my bewilderment.

◻ ◻ ◻

Forty days passed between Maman's death and my half brother Yusof's visit. I could hear his conversation with my father from the courtyard.

"Are you sure Iran won't be a burden to you and Azar?" Baba asked.

Azar, Yusof's wife, was one of our father's nieces. She was among the first group of girls to graduate from the French School in Tehran. I never forgot the first time I laid my eyes on her—it was right after our move to Shiraz. Yusof brought her to our house to meet everyone. I opened the door to them. For a minute, I thought the king and queen were standing before me. Yusof in his military uniform and Azar like a farangi lady, stood shoulder-to-shoulder. Her huge white hat shaded her face. Her gloves and her pink, fitted dress were a perfect match for her olive skin. Her open-toed shoes were unusual.

"This is Iran!" Yusof said, making the introduction.

Azar stepped into the courtyard to acknowledge me; she forced a smile. Her eyes were like those of a trapped gazelle, waiting for some savages to attack her. I led them to Baba's room. Maman was sick and would not show her face to them. It was rude of her. We never, ever refused to go before our guests.

From that day on, Azar became my role model. She was a good example of an educated girl without a rich

128

father. In reality, she had no father. He had fallen ill with an incurable disease when Azar was a little girl. She had no siblings either. With the help of her uncle, the king's physician, and her mother, a skillful dressmaker, Azar was able to finish the only French school in the country. The girls who graduated from this school could speak French fluently. Its hefty tuition, however, was unaffordable to most people.

"Of course not!" Yusof's response brought me back into our courtyard.

"But, promise me as soon as you get to Abadan, you'll sign Iran up in the eighth grade. Here schools started a week ago."

"I give my word! Iran will have a comfortable life. I'll take good care of her as if she were one of my own. This is my help to you. You have a heavy burden on your shoulder." Yusof stopped. He lowered his voice. "You have too many mouths to feed."

I entered the room to put Baba's ghalyan before him. Yusof whispered to him, "What do you think about Shirin khanoom's brother, Hassan?"

"What about him?"

"He betrayed us." Yusof sounded angry.

"How did he do that?" Baba raised his voice.

"He refuses to sign up for the draft, and he's a *fugitive*. The government's looking for him."

"To my eyes, he's a hero. He refused to shake hands with this royal devil. I wish I could've done the same." Baba's stern voice made me uneasy.

"His Majesty needs all of us to unite behind him to climb the mountain of modernization."

"But, our king—this Hungry Soldier—hasn't done a damn thing to bring us together: the *bazaaris*—the tradesmen, the educators, the mullahs, the insolvents, and the array of tribes. The only thing he's done is to liberate women, allowing them to kill the babies in their wombs!"

Baba's words pounded my ears. I wished I were a boy. Then, Maman would never ask me to keep her secret— my trip to Marta and getting that root. She trusted me as a woman to a woman.

"Iran," Yusof's voice startled me, "gather your possessions. I'll come tomorrow before sunrise to take you with me."

□ □ □

The hustle and bustle of the harbor sounded like passionate music to my ears. A petroleum tanker had cast its anchors at a distance, waiting to be filled with our black pearls. This southern city, Abadan, sat at the tip of the Persian Gulf. The vast horizon touched the blue sky. The sea looked delicious—I relished the taste of its salty air on my tongue from the moment I arrived. Standing on the shore barefoot, I felt as if I was at the center of an important moving wheel. I yearned for Jahan, my baby brother, to be with me. Instead, I kept Hafiz's *Divan*, my souvenir of Maman, closer to my chest. For the first time, I knew she was in a better place than I was. She was united with her beloved Hafiz.

Yusof's voice broke into my thoughts. "His Majesty's plan is to build our first oil refinery here in Abadan. Since the Qajar Dynasty, starting with Naser Al-Din Shah until now, we've sold our crude oil to the West. They've refined it and sold it back to us."

"So, we save some money, won't we?" I interjected.

"Bravo!" Yusof cheered. "Our king's determined to make us as modern as the West."

Modern! Yusof's words sounded like he was veiled with the blanket of illusion. If our women believed that they could be healed by gypsies like Marta, how was it possible for His Majesty to make us like Western men and women?

However, I still went on believing that I was safe in a stormy harbor because His Majesty Reza Shah was our king and Yusof was one of his watchdogs. The break of a wave at my feet left the grit of sand in my mouth. That night, we reached his house.

Yusof, a high-ranking officer, had a spacious house, two cars, a driver, and a male servant. Jamal was one of those illiterate farm boys who had enlisted in the army, and he was assigned to Yusof's household. He was their boss-boy. They had a live-in nanny for their daughter Hoori, a chef and a maid. They had more people working for them than family members.

During the months to come, I grew to dislike Azar, Yusof's wife, more and more. On several occasions, she whispered to him, "Too bad! Why did Uncle Ali have to marry that peasant girl?"

Azar planted the seed of hatefulness in my heart every day. Upon my arrival, she assigned no room to me. They had at least two or three furnished ones; however, I had to sleep on the floor by Hoori's bedstead, to keep an eye on her as if I was her sitter. "Hoori's nanny must get plenty of sleep at night," Azar said, "so she can be alert during the day."

She even ordered me to eat with the rest of the workers in the kitchen, as if I were not her husband's half sister. This insult covered my heart with a thick black cloud. I contemplated it for a long time until one day I gathered all of the workers together and said, "From now on, when I return from school in the afternoons, I'll come here to be with you all."

"To do what, Iran khanoom?" Jamal stared at me with his dark eyes.

"To keep an eye on all of you." I tried to have a firm tone of voice and sound like a leader. "Poor Azar khanoom is too busy, so she asked me to be her eyes and ears. Keep this a secret."

"Still I don't understand," the chef announced.

"To start with, I can teach Jamal how to read and write." I turned to Jamal, "You've heard what His Majesty says—'A person who can't read or write is like a blind person'."

"Iran khanoom, why are you eating with us?" the maid asked.

"I love you all. I do want to be close to you all."

"How come you don't have a room of your own?" Jamal stared at me.

"Enough!" Clapping my hands. "Let's go to work."

Since my arrival in Abadan, every day, Azar had an excuse to avoid registering me at school. For a couple of weeks, she had to wait until her paperwork was complete. She was going to be the French teacher at the high school. Then Hoori was sick, and her nanny needed an extra hand. The only solution to their problems was to hold me back from school. At last, I asked her one day, "Azar khanoom, when do you think I can go to school?"

"Soon, soon. I must run—it's getting late," she said and slammed the door in my face.

One night after Yusof came home, I said, "Yusof khan, I miss Shiraz and want to go back."

"Shiraz! Not a good place to be these days."

"Why not?"

"They have an outbreak!"

"Outbreak of what?"

Yusof ignored me and went back to reading his paper.

"It doesn't matter," I told him. "I've missed Jahan, and I can accept whatever my destiny brings me."

At last, one night when everyone had gone to bed, I tip-toed to the courtyard, sat on the gravel, put my back to Yusof's jeep, and waited for him. All night long, I kept my eyes open while my ears were tuned to the howling of the wilderness. Early morning, before the sunrise, Yusof's voice woke me.

"Iran, what are you doing here?"

I rushed to stand up. "Good morning!"

"Good morning!" Yusof answered with a worried look.

Trembling, I said, "I'm not registered at school yet. I stay home every day. Why can't you send me back to Shiraz?"

"I told you why not. It's dangerous to go to Shiraz these days!"

"I know. If God wants me to die like my mother, I will."

Yusof, with eyes as black as Baba's, stared at me, and muttered, "Let me write to Baba, and see what he says."

He hastened inside his car and the driver drove him away. I was left standing with some dust in my face.

When I finally started the eighth grade in Abadan, the other students were ahead of me by more than two months. I was behind in all the subjects including French, which was taught by Azar. She browbeat me in front of the students every chance she had. "Iran, you're simply a dumb student. We must marry you off!"

I lowered my head, remembering Maman Shirin's words: "Iran joon, don't you ever stop going to school. You must grow up to be a khanoom, a lady."

¤ ¤ ¤

A few days later, Yusof gave us the best news of my life.

"We have to move back to Shiraz. I've been transferred."

It was then I understood God's greatness.

During the next ten days, with Azar's supervision, the workers packed their furniture—all had been brought from Italy—their colorful rugs, and their silver dishes, which were Azar's dowry. Whenever I attempted to pack my own belongings—five or six dresses, colorful seashells I collected for Jahan, Azar screamed, "Not now, not now." At last, her blood boiled over, she lost her control all together, and screeched like a peacock. "Those colorless dresses can't be mixed up with our nice things. *Wait.*"

I waited and waited. When the last small chest with a few odds and ends was about to be closed, the male packer listened to my plea, dumped my belongings in, and sealed it.

We reached Shiraz late at night. The next morning, when Yusof went to report to work, he heard grievous news. In the middle of the night, some rebels had ambushed the military trucks and stole every case except one! When they opened it, they saw a few odds and ends, my clothes, and few seashells.

"If we had known," I heard Yusof say, "we would have mixed Iran's clothes with ours. Then, the robbers would've taken nothing."

God was just. I knew.

10. Love

Shiraz, Persia, 1941
Iran (17)

Since I came back from Abadan, my father treated me as the lady of the house and gave me money. I was in charge of the household.

"Iran joon," he said, "every day, write a ledger listing what you buy, and how much money you spent." He gave me a notebook, and ten tuman bills. "This is enough for one month's expenses. Make sure to have some left over at the end of the month."

These days, typhoid fever stretched its black wings throughout the country. It had a strong presence in Shiraz. Thanks to Baba, he walled all of us in the safety of our house. As soon as he read in the newspaper about the death of some children, he ordered my younger brother, Amir, to close the water passage between our house and the rest of the city, and to cover the pool.

"Iran," Baba instructed me, "every morning boil the water from the pool for everyone to drink—from now on, no water from outside."

"Not even *shahi-water?*" It was the drinking water delivered to us each day.

"No!" His firm voice nailed me to the ground. "Boil the water from the pool before drinking it."

Like a mill, I ground Baba's plan to perfection. Every day before going to school, I repeated, "Mamani, boil the water before giving it to the children."

Days went by fast. Sometimes, I even forgot my weeping heart, or to think of my mother, Shirin. Meanwhile the grief of her death seemed like a molehill compared to the grief of the whole world. Germany, like a *ghoul*, Godzilla, was devouring Europe. The combat had begun on the other side of the globe, but in recent months, this demon even tried to swallow our next-door neighbor Russia, too. Thanks to His Majesty Reza Pahlavi, he kept us inside our walls. The bloodshed spread all over. Praise God that in our homeland, we only dealt with a shortage of tea and sugar—they were rationed. We had to change our tradition and were no longer able to have a cup of tea with our flatbread and goat cheese for breakfast. I woke up every day before sunrise with our grandmother, Zahra. She performed her ritual ablution before her prayers, and I boiled water, not in our huge samovar, but in a small kettle, to make tea for Baba, and I did the same when I returned from school. Most days, we served boiled vegetables and beans instead of lamb stew and rice with saffron. The food was barely enough for all thirteen of us. I, as the oldest child, had to stop eating before I felt half full. Sometimes I skipped a meal or two to make sure the younger ones had enough. As a habit, Baba had his dinner in his room late at night after everyone had gone to sleep. His dinner was a small lamb shank. The neighborhood butcher saved it for him, knowing he was from a royal family. I was in charge of cooking it to his taste.

One night, while we were eating, Baba walked in, picked up the three-year-old, Jahan, put him on his lap, and sat by the sofreh. He turned to me. His eyes were gloomy and dull. He said, "Yusof has brought me disturbing news."

"What?"

"His daughter, Hoori, is dead."

In her black dress, Mamani burst into tears and said, "Allah knows, when a child dies, her mother wishes she could go to the grave with her."

I wondered whether God had given them what they deserved. The rich people always thought they were above the needy ones. Today, God showed them the truth about all of us—that we were all humans, regardless of how rich or poor we are.

Still I turned to Baba and said, "Why couldn't they do something to stop it with all the money they've got?"

He shrugged his shoulders and reiterated exactly what I was thinking: "When it's our time to die, rich or poor can't do anything about it."

Hoori's death melted down the seed of hatred that Azar had planted in me when I used to live with them. The Almighty always took care of the paupers.

Mamani Zahra wiped her tears. "She was the same age as Jahan, wasn't she?" She then glanced at Jahan, and murmured, "Thank Allah, at least, He left you all for me, to remind me of Shirin, my beloved daughter. Allah, bless her soul!"

"Baba," Amir said, "why is there war everywhere?"

"We don't know exactly."

I was baffled. If my father, Ali khan, didn't know, then who would?

"Baba," Amir jumped in while Baba was drowned in his thoughts, "actually, it's very clear."

I turned to Amir, wondering how he knew.

"Oh!" Baba touched his chin, turned to Amir, and stared into his eyes while Amir continued.

"Reza Shah believes that we are descended from the Aryan race …"

"My history book says," I cut off Amir, "that in ancient times, the Aryan race was divided into two groups. One went to Europe and settled in today's Germany. The other group came to Asia, and settled here. They called this land 'Iran', derived from the name of their race." I then chuckled, "Just like my name."

"I know your mother's reason for naming you 'Iran'," Mamani said, entering our discussion and surprising us all. "I remember as if it were yesterday. Shirin was excited the day you were born." She raised her head and looked into my face with teary eyes. "She read in the paper that our king wanted the Western world to know us as Iran, and not Persia because …" Mamani Zahra was lost, so I rushed in and finished her thought.

"… The Persian Empire didn't exist anymore. His Majesty had made a modern country of our homeland …"

"Both of you are right," Baba said, pointing at Amir and me. He looked around as if he wanted to make sure no one else was listening, then lowered his voice and grumbled, "It's rumored that this Hungry Soldier wants very much to support the German leader …"

"Hitler!" Amir gasped.

"Be quiet, Amir," I scolded. "I want to know what's going on in the world."

"War, war, war—that's what's going on all over." Baba's hostility toward the regime was boiling again. His face was slashed with wrinkles. With his droopy eyes, he looked like an old, wounded lion, grasping for air when he continued. "This so-called *king* of ours is another tyrant, just like Hitler. Neither one thinks twice about washing his hands in a basin filled with the blood of innocent people."

"Except," Amir, wise as a sage, said, "the reason for Hitler's war is that he believes his people are above all other nations and races. He has his people's interest in mind." Amir paused, shook his head. "But our king, as a servant to the Western world, is killing his own people. The ones who do not want to obey him ..."

"Remember, Amir!" Baba said. "Killing is killing. To God's eye, it doesn't matter our reason for taking a life. We're all humans regardless of where we're born. To His eyes, whoever kills is a murderer."

Baba's words pounded into my ears. I wondered if he knew about my secret trip, which caused Maman's death. *Am I, then, considered a murderer?* I wondered.

◻ ◻ ◻

On that bright summer day, the sweet smell of roses filled the air and made us all forget about the war and the typhoid fever. The month of Moharram, the season for grieving over Imam Hossein's death, had begun. I pleaded to Mamani Zahra to let me go to the mosque to listen to rozekhani, the recitation of the Tragedy of Karbala.

"As long as you cook your father's dinner, wash the dishes, and take everyone's mattresses to the roof."

"Mamani, you know I do all my chores in no time, like a whirligig."

"Yes! Unlike your sister Pouran."

"I do miss her. I wish she were here with us."

"Well, Allah etches on each of our foreheads a different destiny, and it can't even be washed away with *zamzam* water."

"What's zamzam water?"

"Iran joon, as a Moslim girl, how come you don't know

this? This water comes out of a holy well near Karbala. We Moslims believe Allah made the water gush from the ground for Ebrahim's infant son Esmael, the ancestor of our Prophet Mohammad, many years ago."

"Now, I remember!" I exclaimed. "Hafiz, Rumi, and other poets mention zamzam water in their poetry. But they mean this water exists only in heaven. If anybody could find and drink it, he would be immortal."

"Well, they're not good Moslims!" Mamani Zahra said distastefully.

"Mamani, they're Moslims, but they're Sufis," I protested, then looked into her teary eyes, as she continued.

"I hate to see Pouran go to Tehran with your brother, Yusof. To me, you are all branches of my Shirin."

I frowned and said, "I hate it even more. They married her off right away, without sending her to school."

"I wish your father had never agreed to send her there," my grandmother said, drying her eyes. "Iran joon, are you sorry that your younger sister is married and you aren't?"

"I don't know," I shrugged. "What I'm certain of is that I want to become like Azar—a khanoom farangi."

"Like a Western girl?"

I nodded, yet inside of me, I heard another voice. I could never be like Azar and marry a high-ranking officer. *Impossible!* With so many siblings to look after and without even enough money to eat a full meal, no man would be eager to wed me. Azar had been very lucky. It had been God's will not to give her so many brothers and sisters. I wondered how Mamani Zahra could not see the drastic differences in our destinies. I imagined even our king could not see it; or even if he saw it, he could do nothing about it. No one could do anything to change the Almighty's will, or a person's destiny.

At sundown, when my friends came to the door, I

swiftly put my chador under my arm and ran out before Mamani could remind me of something else to do. At the entrance to the mosque, we took off our shoes, shoved them into pigeonholes, put on our chadors, and walked in. We met other girls who had gone ahead of us to save us seats next to the dingy curtain. It separated the men from the women. If we were not prompt, we young girls had to sit in the last row on the rocky ground without a geleem, a flimsy old rug. When the first mullah finished leading the dusk prayers, some women could spare a few shahi to have tea with sugar cubes. Soon, they sipped their tea and their mumbles filled the room. It reminded me of our hammam, the public baths. The women went there to wash their bodies and came here to cleanse their souls.

As the new mullah began his preaching, he asked the audience to send a salavat to Imam Hossein's soul. We all joined in, chanting, *"Allaho masala ala Mohammad va ale Mohammad."* From the men's side, one voice lagged behind the rest. So, the last word, *Mohammad*, reached me very loud and clear. When I heard the same voice three times, my body filled with affection. This heavenly voice had to be for me. It was like a breeze sent from heaven. I yearned to see the man behind this blissful voice.

Throughout the month of Moharram, I made a habit of going along with the neighborhood girls to the mosque. In my heart, I was counting every moment of the day until I could hear the stranger saying *Mohammad* one more time. Like a fish caught in a net flapping to get back to the sea, I waited for the evening to rush to the mosque. Night after night, I combed the crowd with my eyes to put a face to his voice. At home, I begged God to help me find him.

One month passed, the month of mourning was over, and still I had no luck finding the young man behind the voice. At last, one day when we came out of school, my friend Tooba whispered to me, "I wonder why my brother's here!" I looked at the young lad across the street. Our eyes met. I felt the whole world had stopped. His immense black eyes reeled me in—they filled me with joy like a released bird. Somehow, I felt he was the same lad behind the voice. I turned to Tooba, my closest friend. Her face, like a miniature painting—her eyebrows, eyes, nose, and her lips appeared to have been painted on her face—very minute, yet complete. Everyone told us we resembled each other, like sisters. "Better than sisters, we're doost, always," I answered.

"Iran, look!" Tooba shook my shoulder and, in her wholesome Shirazi twang, murmured, "Here's your mystery voice standing across the street."

I wondered. I had talked with no one about my yearnings to find the voice in the mosque. It was my secret and I dared not reveal it to anyone. Instead, I giggled, "How do you know?" Without waiting for any answer, I ran toward my house for Tooba not to hear the loud thumping of my heart. Our homes were on two separate paths.

Soon, seeing the lad on my way home at the end of the day became a pleasant ritual. I whirled through the day in anticipation of the delight waiting for me at the end.

Like a lighted candle attracts butterflies, he drew me to him. He was my Majnoon, my lover, and I was Laily, his beloved. Then, Maman's face flashed before my eyes. "Iran joon, I never knew how it felt to love a man. The only love I feel is for Hafiz. I wish ..."

I felt sorry for her. She never experienced the yearning to be close to a man and not to care that his flame of love might burn her.

Many days went by without any words between my *Mohammad* and me. I, however, cherished the way he looked at me. His round face shone on me from the moment I saw him until I passed him on the street. I could feel his eyes peeling off my clothes and kissing me all over. I was in paradise.

Like a trained dove, every morning I flew outside. Every day, Tooba appeased my thirst by pointing him out to me. "Hey, look! Your *Mohammad* is here again."

At last, one day, she confessed, "Iran, my brother comes here for you."

"For me?" I whispered. I felt like snow, melting under the sun's heat. I was embarrassed—it was as if Tooba had ripped off my invisible veil.

"But I care for the fellow in the mosque with the heavenly voice!"

"Iran, he's my brother, and his name is Morad."

The following day, during the break, Tooba shoved a piece of paper in my hand. I felt my heart pounding in my ears. With my shaking fingers, I opened the envelope. My eyes stuck at the beginning: "Angel face, my beloved Iran …"

"He called me 'Angel face'!" I whispered to Tooba and continued reading: "I saw you with my sister and fell in love with you. Each time I went to the mosque, it was only for you. To know you were on the other side of the curtain catching my words …"

"Tooba, I see your brother every day. Doesn't he go to school?"

"When my father died, Morad as the firstborn had to go to work at the blacksmith shop to be of help supporting us."

I glanced back to the note: "I love you so much that I want to send my mother for *khastegari* …"

"Oh, my God, he wants to marry me!"

"Morad broke the news to us last night." Tooba hugged and kissed me. "I can't wait until you're my sister-in-law."

Both of us jumped up and down, drowning in our happiness.

"But," I sighed, "my father will never give me permission!" My father came down from a royal family, the direct descendant of Naser Al-Din Shah of the Qajar Dynasty, and would never allow me to marry a blacksmith. I ran to get away from Tooba. *He would never allow it.*

¤ ¤ ¤

After school, on my way home, I could picture my conversation with Mamani Zahra: "Tooba and her mother want to come to our house. They're asking for my hand for her brother."

Mamani would ask, "What does he do? Can he afford to buy you a house?" Then, without any hesitation, she would say, "You know your father. He'd never give you to a lad who takes you to his parents' house to take orders from his mother!" I cared not where Morad would take me. I loved him. By the time I reached our house, I was ready to reveal my secret to my grandmother, and even to my father.

I opened the door. I could not believe my eyes. Our house was in shambles. It looked like a battlefield. Mamani ran out of her room, beating her head and crying, "Allah, help us! Why do you cut off your blessing from us?"

"What's happening?" I stiffened.

My brother, Amir stood in our courtyard and responded, "Time to move again!" His words hammered my head.

"Move!" I lamented. "Did you say we're moving?"

"Yes."

Mamani rushed to carry out some pots and pans from

the kitchen, and like a rock, I was glued to the ground. I looked up to prevent my tears from rolling down. The orange red horizon reminded me of my burning heart.

"Iran, don't stand there as if a jinni struck you." Mamani's voice brought me back to our courtyard.

"Where to?" I muttered.

"Tehran, silly!" Amir answered.

"But why?" I could hear my wailing.

"Haven't you heard?"

For the last few months, I had heard nothing. I was consumed by thoughts of Morad's love.

"Reza Shah's sent to exile," Amir roared.

"By whom? He is our supreme power. Who dared?"

"Not exile," Mamani corrected Amir in a soft tone. "He abdicated for the sake of his son, Mohammad Reza Pahlavi. He is our king now!"

"You all love to smudge the truth," Amir erupted. We could see the foam of anger on his lips. "Everyone knows. Reza Shah intended to cooperate with Hitler. He refused to give permission to British forces to come through our land to fight the Nazis in Russia. So, after twenty years of ruling, the allies kicked him in the ass and banished him to an island."

"His Majesty," I defended our king, "refused to allow foreign soldiers to come onto our soil. He's a patriotic soldier at heart." I burst into tears, and each teardrop pierced my heart.

"Are you crying for us, or for His Majesty?" Amir grinned. "I'm sure he stole enough money to prevent his living in misery."

I ignored Amir and rushed to my father's room. I confronted Mamani, who was busy putting Baba's books in a box. "What are you doing? Where is Baba?"

"Gone to Tehran! This morning, right after you left,

a telegram came. Ali khan had to report to the office in Tehran. Why are you crying?"

"Nothing." I wiped my tears.

"It must be difficult for you to move away from your friends. Above all, from Tooba."

"Mamani, can I go to her house?"

"Just come here and help me pack."

"Please, I won't be long. I'll bring her with me to help."

"Hurry up! Go as the speed of wind."

¤ ¤ ¤

In Tooba's house, she and I decided to ask Hafiz to untie the knot of my love. We believed Hafiz was omnipotent. When we made a wish in our hearts, his poetry would manifest the right solution. I dared to ask him if it was in my fate to marry Morad. I then opened Divan, and the words danced before my eyes. My tears blinded me. I could see no words. I threw the book to the corner and turned to Tooba. "Tooba joon, how can I leave Shiraz?"

"Iran joon, it must be torture for you to even think about moving to Tehran. We've got to come up with a plan."

"What plan?"

"How about," Tooba said, "my mother and I come to ask for your hand right away. Let's say, tomorrow afternoon?"

"My father's gone to Tehran!"

"If we get your grandmother's consent, your move to Tehran can be delayed."

¤ ¤ ¤

When I heard a knock at our door the next day, I yearned to disclose my secret to Mamani but no words came out of my mouth. I could answer back to my teachers, my principal, and the other girls in our school. But my tongue was tied up when I thought of talking about my feelings and my love for Morad. I was baffled.

Amir rushed to the door.

"Grandma! Tooba and her mother are here," he screamed from outside.

My thundering heart prevented me from speaking. Mamani pulled her chador over her head, and went to the door.

"Khanoom, we're almost packed, waiting for the trucks to move us to Tehran."

Tooba's mother murmured something to Mamani when, like a torchbearer, Amir ran to them and yelled, "Khanoom, what does your son do?"

"He's an apprentice at the blacksmith near our house."

"He doesn't make that much money, does he?"

"No! But enough!" She held her head down.

"Now, he fancies marrying my sister!"

"He loves your sister, Iran khanoom."

"Well, my sister isn't allowed to marry a man who can't afford to feed her."

"Amir, stop it." Mamani jumped in.

Amir's words came down on me like an axe on a piece of lumber. I wondered, *My father isn't dead yet. Why is Amir acting like my father? Why can't he let me decide!* I yearned to rush outside and scream at Amir and reveal my love for Morad. I wanted to grab him by his shirt collar and scream in his face that it was not his duty to choose a husband for me. Instead, I did nothing. No words came out of my mouth—as soon as my mind urged me to do something, the ocean of my soul washed away my intentions. He was there to fill up my father's place. I wondered if I could ever forgive him for not letting me have a voice!

◻ ◻ ◻

During the following months in Shiraz, the typhoid fever gained immense strength. Our schools were closed. The roads were blocked so we heard no truck coming to take us to our father in Tehran. We were prisoners in our own homes. We could only listen to the news on a radio. It was a big box that Amir had borrowed from a friend. He said, "It's important for us to know what's going on with the war." We listened. The Allies' forces roared into our land. They entered from the south, through the Persian Gulf, and marched on to the north, the Caspian Sea— the largest lake in the world. They crossed over to battle the demon force in Russia. Winston Churchill had called Persia 'The Bridge of Victory'.

"In return," Amir murmured, "the Allies have made sure the young king's crown was nailed down, just as long as he doesn't disobey them like his father did."

"Amir, you sound like His Majesty is the Allies' puppet."

"Of course, he is." His cheeks were red in anger. "We, the people, have no control over who we want to be our leader. We are treated like sheep herds and donkeys."

Day after day, when the foreign forces did not leave our land, Amir grew more and more wrapped up in our nation's shroud of freedom, and I was lost in my love for Morad.

My adoration for him was like air that I breathed. My only solace was that sometimes I sneaked out of the house telling Mamani that I was going to the mosque in our neighborhood. But, in reality Tooba, as a messenger between Morad and me, made arrangements for me to go to their house to see him. Most of the time, she made excuses to leave Morad and I alone. Even though I felt the storm in my heart, feeling shy, I was pleased that Morad could hold my hands and caress them. After a few times, he and I became brave. One time, he even touched my breast over my silk shirt giving me a sensation as if I were a dove soaring to the sky. At that moment, I wished he would be my husband, so he could rip off my clothes and kiss me all over, especially between my legs. Then, I would show him how much I love him when our flesh touched and we were connected. We could experience our delicious love in this crazy time when the world was filled with disease and abhorrence. If I were fortunate, the fruit of our love would be a baby, and I could taste the motherly love in this life. I knew. On that instance, I could give my life in exchange to be with Morad as his wife.

However, when he continued stroking me, I jumped, ran to the other side of the room, pulled my blouse down, picked out my purse and like a dumbfounded person rushed out of his house.

I stopped going to see Morad. I did not trust myself that next time when I was alone with him, I could resist the temptation of showing my love to him.

I lived like a zombie. My mind was shut off to the world around me; especially that there was no letter from Baba, Ali khan. All the communications between us were severed. I was a dreamer, hoping that soon the war would be over and I would contact my father to get his permission to marry Morad. *Morad is Iran's husband!* I screamed in my head. In my heart, however, I knew it wouldn't be possible.

Day after day, I was firmly believed that Maman Shirin was watching over us in heaven. It seemed as if she did not like the way my siblings, ages five to ten, were treated. One by one caught the typhoid fever. It was too much for Mamani and me to handle. We had to take them to the hospital where its walls could cry blood. The soiled mattresses on the floor were crowded with moaning and groaning people praying to God to take them. At last Ezrail, the Angel of Death, came and released most of them from their misery, including my beloveds. Each day, I had to carry the news of death to Mamani Zahra and Amir. Jahan, my baby brother, was the first one to go.

Without my father, our protector, I had failed to take care of my siblings. I had loved Jahan as if he were mine. I wished all five of them had worn the same talisman around their necks as I did; I wished they had been saved from the evil eye.

It seemed that even Morad's love could no longer soothe me. As the result of God's wrath, I felt numb, as if my soul had been sucked out of my body. Mamani stopped eating. She wanted to go to the other world where her daughter and grandchildren were. "Allah, take me too," she kept screeching. On the second day, Amir brought a mullah. I led him to her room. He addressed her. "Khanoom, by abstaining from food, you are taking your own life. And to Allah's eye, you're a sinner. Break your fast, accept your fate, and take care of Iran."

"If we had been free of foreign soldiers in our land, we never would have the plague!" Amir bellowed. I looked into his jet-black eyes. I thought I saw all of my family members in them. To me, they were not gone at all. I still had him. I knew at that moment my sisterly love toward him would never be extinguished.

¤ ¤ ¤

At last, our waiting was over. We received a letter from my father that we need to be ready to be transported to

Tehran. The day before leaving Shiraz, I met Morad in the garden where Hafiz was buried. I did not dare to meet with him in their house, since I had promised myself that I would never put myself alone with him in a room unless he was my husband. So, as before, Tooba had secretly arranged our rendezvous. If even one person discovered it, she could gossip throughout the town and no one would believe I was worthy of being the nobleman, Ali khan's daughter—*not knowing I had gone so far with Morad!*

"Iran isn't a lady," the women around town would say. "Not a descendant of the royal family. She's a *scarlet woman!*" I could hear their murmuring, "Who is the lad with her? Is he her brother, or her husband?"

I could not even imagine what Amir would do to me if he was aware of what I had done with Morad.

◻ ◻ ◻

On that day, Tooba came to our house, and we told Mamani that we would go to the cemetery for me to say my goodbyes. Then, from there, we could rush to Hafiz's garden to meet Morad.

When Tooba and I entered the garden, the sturdy palm trees, the smell of roses, and the thin sound of flute transported me to heaven. I imagined that I was Laily, and with Morad as Majnoon, we were taken to a refuge in an oasis. Then, forever no one would disturb us.

Tooba and I hurried to the tomb to send a prayer to his soul. Right away, I saw Morad standing there, staring at the tombstone. I glided by him wishing to quiet my heart before anyone else could hear it. Muttering the words carved on Hafiz's tombstone, I read, "... no one dies if he fills his heart with Love ..."

"How are you?" Morad murmured in my ear without

looking at me.

I felt my body was on fire when I gazed into his eyes. I knew well that no Moslim girl was allowed to stare into a man's eyes. It was a bold move on my part.

"Let's take a walk through these beautiful trees," Morad suggested with his two bright eyes full of love for me.

"I'll sit here," Tooba said, "to send a salavat to Hafiz's soul. You two go."

We walked through the trees among the bushes of red roses; Morad's white shirt sleeve caressed my blue dress. The blaze of love in me grew higher and higher. "It's too bad you're moving to Tehran," Morad said.

With a knot in my throat, I could not say a word. Behind a sturdy tree far from any eyes, our lips touched.

If Amir knew I had kissed a lad, he would kill me. Like a person struck by a lightning, I ran while whispering, "Morad, you're the love of my life."

The next day, the truck arrived. They loaded our belongings, and took Mamani, Amir, and me to Tehran. I left my heart with Morad. From Shiraz, I carried the memory of the time we spent together wishing he would be my husband soon!

11. Actress

This afternoon, when my brother Amir spoke with me, I did not feel any resistance toward him. Perhaps he sensed that over the years, the fire of my anger had sunk to the bottom of my heart. There was no other way. I felt that my love for my brother stayed alive and never diminished, but my love for Morad was losing strength like a sun hidden behind clouds.

"Iran, this is for you!" He extended a stack of papers to me. "Would you like to act with me in a new play?" His eyes and mine connected.

"A play?" I said, amazed. "But do you think Baba will let me?"

"I play the leading role. I can decide who plays the leading female actress."

"What's the play about?"

"I've not read it yet. But I know its author, Nima."

As a young man, Amir liked to act. When our country became modernized, stage performances were very popular and Amir acted in several plays. The small morsel he earned was a help toward his school expenses. Unlike

153

him, I never dared to reveal my secret that I too would love to act. I was afraid of my father's reaction. I knew. The daughter of a nobleman was not allowed to do what her brother could do. I could not follow my heart and join a group. Boys followed their dreams wherever they took them. Of course, until our young king came to power, we had no female actresses. Instead, men dressed like women and acted on the stage.

"Do I get paid?" I asked.

"This isn't a professional play. We want to perform for one night to see how people like a play written by our own writer …"

"Isn't this a translation of Molière or some other farangi playwright?"

"Right."

Apparently, he read the fear in my eyes when he said, "Don't worry. I'll talk with Baba."

On his way out, he left me the play. I had no strength to quiet my desire any longer. The fire of traveling to Paris and becoming an actress began to rise up in me. I always believed that underneath my skin, there was a perfect actress just waiting to step out. I felt my fate was to be a famous actress. I dreamed of embarking on new adventures in different parts of the world. I would be even better than Yusof's wife, Azar. She could never leave the country. I would become the first girl in my family to travel abroad alone. My life would be a splash of spices! I stood up like a cedar tree and imagined what people would say: *"Iran, a girl from a poor family goes to Paris! Incredible!"*

With a boiling enthusiasm, I read the play. It was a modern comedy. It showed a couple who had a maid and a servant. The wife had a stinky suspicion that her husband was in love with the maid and was trying to find a reason to get out of their marriage. To get back at him, the wife tried to seduce the servant. However, in the end, the servant and the maid revealed their love for each other and left the stupefied couple to themselves. It was not conceivable that the play could take place in our country among religious families.

The last page had the cast's names. Amir was the servant. I would be the wife. I did not, however, understand the question mark in front of my name.

◻ ◻ ◻

"Bravo Iran!" The standing ovation the crowd gave me nearly transported me to heaven. I bowed to them, thinking I had to be dreaming. In the first row, my father, Ali khan sat with his stern face, covered in clouds of sadness. Those days, he confined himself to his room. To see me on the stage had to be special for him. Tonight, he even put on his dashing suit and blue tie. In his farangi outfit, he trumpeted his nobility to everyone. My mother's twinkling eyes loomed in my mind. I yearned for her to be here too, so I could see in her eyes the pride she would feel for me. If only I had refused to go to the gypsy's house, today she would be sitting beside my father. Then, she could watch me perform on a stage with no chador, or even a head scarf. These days, we women could choose whether to cover our heads or not, thanks to our young king, Mohammad Reza Pahlavi. Mamani Zahra was happy about the new rule. She said, "Thank Allah, these days when I follow Allah's law and wear my chador, no ajan beat me up like a donkey."

"*Marhaba!* Bravo!" There was no end to the crowd's enthusiasm. My brother Amir joined me on the stage. Both of us held hands and bowed to the audience. Since we had started rehearsing, I had felt as free as a bird. No

155

more thinking of Morad, Shiraz, and our sinful actions—
all were dissolved like salt in water.

When I walked away from the stage, my satin blue silk
dress glided over my curved figure. Its collar hugged my
neck; it fitted my waist, and its sleeves were cuffed like a
man's shirt, at the wrist. Its skirt came down to my ankles.
It was Mamani's creation. She made sure to protect me
from "*the men's hungry eyes.*"

"Iran khanoom, you were magnificent," Nima, the
playwright, said behind the stage. He looked at me
through his black-rimmed glasses and his ruddy cheeks.
His brisk gait, aloof manner, and his impeccable dark suit
gave me the impression of a man with unmistakable self-
confidence. If I hadn't left my heart in Shiraz, perhaps he
would have been a perfect husband for me. But there was
no husband for me except Morad.

"Iran khanoom!" When Nima moved, I saw a huge
man with a white turban approaching me.

"Mr. Raji wants to talk with you."

His Indian drawl made me gaze at his beard when he
said, "Tonight I saw your unbelievable performance."

"Thank you!"

"I own a group of performers." He rubbed his hands
together. "We travel to different countries to perform."

Paris too? I wanted to ask. As a woman, I was supposed
to be humble and not speak very much.

"What Mr. Raji's saying," Nima jumped in as if I
needed a translator, "is that he's impressed with your
performance and he wants to hire you to join his group."

Mr. Raji nodded. "Yes, you're born to be an actress—
and you're pretty too." He wet his lips.

"But Iran khanoom has no acting experience." Nima
diverted Mr. Raji's stare from me to him. "This was her
first and only performance."

Meanwhile I put my hand over my lips and pressed hard, keeping my mouth shut. I didn't want to say anything that would jeopardize my luck.

"I'm leaving tomorrow afternoon with my performers. If you decide to join us, I'll be in front of the main door to the bazaar." Then he rushed away.

"Iran khanoom, you're not possibly taking this foreign man seriously!" Nima's sharp, brown eyes watched me behind his glasses.

"Why not? Wouldn't it be wonderful to perform in Paris?" I said gleefully.

"A beautiful girl, all alone in faraway lands. It's so hard to imagine." Nima scratched his head and rushed out.

On our way home that night, I chose not to break the news to my father. I felt there was an unspoken tunnel between us. I wanted to talk with Mamani first. I admired her strength in life, even without any education. Like a stormy river, her life carried her through the highs and lows, though I was not certain that her life had any true highs. To my surprise, she was content to obey God's will. She lived according to Allah's law. These days, she was the only one in our home to kneel down on the mat five times a day, praying for us. "I possess the key to heaven," she kept saying. The best news for her was when last month, her son, Uncle Hassan, was no longer a fugitive and came to visit. Our king had forgiven most of the outlaws.

Imagine—tomorrow night at this time, I would be in a foreign land. I would be free as a bird, unlike my sister, with a husband and children.

The next day, when I carried the boiling water in the samovar to make tea for our breakfast, Mamani had finished her morning prayers and was sitting by the sofreh. Without any eye contact, while I was busy putting a tablespoon of tea leaves into the white porcelain tea pot, I said, "Mamani, last night the most interesting thing happened to me!" She kept quiet as I explained about Mr. Raji's offer. After putting the tea pot on top of the samovar, I turned to her. She was holding her holy beads to her chest with a flame of anger in her face. "Do you want to go away with a farangi man?"

"Wouldn't it be wonderful?" I said with joy.

"Iran," she dried her eyes, "you're the only one Allah left for me. A girl must marry to have children, not run away from home like a gypsy."

"Mamani, why didn't you remarry after your husband died?"

"You're old enough to know!" She stared at me with her gloomy eyes, took a breath, and hid more of her white hair under her chador. "Men, especially the noble ones, think of a woman as a clay bowl. After she marries and gives birth, she is nothing but a cracked bowl—not worth drinking from." Mamani Zahra frowned.

I laughed and said, "Are you telling me you must stay a widow for the rest of your life and no man wants to marry you?"

"Something like that." She looked down and continued counting her holy beads.

"Mamani, what do you mean I will be like a gypsy if I go abroad?"

"Well dear, this isn't something I can give you permission for. Ask your fa—"

Before she could finish, I was on my way to his room carrying his tea on a tray. I could not deny my happiness. After hearing Mamani's reaction to my future dream, I put all of my hope in my father, Ali khan, the nobleman. I hoped he could see the dreams in my eyes and would grant me permission to chase my fantasy.

When he saw me at the threshold, he stopped reading his newspaper and raised his head. "Come on in!"

I entered, placed the tray in front of him, and sat beside him on his mattress and stared into his eyes. I expected to see his eagle eyes piercing my heart. For the first time, I could see no light in them. He was an aged lion. There was no battle for him to win. He was counting his days.

After I explained Mr. Raji's offer, he asked, "Is Amir going with you?"

"No. He only gave this offer to me."

He then took a sip from his tea. "Even if I grant you my permission, do you think it's appropriate for a girl to go off among strangers and live like a gypsy?" Then, without any hesitation, he opened his newspaper.

At that moment, I was crushed. My grandfather, Mehdi khan, lost his life for us to have majlis. Our previous king, Reza Pahlavi, that brave man, even went against our religion and liberated us women and ordered the abolishment of veils. Our present king left us free to choose whether to listen to our tradition or heed to our own voice. But as a girl, I was still forbidden to decide for myself and pick any path in life I wanted. My father had the power to smash my dream in an instant. It did not matter how much freedom our king gave us. We women never could stand on our own. We would always be like branches hanging from a tree. My mouth was muzzled and I had no strength to remove it.

¤ ¤ ¤

After my father dashed my idea of travel, I was stuck in my house in Tehran. We had rented three rooms in Malik khanoom's house. "Ali khan," she said, "I know what you're going through. Just pay me for three rooms, and I will not rent the rest of the rooms." All seven rooms around the courtyard looked like they were hugging the quadrangle. On the north part of the house, a long set of stairs snaked into her quarter, along a balcony with several rooms.

According to our neighbors, Malik khanoom was a widow. She was nine when she was joined in matrimony to an old, but wealthy man. One night, he went to bed and never woke up. They had no idea from where she moved to Tehran. But, according to her maid, she was born in a harem from which she and her mother were expelled. When her mother died, she took over the hidden chest smuggled out by her mother.

We seldom saw her. Sometimes she looked down on us from her veranda, but she never left her area. She had a full figure with milky skin. Her massive breasts were often on display—she wore low-cut dresses and never bothered to hide her cleavage. She never talked with me or Mamani Zahra. Once in a while, she would stop by Baba's room to talk with him behind the closed door, and most of the time she invited my brother Amir to dinner. In the beginning, I could hear him coming down after dinner late at nights, but recently I heard nothing at all.

I spent my days taking care of Mamani and Baba. I had no school to go to. My father could not afford to pay for my schooling. Uniforms, books, papers and ink were scarce. Baba could only pay for Amir. Besides, every house needed a housewife, and this task landed on me. All four of us were living on Baba's meager retirement money.

Every day, while I washed and cooked, I cried. Since my father did not give me permission to follow my dream to become an actress, I understood my life was destroyed. I hated that I had been forced to abandon the graves of my beloved mother and siblings and to leave my love, Morad, in Shiraz, to live in this sad house. There was no way of escape. I was not brave enough to leave everything behind and follow my dream. Like a candle I was slowly burning down to nothing.

¤ ¤ ¤

One day, at the sound of knocking, I opened the door. To my amazement, the playwright, Nima, stood before me in a crisp, white shirt.

"If it's Nima, let him in," my father yelled.

Nima and I walked to his room. I felt safe beside his tall, slim figure, as if he were a cypress tree providing me with shade.

As soon as Baba saw him, he sat straight up on his mattress and asked, "Nima, what's happening on the streets?"

Nima took a spot on the floor in his well-ironed khaki trousers and wiped his forehead. "Ali khan, good news!"

I was supposed to run and get him a glass of iced water. Instead, I stayed in the room to hear what the good news was. I noticed my father's eyes sparkled. "Tell us!"

"Our waiting and persistence has finally born fruit." A shadow of a smile crossed Nima's face. "Now, Mossadegh is an elected representative from Tehran to our majlis!"

"Yes, these days, we hear a lot about him—even though he went underground shortly after this Stooge's father was put into power!" Baba said with a low voice.

"Ali khan," Nima's excitement was clear, "you should remember him! Mossadegh's from your dynasty—Qajar. Since he could not work with our former dictator, Reza khan, he went on practicing law in his hometown, defending the poor people's rights without charging them."

"I don't remember him. He must have been educated abroad."

"Yes! Now he's extending his hand to our king, the Puppet of the West." Nima took off his slippery eyeglasses and placed them on the floor. "Mossadegh's genuine in his desire to serve the people. He'll bring us freedom. We've been robbed of it for a long time."

"At last, there is a ray of sunshine upon this nation!" Baba sighed.

"Ali khan, we love his ideology." Nima pulled his sleeves up and waved his hands in the air, as if he could not sit still. "Mossadegh is a nationalist. He's urging people to unify, so we can clean out the British forces from our homeland."

"Those foreign intruders, they never left our land, even after the war was over!" Baba yelled as if Nima had injected him with some new blood.

"Yes!" Nima concurred. "They're still in control of our oil and the refinery in Abadan. Mossadegh wants to put our people in charge, not those aggressors, the British ones."

"Then he is truly a flag-waver for our nation."

"Believe it or not, Ali khan, he wants to nationalize our oil and—"

I could no longer keep quiet. "Nima khan, what do you mean?"

He turned to me. I noticed his twinkling eyes. "Iran khanoom, since the time of Naser Al-Din Shah, the British and Russians found out we have black pearls. Then they began to bribe our kings. Our shah gives away our petroleum for a fraction of its price." Nima tapped on the floor with his left hand. "The Westerners, the buyers of our oil, do not enter into negotiation with our representatives. Instead, they sign an agreement with our kings as their servants." He paused. "Hopefully, Mossadegh will change all that!"

My father turned to me. "Our king is the one who has his own interests at heart, not the people's."

"Our king rules over us," I said, "so, on behalf of his people, he enters into all treaties with foreign countries. Besides, Mossadegh's only a representative and doesn't have any power to do anything!"

"Iran khanoom, you're right. He doesn't have any power now," Nima said, wiping his glasses, "but he's the first man in our history to assert what's wrong with our government."

"What is—" I started to say, but Nima raised his hand, signaling me not to continue.

He went on, "If we had elected our leaders, we would have a democratic regime. We all remember less than ten years ago the Allies put this young puppet in power and got rid of his father." Nima's mood shifted from excitement to edginess, and I felt the brush of his anger.

"Nima khan," I said, "then, the Allies chose our shah, so they can control our oil!"

"Of course!" Baba's stern voice sounded in our ears. "That's why first, the British brought that Hungry Soldier." He dried his lips. "And then they gave the crown to his son, this stooge!"

Nima grumbled in agreement with my father. "Of the measly money that this traitor gets for our oil, part of it goes to build extravagant palaces to pay for the lavishness of the royal lifestyle, and the rest is stashed in his Swiss bank accounts!"

"Not much left for the poor nation!" Baba grumbled.

Nima had to be right, I thought. Since Naser Al-Din Shah, who built the Golestan Palace, every king built one new fortress for himself and his family.

"And the king turns a blind eye and deaf ears to our poverty." Amir's strong voice startled me. He continued as he walked in. "Most of our people are drowning in destitution!"

I was devastated. How was it possible? Our king, the shadow of God, betrayed his people like this? I was baffled.

"Iran khanoom," Nima turned to me. His look warmed my heart. "I wish I could stay and tell you all about our hero, Mossadegh. But he's giving a speech in front of the bazaar, and I have to go." He shoved his white handkerchief back into his pocket.

"I'd love to come with you to hear this great man!" Amir said.

The sound of their footsteps made me understand how I yearned to go with them. I desired I could hear Mossadegh in person. But I knew well there would be no women there. Men were free to go, listen, choose, and vote. We women had to sit, wash, cook, clean, and bear children, and when we became old, like Mamani, we could only pray. But we could utter no words in public— our mouths were covered with invisible muzzles, even though our veils had disappeared.

□ □ □

If Mossadegh was *a ray of sunshine* for our nation, Nima brought sunshine to our home. My father's frail body came to life whenever Nima walked into his room; as if he were a dying tree and Nima were his gardener. Baba called him our newsman. My father and brother, Amir, sat together with him. They put him on a pedestal and paid their undivided attention to him.

One day, Nima brought us a newspaper with the title, *Defa-e-Moshtarek*, All United.

"See, I've published my own newspaper. Mossadegh inspires us all. He's leading us to the path of freedom and unity." With his subtle smile, he gazed into my eyes.

Freedom! The word sounded strange coming from a man. I always thought our men were free to do whatever they desired. They could go wherever they wanted to go, or say whatever they decided to say. They had never worn veils or invisible muzzles.

"At least we know someone's fighting for our freedom!" Amir said with joy.

"In this land, men are free!" I said as I stood up to bring some tea or watermelon for our guest Nima.

"Iran khanoom ..." He stared at me; his eyes lighted up my heart. He reached to me as if he intended to take my hand. "Please, don't go." He swallowed. "On the surface, it appears that way, as if men are free!"

I sat back down and said, "Yes, you don't have to get permission to open your mouth, or state your opinions."

"Iran, please!" Amir said, looking agitated.

Nima let out a sigh of irritation. "I am not free to publish everything I know in my paper. I cannot write about how corrupt our royal family is! But, with help of Mossadegh, perhaps one day ..."

"Iran, do you really believe we men are free?" Amir asked. "If anyone opens his mouth and expresses any opposition to the regime ..."

"Then our bodies would be placed in the bottom of the salt lake on the way to Quom!" Nima murmured, lowering his head.

I was embarrassed by my naïvety. I looked at the headline: *"Mossadegh for Prime Minister!"*

"Is he now our prime minister?" I asked in a humble voice. Politics was the realm of men, and I was embarrassed by my lack of knowledge.

"Not yet! Our majlis elected him, but the shah's signature is needed." Nima continued in an irritated voice, "And of course, this tyrant is in no rush to sign it!"

"It's too bad," Baba added. "Our recently assassinated prime minister was from the Qajar Dynasty! I knew him!" He then sank into deep thoughts, disconnected from us, as Amir's angry voice thundered in the room: "Well, he was a handpicked puppet to the shah, just like your brother was as the personal physician of the previous king. In the majlis, this prime minister blew his horn against Mossadegh's push to nationalize oil."

"Our prime minister was killed by a clergyman." Nima's soft voice filled the room. "This means the clergies are also in opposition to the shah. We, as a nation, have come together from all different groups. We are united behind Mossadegh." Nima raised his hand as if he was in a demonstration and continued, "Being *united*! This is what we must have. It's like air essential to our existence. Without it …"

I cut in, "Do you mean all different groups, such as clergymen, bazaari—"

Baba interrupted me, "What exactly our previous leader had to do when he came to power twenty plus years ago, he had to *unite* our people, not to *tafragheh*, to make us an enemy with each other!"

"Tell you all the truth," Amir's voice jarred me. "We don't need a king!" Amir ran his fingers through his jet-black, curly hair. "The king is the root of our miseries."

"Amir, what are you saying?" I stared at him in disbelief. "Generation after generation, we've had kings and prime ministers. A nation without a king is like a body without a head!" I felt brave enough to express the truth in my heart.

"As long as the king doesn't have any power," my father said in his weak voice, "we must have a regime like England."

"Where the queen can reign like a king," I said.

Nima removed his glasses. "Or like in America, where they elect their president and their representatives." He stared into my eyes. "Isn't that wonderful, Iran khanoom? Americans, men and women, go to polls and vote. They always give a new chance to a different political group— unlike here where the power stays in one person's hand, and then it's transferred to his son." He put on his glasses. It seemed each time he talked about our government he preferred to hide his eyes behind his glasses. "I yearn for a government," Nima continued, "to warrant every individual's liberty, root out poverty and bring our lifestyle up to the standards of the Western world."

"God knows," Amir said, "we have enough black pearls for everyone."

"You young ones," my father said, and we all turned to him, "bring any government you want. But make sure the mullahs and clergymen do not take over this country, for they would take us back to the dark ages ..." Baba pulled the blanket over his shoulders and closed his eyes.

"There are other countries," Amir jumped in, "that don't have a king. They do much better than we do!"

"Like where?" I asked.

"Russia, for example! Their regime is communist. The wealth of the country goes to one bucket—then, it's divided fairly among everybody."

"Amir, how do you know this?" I said in disbelief.

"Iran," Amir lowered his voice, "I think I can trust all

three of you!" He pointed at each one of us.

Nima and I nodded. Baba opened his eyes and stared at Amir.

"Of course!" I said.

"I'm a member of the Communist Party, *tudeh*."

I hit my cheek. "Amir, you know how this party is a despicable creature in the eyes of our king!"

And Nima followed. "Watch out, Amir! There's a direct order from the shah to execute any member of this party if they're caught."

"Without a trial?" I asked, gasping for air.

"Whatever you do, take very good care of yourself." We all heard Baba's words.

"I'm not scared of death!" Amir's fearless voice rang in my ears.

"Amir's partly right! There're two things tying this country down." Nima pushed his slippery glasses back to his nose. "One is this absurd monarchy—"

"And the second is our ridiculous religion!" Amir finished Nima's thoughts.

After listening to these men, I knew my world was shattered. They disarmed me and destroyed my core beliefs. But, I refused to keep quiet. "Islam and our king are like blood flowing in our veins! How can you tell Mamani her prayers don't matter?"

"Well, you see that they don't!" Amir mocked me. "With all her prayers, our mother and siblings died. If there was a god, why didn't he do something about it?"

"God doesn't make a good life for us!" Nima broke in. "It's up to us!" He then turned to me again. "Iran khanoom," Nima's eyes behind his glasses gazed on me with pity. "These futile beliefs are what the mullahs and the supporters of our king drilled into our heads to rob us of our freedom and wealth."

That day, I wondered who had the key to the truth, the clergymen, the nationalists, the Communist Party, or our shah, Mohammad Reza Pahlavi.

¤ ¤ ¤

In the days to come, Amir changed a lot. Mamani and I seldom saw him. He ate with us no more. At nights, if he was at home, he ate upstairs with Malik khanoom, our house owner. Most nights, when everyone was asleep, men were tiptoeing through our courtyard on their way upstairs. The glow of their kerosene lamps kept me awake in the corner of the courtyard, in our mosquito net protecting Mamani and me.

I was baffled by these men. Was Amir involved in a conspiracy? He was against our king, I knew. Was he against Mossadegh too? It appeared that way. Unlike Nima, I never heard Amir say anything in support of Mossadegh. I wondered what exactly he was up to.

¤ ¤ ¤

One Friday, when Yusof, my step-brother, came to visit our father, he asked me on his way out, "What's the matter, Iran? Why are your eyes swollen?" I gazed into our cloddy yard. No words came out of my mouth. I felt I was still that young girl who lived with him and his wife Azar in Abadan.

"Where is Hassan?" he asked as if he was ordering his soldiers around. Uncle Hassan entered the room, and Yusof addressed him, "Tomorrow, go with Iran and register her at the Teacher Training School." He placed his hat on his head. "Thanks to His Majesty, this school is available to girls with some high school education. It's not far from the bazaar and it's free. They pay for everything, including materials. In two years, Iran will be a teacher with an income."

"But …" Hassan started to object.

Yusof interrupted him in a harsh voice, "Now it's no longer an age in which only men work. Women must also work." Without another word, he dashed out of our house.

◘ ◘ ◘

As a future teacher, I was pleased to get up every day and go to my school. I did not care that I would neither obtain a diploma, nor go to the University of Tehran and sit beside male students. After the two-year training, I could only teach at elementary schools for the rest of my life. I could never be like Azar, Yusof's wife, who spoke French and taught at high schools. Still, I was better off than most girls. They could not even read or write. They would never earn any money in their lives. Their husbands had to support them.

The most exciting news came to us when we heard our king would visit our school within the week. I went to my principal and told her, "For His Majesty's visit, I would love to be the school representative to welcome him to our school."

She looked at me warily. "Why?"

"I'm not afraid of large audiences. I love to act and having him here would be like being on stage again."

"Let me see!" The principal looked me over with her foxy eyes and said, "Your almond shaped eyes with your slender nose are perfect. Tell me; are you from the previous dynasty?"

I looked down to hide my embarrassment. She thought she was at the bazaar buying a cow.

"With your wide connected eyebrows," she broke my

thoughts, "You must be ..." She then gazed at my hair. "Did you go to a beauty salon to get those beautiful curls?"

I shook my head. "We can't afford ..."

"Then how did you do them?"

"I used papers. For each curl, one piece."

"Hopefully not from the notebooks we give you!"

No words came out of my mouth.

"You are beautiful! Hmmm!" She scratched her chin. "I guess we can present you to our king. But I don't think you can speak to him. Commoners are not allowed."

"Why not?"

"Perhaps you can give him a bouquet of flowers!"

"Not even a welcome message?"

"Who do you think you are?" she said with contempt. "Ordinary people are not permitted to address His Majesty!"

The sound of the bell saved me.

□ □ □

On the day of the shah's visit, for the first time in a long time, I felt sugar was melting in my belly. The night before, I could not sleep. I closed my eyes, but my mind would not leave me alone. I did not even know what I would say. Then, I realized. Our principal was right—a commoner was never allowed to address a king.

While I was walking to school, I pretended to be calm. We were aware. Our queen, the sister of the Egyptian king, had returned to her country. For a while, her brother refused to release our former king's body, which traveled through Egypt, unless our shah would send the queen's divorce decree. In due course, he did.

Whenever I replayed the events of that day in my mind, it all happened so fast, in the blink of an eye. At last, His

Majesty stepped out of his jeep. My principal was standing behind me holding my shoulders, and she nudged me to go forward. I could only hear the sound of my pounding heart, but as soon as I saw his bright young face, the hand of God took over. I stepped toward him with a bouquet of colorful flowers. He wore his usual khaki outfit, which was very similar to that of a soldier. It was obvious, however, that his was woven with different threads. He was like no one else. With the Almighty's will, his father became a king and took the crown from my ancestors. Today, this man was the king and my father was a commoner.

We knew the shah had been educated in Switzerland. He was a dashing young man, very soft-spoken. Even though I stood only a few steps away from him, I could not hear what he said to his soldiers. I opened my mouth to express my joy at meeting him when one of his cohorts murmured in his ear and led him away from me. With my feet solidly on the ground, in a loud voice, I said, "Your Majesty." He stopped.

"Whatever they tell you about how they are using the funds to further our education is not true!" I read in his eyes, *What do you mean?* I was baffled with myself—I could not understand how I could be so bold, as if my mind were not in charge. The words came out of my mouth without my control. I was determined to attract him like a rose charms a bee.

I swallowed and continued. "We do not have enough books, papers ..." I could not finish my sentence. Our principal pulled my coat. "Iran! Stop! Stop!"

I turned to her. "Leave me alone, I want to talk with my—"

His body guards were successful. They took him away from me and our principal pushed me to the crowd away from him and his car.

After his visit, as soon as His Majesty sat in the car, I pushed my way through the men protecting him. In an angry voice I screamed, "Let me go! I want to talk with His Majesty!"

But, the principal, the one closest to his car and the guards, tried to yank me away from him. I was oblivious to their efforts. Like an insane person, I was wiggling my way out when His Majesty's calm, reassuring voice said, "Let her come closer!"

I was even more shocked when he changed his seat to sit closer to me. I knew he was impressed. So I became even bolder.

"Your Majesty, please forgive me." I looked into his eyes, and he looked into mine. In a flash of a light, I thought I heard him say, *"Iran, you're the most beautiful girl I've ever seen. Get into the car, and come with me to my palace. You're my queen!"*

Instead, I heard, "I'll send my own envoy to look into the matters at your school." *So simple!* Right away, his car and his companions' motorcycles sped away while I was still standing on the gravel. I understood that Allah had forever closed the door to me becoming a queen. My mother, Shirin, used to say, "Allah inscribes one's fate on her forehead before sending her to this world." So it was not etched on my forehead to be a queen, just as it had not been etched onto Mamani Zahra's forehead. Fate had to be playing a game with us.

We had to be nothing, to remain commoners as long as we lived.

¤ ¤ ¤

One day, during my second year of school, I heard a whisper in my ear as I was walking by the bazaar. "Iran joon, how are you?" I turned around. At first, I thought I was dreaming of Morad again. Day after day, I fantasized he had come to Tehran, and today was no exception. I shut my eyes tight.

"Iran joon, open your eyes!"

Morad was standing before me in new white starched shirt, black pants, and shiny leather shoes. He no longer wore the clothes he used to wear in Shiraz—the washed-out shirt, pants, and the fabric shoes. For a moment, I thought I had turned into a stone. I never expected to see him in my life again. He had to read my astonishment in my face. "I live in Tehran now."

"Where's Tooba?"

"Everything's happening here." He gazed into my eyes. "I couldn't forget you."

I yearned for him to hold me in his arms and kiss me the way he did in Shiraz. I swallowed the knot in my throat, stared into the dirt on the ground, and murmured, "You can't talk with me on the street like this! What would happen if one of my relatives sees me talking to a strange man so closely?"

"I saw your performance," he said. "You're really an actress!" Before I could open my mouth, he whispered, "Come this afternoon to my house to see Tooba and my mother!" He shoved a piece of paper in my hand and disappeared into the bazaar. The address written on the paper was not very far from where we lived. I wondered if at last God had brought my love to me. In recent years, I had rejected all my suitors. I could not wait to get home to share my news with Mamani Zahra! Perhaps this time my father would forget his noble blood and allow me to marry Morad.

"Mamani, guess who I saw today?" I blasted when I walked into the room.

She stopped counting her holy beads, and in her calm voice asked, "Who, dear?"

"Morad! He lives here now. His house isn't very far from us. He wants me to go there this afternoon!"

She stopped rolling her beads. "How do you dare to go to his house?" Her kind voice turned harsh. "A young girl … alone … what has this world come to?"

"Mamani, I'm his sister's friend! Remember, in Shiraz, I used to stay overnight at their house!"

"That was before we knew he had his eyes on you!"

"The way he was dressed today, he must have found a good job, earning lots of money. Now, I'm sure he can afford a wife."

"Money isn't everything, Iran!" Mamani picked up her holy beads and started counting them again. "He doesn't have a decent education, nor is he from a respectable family. You're from a royal family—don't you ever forget that. Your father won't allow it!"

"I know. He wants me to marry Nima, our newsman. I see how he perks up whenever he comes to our house."

"Justifiably so!" she said raising her voice.

"Mamani," I increased my voice even higher, "I *love* Morad!"

In the past, I never dared to confess my love for Morad. Today, I revealed my secret for the first time. The words jumped out of my mouth without my control. "Mamani, remember the day in Shiraz when Amir threw Morad's mother and sister out? None of you understood how Amir shattered my soul." I felt the warmth of my tears on my cheeks. "I should've run to Amir and confessed my love for Morad. But I was not brave!" I wiped my face with my hands and looked into Mamani's eyes. I read their burden of sorrows when I continued. "Today after seeing Morad by the bazaar, I can sit aside quietly no longer. I'm ready to trumpet my love for him to the world." I looked again into her sad eyes. "Nothing or nobody can change my mind!" With that, I marched out of the room.

However, I could not calm the storm inside me. It would be too bold of me to go to his house all alone. Somehow, I knew my grandmother was right. No young girl could dare to go to a man's house. But his mother and Tooba were there, I reasoned with myself. Then, later on, they could walk me home. A girl and a man were not supposed to be together without a chaperon. Besides, I was confident. I was strong and Morad did not have the audacity to do anything improper. Over the years, my father had dashed the powder of wisdom on me. He talked frankly with me about the proper way for a girl to react to a man's desire. Whenever we walked together in the street and a young man stared at me, Baba uttered, "Iran, you have the control to decide whether or not to encourage a man to look at you with lust. If you do not encourage his behavior, he will give up and go on to his way. Don't ever forget! You are in charge."

Therefore, I was confident that no harm could come to me in Morad's house.

¤ ¤ ¤

Morad opened the door to me. "Come in!"

It was a small house with a triangular yard.

"Where is Tooba?"

"Come in. Mother's here!"

"Iran khanoom." His mother came out of the kitchen and led me to the room next door to it.

I was shocked. She neither hugged nor kissed me. I

sensed her coldness. Clearly, she had not forgotten my brother Amir's behavior toward her.

"Is Tooba here?"

"No, dear! Didn't Morad tell you? She's a married woman now, living in Shiraz. I came here to be with Morad …" She paused and led me in. "Did Morad tell you?" She lowered her voice.

"What?"

His mother smiled. "The other day, we celebrated Morad's betrothal to the hajji's daughter."

"Hajji's daughter?" I felt my life was sucked out of me in an instant.

"Iran khanoom, are you all right? You look pale! Sit down!"

"I'm fine …" I lied.

"Let me get you some tea!" She rushed into the kitchen.

I wanted to get up and run out. I was appalled. Morad had neglected to mention his future wife. I did not understand then why he invited me to his house. On the other hand, this morning, I could read his love for me in his eyes. Morad walked into the room; his voice jarred me. "Iran joon, it's good to see you here in my house!"

My heartbeat escalated. I tried to quiet the nagging voice in my heart, which reminded me of my promise not to be alone in a room with him again. I felt sweat beading on my forehead. I took my handkerchief from my purse and wiped it off. I was trembling. I did not want to confront him right away—I wanted to see whether or not he would tell me about his betrothal.

"Business is good here!" he said.

I looked down, entranced by the obscured red and white patterns on the rug. He came closer to me and reached to raise my chin. "Look at me!"

With a harsh move I jumped up.

"Iran joon, what happened?" He stood beside me.

"You must have a good job to have such a nice house …"

"I work for a hajji in the bazaar."

"And he pays you so much that you can buy your own house?"

"He likes me a lot—he even wants to give me his daughter!" he grinned.

I felt a wave of fury roll over my body. "Wants? Is she pretty?"

"I love only you, Iran joon!" he whispered.

I dared not confront him and ask about his engagement. I was drowning in a sea of confusion. I had no courage. I yearned to spit in his face for lying to me—that was the punishment for lying. But I did nothing. I was not surprised that his words of love for me left me cold. Nothing was like it had been in Shiraz. I tried to keep my cool and let him confess to me.

His voice broke my thoughts: "How come you haven't been married yet? Hasn't Amir found a rich man for his sister?"

I despised his crafty smile.

"What's he doing now?"

I kept quiet.

"Is the rumor around town true?"

"What rumor?"

"That he hosts secret political gatherings?"

"Secret gatherings? What do you mean?" I tried to hide my anger by wrestling with my purse handle.

"He's gone too far. Being against His Majesty, I mean."

"What are you talking about?"

Morad raised his voice. "He's a member of the Communist Party!"

I could see the fire of anger in Morad's eyes. "We have our eye on him and know every move he makes!"

I concealed my fury the best I could and asked, "What about us?"

"Your family, especially Amir, has been against me before, and without a doubt, now we're each other's enemy! He's *Tudehi* and I'm *Shahi*."

"I thought Mossadegh wants to work with all groups and unite the nation?"

"If Mossadegh imagines our country without our Shahan Shah, then it'll be the end of Mossadegh too."

I pressed my long nails into my palm and asked, "At what price?"

"Any price! Even if we have to kill everybody, including Mossadegh!"

Before my eyes, Morad had transformed into a monster. I wondered how I could have loved a man with such a dark heart. I could tolerate him no more, and rushed outside where the breeze from the Alborz Mountain soothed my soul.

◻ ◻ ◻

A few weeks later, my family members and I were sitting in my father's royal family mausoleum. We were listening to a mullah reciting part of the Koran. That morning before sunrise when Mamani got up for praying, I also got up to prepare Baba's breakfast. I took Baba's tea to his room. My several knocks went unanswered. I tired of waiting and walked in, placed the tray on the floor, and went to his bed where he lay, eyes closed. I said to wake him, "Baba joon, your tea!"

A morbid feeling came over me. I shook him gently. I put my hand on his forehead. It was cold to the touch.

I ran out and called, "Amir, hurry, hurry. Something's wrong with Baba."

He ran in the room, immediately flew out and said, "I have to fetch a doctor."

I sat on the ground weeping quietly. Mamani came and sat by me too. My heart was telling me that something dreadful had happened. It seemed ages until Amir and a doctor arrived.

"So sorry! Your father's in heaven now," the doctor asserted when he walked out of Baba's room.

Mamani and I hugged each other and our crying intensified. As a Moslim tradition, we had to bury our loved one before the sunset. Through the doctor, the burial happened very fast. Amir went and let Sima, my half-sister, know, and she informed all the other relatives.

When I looked at the fresh dirt on his tomb, I refused to accept that Baba, Ali khan, had left this world. I wished my father had taken me to the grave with him. Being six feet under would put a stop to my bewilderment. Here, as a woman, I had lost my father, mother, and five of my siblings to death. My love for Morad was instantly shattered when I learned he was going to marry a hajji's daughter. If he loved me the way I loved him, he would have resisted the marriage. It would have been much easier for him— he was a man. *Thank Allah!* I was lucky. My father's words rang in my ears: "Iran, you must decide—not me. I'm not the one who will live with the lad."

"Iran joon," Sima crashed my world. "Why aren't you married yet?" she asked. Her husband, who had been educated in Paris, said, "Now that Ali khan is gone! A girl needs a protector!"

Husband! I thought Morad would be my husband. But that dream of mine had also turned to ashes. And the way he talked! He supported our king wholeheartedly.

He turned a deaf ear to what other people wanted. I was afraid for Amir. I knew. The shah destroyed anyone who opposed his power. Rumor had it that he was looking into some way to get rid of Mossadegh, our elected prime minister. My brother, Amir, was sold to his Party. My uneducated Mamani devoted her life to Islam. But I had no idea to which group I belonged.

"Thank God," Sima murmured in my ears, "at last my father is beside my mother." She wiped her tears. "Now, both are together again!"

Wealthy people lost all touch with the way the rest of us lived. I could bet Sima's world was as quiet as a morning breeze. She did not care if she bruised my soul with her remarks. I was relieved that my mother's grave was in Shiraz at a public cemetery, not a place like this. Thank God, she was not mixed in with these heartless rich people. Here, every grave was raised like a platform, so different from how our Prophet, Mohammad, had instructed us. The marble on one tombstone looked more expensive than the next. The sparkle of gold calligraphy on each was an exhibition of the family's wealth. The affluent ones did not bother to follow any rules, even God's. This place was dedicated only to people with royal blood from our previous Qajar Dynasty. It was not for my mother, Shirin, or even for me, since I only had half-royal blood. I understood the war in me was the battle between fire and water. I had no idea which one to choose.

Today, the mystery of life dismayed me. It seemed I was the only one with an internal conflict. I could not marry Morad, for he was not from a royal family, nor would the king take me to his palace, for I was no princess. When I looked around, I felt lonely amongst the crowd. Amir was so dedicated to his party that he was willing to sacrifice his life. He had no internal battle. But not me! Before I listened to my heart, I had to decide what people would say about anything I wanted to do. I was gagged as if by a muzzle.

◻ ◻ ◻

Soon after my father's death, Nima, our newsman, stopped coming to our house, and Amir became more engaged with tudeh's secret meetings.

Amir used Malik khanoom's empty rooms to conduct secret get-togethers with the members. Mossadegh was our prime minister and had tried to cleanse our land of foreign footsteps by taking the power from our king.

I read in *Defa-e-Moshtarek*, All United, that Mossadegh had appeared before the international court in Holland asking for the immediate withdrawal of the British forces from our homeland. He attested that his desire was to create a monarchy regime like Britain. When I folded the paper, I saw the headline: *"Mossadegh Is Determined to Cleanse our Land of British Aggressors."*

"Iran joon," Mamani spoke up emphatically, "it's time for you to choose a suitor and get married! The only wish I have is to see your children before I leave this world."

"Mamani, I don't have to get married! Soon, I'll be a teacher, have an income of my own, and can take care of both of us." I loved to disagree with Mamani, but I knew better. I had to decide on a suitor sooner or later. No girl my age could get by without a father or husband for long.

"My dear," Mamani corrected me, "we women come here to marry and give birth, so our children can live our legacy! If a girl doesn't have any children, she hasn't paid her dues to Allah!"

"I fell in love once. According to you and Amir, he wasn't good for me. It must not be written on my forehead to marry!"

"Nonsense! Every girl's fate is to marry! What about our newsman?"

"Nima? He is a nice man, but ..."

"A girl is not supposed to feel anything toward any man who has no relation to her," Mamani cut me off, "but when she weds and gives birth, she learns to love her entire family!"

Perhaps Mamani had a point. If I had one or two children, I would be busy raising them. Maybe then I would forget the bewilderment in me.

In my silence, she said, "I should have a talk with Amir!"

◻ ◻ ◻

The year 1953 was not only etched in my life, but it was engraved in our nation's history. I was taken aback when my brother Amir told Mamani, "We'll be lucky if Nima's interested in Iran!"

In reality, Nima was more than interested in me. One night, Amir brought him to our house for dinner. Afterwards, Amir left Nima and me in the room to help Mamai in the kitchen.

"Iran khanoom ..." Nima looked directly at me. His eyes behind his glasses were beaming with love for me. "I hope the invitation was from you as well!"

I nodded.

"I had a talk with Amir earlier, and he gave me his permission to ask you ..." He swallowed. I had no idea what he read in my eyes, but he took my trembling hand in his soft, artistic hand. "Iran, I hope you agree to be my wife. I wanted to ask your father for your hand several times, but I could never get the words out of my mouth." A subtle smile covered his face. "I'm happy that Amir encouraged me to talk with you tonight."

I could not force my mouth open. Somehow, I turned into that scared little girl again. I could not put my feelings into words. I was disappointed with my destiny, for I wished that, instead of Nima, Morad, the one I had fallen in love with in Shiraz would have asked me to marry him.

Mamani's words stung in my ears: "Nima's a gentleman and he loves you! That's all that is needed for a marriage."

My eyes stayed on the run-down Kermani rug, Mamani Zahra's dowry. She was right. I had to marry and have a family of my own. I knew this tradition covered me like an invisible veil.

¤ ¤ ¤

It took a little longer before Nima could make his father consent to our marriage. I could replay the conversation between him and Nima in my head: "Nima! Why do you want to marry this poor girl, Iran?"

"Agha, Iran is the most beautiful girl I've ever seen. She and I can talk about politics."

"She has no dowry! Why don't you marry your cousin? Her father's rich. Her dowry needs more than ten camels to carry!"

"Iran will be a teacher soon! It's better than any dowry. She'll be independent!"

Today, Nima's father and his stepmother were here. We could not invite any guests, for it was not yet a year since my father's death—even Malik khanoom did not come downstairs. It was a simple ceremony. Nima gave me his mother's ring and I said, "Yes," to the mullah after he asked me the first time. I had rejected our long-lasting tradition of waiting to be asked three times before accepting. I was proudly leaving some of our silly traditions behind.

When I sat on the soozani and looked in the round mirror before me, I felt my churning stomach give way to serenity. The soozani, the tapestry, tied me to Maman Shirin, Mamani Zahra, her mother Fatemeh, and on and on! We were united. I yearned to have a girl so that one day she could sit on this soozani too. I would do exactly what my mother and grandmother had done. I would learn to love my husband.

After the ceremony, Nima lived in his father's house and I continued to live with Mamani and Amir until Nima could find a place for us to live. Some days, he came for a visit and had dinner with us. He never stayed overnight, even though we were husband and wife. Instead, we had to live as if we were only engaged.

As we moved on through the days, we learned Mossadegh had won the case against the British, and the international court ordered that all British forces pull out of our land at once. Mossadegh's picture covered the front page of *Defa-e-Moshtarek*, All United, and other newspapers. Mossadegh even traveled to America, and we saw on the front page he had a visit with President Truman as well. Proudly, Nima said to me, "*Time* magazine printed Mossadegh's picture on its cover and called him 'Man of the Year'!"

He was our hero. Every night, the news featured our prime minister. There was no word about Shahan Shah, except when he would leave the country to go to Switzerland for the winter vacation, or for his summer vacation.

One day, while passing on my way by the bazaar, I was jarred by the sight of men, shouting with their fists in the air, "Mossadegh, feed us!"

That night, when Nima sat down at dinner with Mamani and me, in a gloomy voice he said, "The export of petroleum has stopped!"

I was shocked. "No export, no income for the country!"

"Right! With his accomplice, Britain, this traitor, the shah, has convinced the world that Mossadegh is pro-communist, and the Western world has boycotted our oil!"

"How could they do that?"

"They brought America into their corner! People don't have money, and families are hungry!" Nima turned to me with his sad eyes. "I'm afraid our nation's drowning."

"And it seems no one can do anything," Mamani whispered.

"Above all, theocrats, and even some nationalists, have dropped their support of Mossadegh." Nima tapped his hand on the floor. "They think Mossadegh wants to steer the country in the direction of communism!" His face turned red—he was furious.

"But he's good for the people!" I protested. "Mossadegh's washing away the foreign footsteps."

"Iran joon," Mamani said, "How can he be good? He doesn't practice Allah's law!"

The events of the month to follow proved Nima was right. We were drowning and our supposed rescuers shoved their boots into our throats instead of saving us.

Early one morning, we heard on the radio that our majlis did not have enough votes to re-elect Mossadegh. The shah signed a decree to appoint a military man, Zahedi, to be our prime minister and the head of our army. Afterwards the shah fled the country.

"My Allah!" Mamani raised her hands to the sky, beseeching, "What are we going to do? The *shadow of Allah* is gone!"

That night, when Nima came to our house, he said, "I'm not sure what to think! It's great that the traitor, the shah, has gone away for now." He took off his glasses. "Hopefully, the people will have a chance to get Mossadegh back as Prime Minister." Then, he frowned and murmured, "But, why did the shah appoint his servant, Zahedi, to be the prime minister?"

"Isn't he, like Mossadegh, approved by our majlis?" I asked.

"Far from it! People do not want him. Zahedi is an obedient servant of the shah." Without finishing his dinner, he got up to leave and asked, "Where is Amir?"

"We don't know. He hasn't come home for a few nights!"

"When you see him, tell him to come to my print shop. I'll be there," Nima said, then rushed out.

Late at night, we heard on the radio that Zahedi, with some military men, had invaded Mossadegh's house and arrested him. I was appalled. Our land had become lawless! There was no protection for our beloved Mossadegh. Our hero was thrown out and spit on by the supporters of the shah.

The next day, it wasn't only the weather of Tehran that reached its boiling point, but people's tempers surged as well. On my way to school, I glanced at the bazaar's closed, iron gate. Very odd! I never recalled seeing its gate shut during the day. A crowd of men and youths carried Mossadegh's picture with their fists to the sky, chanting, "Free Mossadegh!"

I stood at a corner, trying to become invisible. There was not even one woman in the crowd. In no time, another group, larger than the first, started shouting, "Long live Shahan Shah, Mohammad Reza Pahlavi!" Among them, I saw some bazaaris with their cloaks and some mullahs in their white turbans. In no time, the shah's supporters collided with Mossadegh's. Soon, the sounds of gunshots filled the air. I wanted to rush into Mossadegh's group to support our innocent men. They had no weapons to defend themselves. Their bodies were falling down, covered in blood. But my feet were glued to the ground.

I wanted Mossadegh to stay and be our prime minister. He was good for our people. For the first time, he was determined to cover us with the blanket of freedom and release us from British aggression. He was determined to give us back the dignity and liberty of our ancient empire. On the other hand, I yearned for our king, the *shadow of God*, to shade us. The etched picture of the king on the wall of Persepolis flashed before my eyes. For over twenty-five centuries, we had been governed by our kings. How could we live without him now? I felt weak and confused.

That night I looked into his sorrowful face and asked, "Nima, why can't the shah and Mossadegh both stay, and work together?"

He burst like a volcano. "Because the Puppet of the West is not a patriotic leader! He's a playboy who only wants to have a good time. I wish the clergy and nationalists would return their support to Mossadegh, and now that the shah's gone, we can elect Mossadegh as our president. We would have a regime as democratic as America's."

"Is that why today there weren't more people for Mossadegh?"

"The shah somehow convinced everyone inside and outside the country that Mossadegh wants to turn Iran into a communist country." He stopped. With his head down he murmured, "It's possible that this traitor has the support of the Western world. There's no way he could get rid of Mossadegh so easily without their help!"

I was puzzled. "Nima, how do you know this?"

"Just guessing!" His unusually stern voice filled the room.

After three days, the country cooled down. On the third day, we learned that the Shahan Shah, the king of kings, had returned to us as our leader.

That hot afternoon, I was by the pool in our courtyard

washing dishes. Our entrance door banged open. Amir entered. I got up to embrace him. "Where have …"

As if I were invisible, he rushed upstairs. His appearance bothered me, for in the past he had always looked neat and clean. Now, his shiny, dark hair was disheveled. His light suit was wrinkled, and his shoes were mud-spattered. I hurried behind him. He could not hear me for I was barefoot.

He opened the door to Malik khanoom's room and she gasped, "Amir joon!" and stared into his yellow face.

"Be quiet! Here!" He tossed a small black notebook to her. "Hide this …"

Before he could finish, we all heard the footsteps of men climbing the stairs. One voice familiar to me yelled, "Where is Amir? We're here to take him!" I turned. Morad and two other men in black suits and white shirts stood there. Morad pretended he did not know me. I wished the ground would open up and swallow me. He turned to Malik khanoom and said, "Sorry for the intrusion, lady. We need to arrest Amir Amirian!" Morad's stern's voice jarred me.

"But why?" I shouted.

"Be quiet, khanoom!" Morad said, without turning his head to me. The flash of handcuffs made me sick.

"No need for this!" Amir said in a calm voice. His look shocked me. He was no longer my younger brother. His unshaven beard gave him the look of a wise man. His calm voice shattered my heart. "I'll come with you!"

Morad barked, "Before we go, we need to search the house!"

"NO, YOU DON'T!" Her voice froze the men. Malik khanoom removed her glasses and closed the book that had been resting in her lap. I read the gold calligraphy: *Divan-e-Hafiz*!

"But, khanoom we're informed that Amir has a notebook with a list of names," Morad protested. "These men are from the *tudeh* party, and we have a direct order to arrest them all!"

"There is nothing here," Malik khanoom said defiantly. "He and his family are my tenants. They don't have the nerve to go against my rules. Out! Out, before I complain to General Zahedi!"

Upon hearing the name of our new prime minister, the two other men each took Amir's arms and pushed him out. Morad, in a flattering voice, said, "Malik khanoom, sorry for the disturbance!" On his way out, he threw a grim look at me. He was oblivious to the tears rolling down my cheeks, or the blood in my mouth from biting my lips.

After the door closed behind them, Malik khanoom rested her head on the Divan and pulled the black notebook from her cleavage. "Iran, burn this right away! You and your grandmother need to move out of here! Why don't you go to your husband's house?"

I saw Malik khanoom's lips moving, but I could hear nothing. The universe had disappeared behind God's fury.

The days became dark. The sun existed no more. The unbelievable political storm destroyed everything, including Amir and me.

Day and night, Mamani and I drowned in our tears and waited for Amir to walk in. When after more than six months there was no sign of Amir, I had to listen to Nima. "Don't wait any longer," he said, biting his knuckles. "I know it's hard for you to admit, but it's very likely Amir's body is with several others at the bottom of the sea-salt lake near Quom. You're lucky. Because of your half-brother, Yusof, being a high rank officer, they didn't come after you and your grandmother."

With tears, I wailed, "I don't understand why one has to pay with his life if he's in opposition to the regime."

"Our leader refuses to put his people's interests in front of his own," Nima responded somberly.

At last, I understood the bitter truth. In our beloved homeland, our shah was our undeniable master, and we were treated like his mules. In our land, immoveable muzzles covered women and men's mouths alike. No one was able to remove them regardless of how many lives were lost. We dragged our hero into the mud and treated him like a villain.

Some of us knew well. Our ray of sunshine had dipped under thick clouds forever.

12. Kaleidoscope

Tehran, Persia, 1963
Mitra (9)

The month of Ramadan was upon us. As a nine-year-old girl, I was not fond of this month. Most of my classmates put on scarves or chador, and fasted. From day one, over and over, they asked me, "Mitra, are you fasting?"

"No!" I had to mutter while walking toward my classroom.

Kobra, in her green scarf believed she was *sayed*, a direct descendant of our Prophet Mohammad. She approached me with the voice of a bully and said, "Why not?"

I paused. I refused to confess. In my house, only Mamani Zahra prayed, but she was too old to fast. My mother, Iran, had to look after my baby sister, Layla, in addition to being a teacher. She had no strength left to fast. My father, Nima, said over and over, "I'm not a sheep to follow my shepherd."

I recalled that even during the month of Moharram, when everybody commemorated the Tragedy of Karbala, my family mourned my uncle Amir's death. I could think of no good reason why my mother, Mamani Zahra, and

Baba thought he was dead. They never saw his body, and we had no grave to visit. According to them, some of the shah's men invaded their house one day and took him away. Uncle Amir was their martyr. The throng believed Imam Hossein was the only martyr—not anyone in my family.

"Hey Mitra!" Kobra sat behind me in the classroom and did not leave me alone. She nudged me, "What are you thinking? You haughty girl, wearing no scarf! No praying, no fasting …"

Mrs. Sami, the teacher who taught us the Koran lessons, walked in. Out of respect, we rose from our seats. She was an eyesore among the rest of our teachers in our school. Her hefty body covered most of the chair, and soon, the smell of rose water permeated the room. Her scent reminded me of Mamani Zahra. Rose water had an odd aroma when it mixed with the perfume from Paris that my mother wore. *Thank God*, she came to our classroom only twice a week. We girls at age nine had to start practicing Islam, praying five times a day, and learn how to read the Koran in Arabic.

She wiped off the beaded sweat from her stern face with her handkerchief. Mrs. Sami, unlike our regular teacher, Mrs. Riyahi, was old and always wore a scarf. There was a rumor that she had insisted on shrouding herself in chador, but the principal rejected her wish. She always took off her chador right before entering the schoolyard. There were no men in our school. The teachers, including our principal, were women, and we students were all girls.

But there was one old scruffy-looking man. He and his family lived on the other side of the schoolyard. Every day, he sat on a stool by the door, protecting us against intruders.

I was scared of Mrs. Sami. Her angry voice and grim

eyes, hidden behind her thick glasses, darted at me each time. When she called on me to read, I could hear the echo of my shaky voice, *"besme Allah alrahman alrahim ..."*

Several times, I noticed that she gave better grades to the girls who had their scarves on, even though they read the Koran worse than I did. In fact, some girls draped their heads with scarves only during her class to show they were as religious as she.

At last, one day, I had no resistance left in me. I couldn't face another day of school without fasting. That night, when all of us gathered by the sofreh, I announced at dinner that, "Tomorrow, before sunrise, I will get up to prepare myself for the fast!"

"Bravo, Mitra joon." Mamani clapped and her full smile revealed a toothless mouth. My mother stopped feeding Layla her bottle, turned to me, and said, "But dear, you're very thin. You don't have enough strength to go without food from sunrise to sunset!"

"Allah will give her strength!" Mamani defended me.

"Most of the girls in my class do!"

Baba Nima chimed in, "Mitra, why do you want to fast?"

"She wants to be a good Moslim," Mamani answered for me and pulled her chador closer to her face. "She's at the right age to start living according to Allah's law."

I knew Mamani had no idea of the reason I wanted to fast. In no time, Maman Iran spoke up: "The person who fasts is the one who prays all year long. You don't even know how to pray!"

I understood fasting without praying held no rewards for us. In an instant, a flash of inspiration came to my head. "I can open my book to the section with *namaz,*" I said joyfully. "Then, whenever I forget a line or so, I'll look at it." I smiled, ran, and brought the textbook.

As soon as Mamani Zahra saw it in my hand, she said, "But you have to pray in Arabic, and this book is in Farsi."

"Mamani, look," I said, trying to dampen the flame of anger in me. I was raised not to speak loudly to my elders. So I flipped the pages before her face. "It has both. Besides, why do we have to pray in Arabic?"

"Those are *Allah*'s words." Mamani sounded defensive.

"Allah's words?" I was confused and turned to my father. "Baba, I thought God doesn't talk. How is it possible He has words?"

"Mitra," Maman Iran subsided the war in my skull, "It's not that God speaks. God revealed our Koran to our Prophet Mohammad, so he repeated the same words in Arabic to us."

"And we *must* repeat the same words," Mamani Zahra insisted.

"Then, we're really memorizing Mohammad's words, and like a parrot we repeat them back to God!"

Baba's face lit up with a rare smile, as if he understood I welcomed him into the arena. "If you're asking me," he pointed at his chest, "one doesn't need to pray in either Arabic or Farsi. God doesn't need us bow to Him and mumble jumble some words that don't make any sense to us."

Mamani Zahra threw a harsh look at him and said, "Nima khan, we're showing Allah that He's our master and that we're thankful of whatever He bless us with."

"Is Islam the only religion with Allah's words?" Baba asked.

"Of course, Nima khan!" Mamani responded.

"No!" Maman Iran jumped in. "We only say so because we are Moslims!"

"At school," I added, "we learned our Prophet

Mohammad endorsed the four other prophets, including Moses and Jesus."

"Yes, Mitra joon," Maman nodded. "And he says after him, there will be no more prophets on earth."

"We, Persians, were Zoroastrians." Baba dropped his spoon to the plate. "Even in ancient times, we never worshiped idols."

"In those days, sometimes even women were among the religious leaders!" Maman Iran said in her sharp voice.

"That's right! If it weren't for our kings' incompetency, the Arabs—a bunch of nomads—would not have conquered the Persian Empire and imposed their religion, Islam, on us." As he said these words, Baba stood up before finishing his rice and meat stew. He walked out with his head down.

"Mitra joon," Mamani conceded, "I'll wake you up tomorrow before sunrise."

◻ ◻ ◻

When the sky was still dark, Mamani shook me to awaken me. Willy-nilly, with my eyes not quite opened, I stumbled over to the pool. I mirrored whatever she did. We washed our hands, mouth, face, arms, and toes. Back inside our room, we put on our chadors and brought one side to the other under our chins. We both faced Mecca, though I was behind her. I knew from then on I was on my own. A woman had to pray under her lips without anyone hearing her. If Baba had prayed like most other fathers, he would have stood before me, reciting the namaz out loud. Then I could do without my book.

By glancing sometimes at my instruction book, I finished my morning prayers while Maman Iran put the warmed-up rice and stew from the night before on the sofreh. I had to hurry and finish eating prior to sunrise, and hearing azan on the radio. We could not listen for the muezzin, for there was no mosque near our house.

At sunset, I prayed for the last time before breaking my fast. When Baba came home, he asked, "Mitra, did you stick to your words? No eating, not even a sip of water throughout the day?"

"Yes, I did it! I don't know how, but I did it!"

I was not familiar with the heavenly joy inside me. The only important matter was that day at school no girls drilled me with their questions.

Mamani said proudly, "Mitra joon, you're pleasing Allah, and He gives you strength."

"You've proved your determination, strength, and discipline." My father's eyes behind his glasses showed immense happiness. "Mitra, I really must praise you, not because you fasted and did something that Islam obligates you to do, but because you kept your word and didn't mind how hard it was."

Baba got up, and from his coat pocket gave me a kaleidoscope. "Look through this and tell me what you see!"

I was fascinated by the colorful geometrical pictures. When I held it to the light and rotated the long part, their shapes and colors changed. I thought for sure I was in heaven.

Thanks to the kaleidoscope, I did not need *shahre-farangi*. Every day, on our way home, we saw the same old man in raggedy clothes standing behind his stereopticon. Every day, he called on us, "Shahre-farangi! For one rial, come and see Paris, Moscow, Rome, and much more!"

Most of the students in fifth, or even in sixth grade, rushed to him and stood in line to give their coins to glance at his cities. I never had permission to buy a moment of pleasure. My mother, Iran, responded to my pleadings, "No, Mitra joon, I'm worried for you!"

"Why? Other girls watch shahre-farangi every day!"

"They're ignorant peasants! Besides, it's possible the lenses carry trachoma." Her almond, jet-black eyes stared into mine. "I just want to protect you!"

"But I want to be like the other girls and see the foreign world."

Even though I argued with my mother wholeheartedly, she never gave in. I always had to keep quiet. I didn't understand why I was too weak to stand up to her. I could have gone with my friends and seen shahre-farangi without her knowing it, but I was a coward, unlike most of the other girls.

I tried to understand Maman Iran. I knew that she and Mamani's lives had been full of hardships. They were enduring life. They had lost many of their loved ones and couldn't have done anything to stop it. Over and over again, they told me about Uncle Amir, who was arrested by the shah's men. He might have been the prisoner of His Majesty. We really never knew what happened to him. His body was never returned to us, and there was no news from him. As the law said, "If we don't hear or see a missing person for seven years, we must assume he's dead."

I recalled hearing Baba murmuring one night to Maman: "These days the Communist Party has gained strength, so the torturing of political prisoners has been heightened."

"What do you mean?"

"They're given hot-boiled eggs as suppositories to prisoners!"

I was horrified.

"I hope Amir didn't have to go through all that!"

Maman responded with her coarse voice. It irritated my ears. If she hadn't had to cry and wail so hard for losing her brother Amir, then she would have a thin, soft voice appropriate for the beautiful woman she was.

"Please Nima! Stop telling me about how the shah's men torture our young men! I don't want to know!" She kept her head in her hands. She barely ever had any desire to discuss her point of view with my father. She kept herself busy with her job, and looking after her husband and two children.

Mamani Zahra, on the other hand, had a huge hump on her back, and spent her time praying or counting her holy beads. She was with Layla and me during the time when my mother was out.

Both of these women were resigned to their fate. They understood that they could not fight the ghoul of government or nature. Nobody could. I had no idea how I would continue living if something happened to my parents. I kept repeating in my mind, *As long as I live, I'll never defy our Shahan Shah! Soon this became my mantra instead of Allaho Akbar.*

There weren't many sounds of happiness in our home except for Layla's *goo-goo* and *ga-ga*. But Maman Iran, by browbeating her so often, stopped that all together. The best I could do was to get close to my father. To be around him made me feel at ease, as if he was made from a different fabric.

"Mitra," he said in a calm voice, "we come to this world only to obtain knowledge."

Every night, his arrival from his print shop marked the best part of the day. I could talk with him about what I learned that day. But, on Fridays or the holidays, he spent most of his time with his books. The shelves in our tiny three-room house were jam-packed with books. Most of them were filled with the translations of Western authors such as Sartre, Tolstoy, Victor Hugo, and only one Iranian author, Sadegh Hedayat. I asked him once: "Why do you have so many books by foreign writers, but only three written by Hedayat?"

He paused and raised his head. "Our mouths are chained, but not theirs."

"Baba, is that the reason you stopped printing your own newspaper, *Defa-e-Moshtarek,* All United?"

He nodded.

Every day, I hurried home to spend my time with one of its back issues. I enjoyed the pictures of the royal family. The women revealed their bare, sensuous shoulders while their skirts covered their legs down to their ankles. Everyone was holding a glass of wine in one hand and a cigarette in another. I read: "The corruption of our society starts at the top."

I wondered if my father was right: that the royal family, including the shah, was corrupt. My mother did not expose her body; nor did any of our teachers or our principal. At that moment, the voluptuous picture of Sophia Loren flashed before my eyes. Every day on my way to school, I passed by a movie theatre. Sophia's life-size picture was on the roof, which made her look as if her hips were resting on a cloud. A pair of shorts covered her thighs partially displaying her sexy legs with a blouse flaunting most of her bust. Her smile showed her white teeth, and even her sculptured lips could not hide them.

So, our princesses were westernized and Baba called it corruption.

Eventually, there were no more volumes of *Defa-e-Moshtarek,* All United, to look at. Sadly, Baba had put an end to printing them. After looking through the books, I chose *Nausea*, by Sartre, to read. I wondered why a Western author had called his book nausea. Was he sick of his life? Why would he be? He lived in the paradise world—the West. And why had Baba bought it? Was Baba also fed up with his life? When my father saw me reading it, he said, "Mitra, whenever you want to read a book, first let me know. There are some books that aren't suitable for your age!"

He was right. Whatever I read from that book made no sense to me. Not all of his books were like that.

Upon finishing third grade, during summer afternoons when everyone escaped the sizzling sun by taking a nap in their cool dark basements, I decided to prove my mother wrong. She kept claiming, "My sleep's so light even a cat's footsteps on the rug can wake me." So all of us, especially Layla and I had to nap beside her. One afternoon, I, like a thief, tiptoed to the other room. I held my breath, not to disturb the air. She did not move a muscle. In the other room, I resumed my breathing. I chose *Uncle Tom's Cabin* from the shelf and placed myself flat on the floor and read about Tom's life. Beneath me, I forgot all about the rough Kermani rug which was the long-standing remainder of Mamani's dowry. Then, every afternoon, as a habit, I proved Maman Iran wrong as I pored over this thick book cover to cover.

I felt sorry for Tom. I learned that in America, people's maids and servants were of a different breed. I could not understand however the reason those black people were called "slaves". Here, I knew that rich people, like my grand father, had maids and servants. They were not a different color, but just like the rest of us. They came from our villages to the capital with the hope to live, and to be fed and clothed by these fortunate rich people. Then, because of modernization, the people like my mother's half-brother, Yusof, were given several lads by the military. Some young men, when they registered for their military duty at age eighteen, were sent to the higher-ranking officers' homes instead of learning military skills. To me this was slavery!

◻ ◻ ◻

Today I had no time to look through my father's books. I had to prepare for a test about the White Revolution decree—the six-point reform bill. Our crowned father was its creator. This bill was His Majesty's magic wand and would take all of us out of the age of darkness and into the light of modernization.

But, as soon as I arrived home and put my sack of books down, Mamani called me: "Mitra, hurry up and take this food to your father's shop before it gets cold!"

"Why? He usually comes home for lunch!"

"Not today. Hurry up! Take this to him."

This was not the first time I had to take my father's lunch to him. I knew the path to his shop. It was past the bazaar in a new part of downtown. Several shops, one after another, were built on a long row.

After I shoved some food in my mouth and washed it down with some water from an earthen jug, I picked up the small steam-tight stew pan. It had two separate containers, one for rice and one for stew. My fingers hugged its wooden handle and I walked to his shop.

I pushed the entrance door open. The press in the back room was roaring, so the gofer, Kamal, could not hear me. He was cleaning the floor. I knew my father's small office was in the back.

I walked in. Father Nima was trapped by the books on his desk.

"Baba, I brought your lunch!"

Like a deaf person, he did not even raise his head.

"It's getting cold …"

Suddenly I felt that Baba and I were not the only ones in the room. The sense of someone breathing on my neck clenched my heart. I turned around. The stern look of three strange men dressed in black suits horrified me.

"Stop that silly machine!" one of them shouted.

My father raised his head, took off his glasses, and said, "Who are you?"

"Just turn off that damn machine," the man yelled.

I could not take my eyes off of them. Each one had a pistol attached to his belt. I felt sick. I closed my mouth tight and listened to my inner voice, *Mitra, be strong.* It was the first time I saw a real gun. In the movies, I watched cowboys chase the Indians, shooting and killing them. John Wayne's picture came to my mind. But he usually shot and killed the *bad guys*! For sure, my father was no bad guy. What would I do if they used their guns on Baba and me? Would this be the end of our lives?

I felt at ease when I heard Baba's voice. "Mitra." He stood up, came to me, put his two hands on my shoulders, and led me to his chair. I collapsed on his seat. At that time, I knew he was in control of the situation, and I wiped off the sweat from my forehead with my bare, shaky hand. Baba, keeping his cool, with a slight push, found his way through the men. They all turned around to watch him. In no time, the roaring print shop became quieter than a cemetery. That silence did not last long. "You are Nima Taheri, aren't you?" One of the men's forceful voices sounded like a cannon firing. "We've heard you print some pamphlets against His Majesty …"

Baba kept quiet.

Before Baba could defend himself, the other two men

started stripping all the books from the shelves, throwing the papers onto the floor. In no time the shop, usually neat and clean, became like a war zone. When the third one joined the two others and went to the room where the print machine was, Baba murmured to me, "Mitra, why don't you go home."

"Can I please stay?"

It seemed unlikely that these men would harm Baba before his daughter's eyes.

"Go home now!"

I wished I could have stayed with my father so both of us would have had the same fate. But I had no strength to oppose him.

He grabbed my arm and led me to the door. I moved stealthily to the hallway. Its floor was covered with books and papers. I had to jump over them like a rabbit avoiding mines.

I ran all the way home. Even the rain splashing against my face didn't bother me. Maman opened the door with teary eyes. "Mitra joon, I was worried!"

Almost in one breath, I babbled out what had happened at Baba's print shop, and asked, "Maman, those men did not wear uniforms. But they were carrying guns!"

"They're the shah's secret service, SAVAK!"

After that, Maman hit her head as she sat in the yard by the door, and cried on and off. She did not even listen to Mamani who begged, "Iran joon, why don't you come in? You'll get sick in this rain!"

But Maman Iran acted like a deaf person and sat there until Baba turned the key and opened the door. It was quite late. The rain had stopped and the darkness of night had covered everything for a long time.

When Baba walked in, he cocked his head. "Iran, why are you sitting here?"

"Thank God! They let you come home!" Maman cried.

"They couldn't find anything!"

Curiosity was boiling inside of me. I wanted to find the truth. So that night when all of us sat by sofreh, I asked, "Baba joon, what were those men looking—"

Before, I could even finish, my father threw his spoon into his bowl and lit a cigarette. It was odd. He usually went to the yard to smoke. He never did that during dinner.

"The shah's men believe I'm one of the supporters of the Communist Party, *tudeh*!"

"This is far from the truth!" Maman said.

"Why, Baba?" I strained to understand.

All of our eyes were fixed on him, awaiting the answer.

He said sadly, "Mossadegh died last night!"

Mossadegh—our one and only elected prime minister! His house flashed before my eyes. I was baffled by the dark windows. It was dusk and no light shone through them. I felt the angel of grief had spread her wings all over this mansion.

One day last summer, Baba showed me Mossadegh's mansion on our daily walk downtown. It was close to our majlis. Its huge garden and tall brick walls surrounded the two-story house.

"The shah accused Mossadegh of treason," Baba said. "Our national hero was put on trial like a criminal, kept under house arrest, and even after his death, this dictator still believes he's a threat to his crown."

"We didn't hear it on the news!" Maman's voice brought me back to our dinner sofreh.

"Yes, the order is no funeral or mourning for him. His family quietly took his body to his birthplace."

The shah's men knew my father was one of the Mossadegh's supporters. Baba's words cut into my thoughts. "SAVAK just wants to make sure that nothing is published about Mossadegh's death, to avoid a public outcry."

Maman started crying. She picked up Layla and paced the room. "God help us. I don't know how I can go on if they take you away, too."

"Don't worry," Baba's voice put me at ease. "They'll never find anything!" He puffed on his cigarette.

I recalled, several winters ago, the smell and warmth of a huge fire in the middle of our yard. Maman was gone to school, and Mamani Zahra was taking a nap. I rushed to see. As soon as my father felt me standing behind him, he turned around, grabbed my arm, and pushed me away. Through his teeth he said, "Mitra, what are you doing here? Go away, go away!"

It had been like a nightmare—my father had never treated me so harshly.

The sound of Mamani's salavat and the noise of her holy beads returned me to the sofreh again. She was sending prayers to the souls of the dead ones.

"Mitra joon," my bereaved mother said, "why don't you go to the other room and study the White Revolution?"

"Our Shahan Shah ordered that the six-point reform bill be placed on the ballot," I said.

Maman nodded. "Within two months we'll have a referendum. Then, each one will become a law."

When I closed the door, I heard Baba say, "Putting this so-called White Revolution up for a referendum is another scam."

I stopped behind the door.

"The representatives have already rejected this ridiculous bill!"

"Wouldn't the shah rebuke them?" Maman asked.

"Even though this dictator handpicked them, they still rejected the bill," Baba said through his teeth.

"Of course," Maman responded, "the uneducated and

destitute people wouldn't dare to do anything against the shah's will!"

My eyelids were getting heavy and I decided to leave the turmoil to the grownups and went to bed.

◻ ◻ ◻

We studied The White Revolution Decree every day at school. Our teachers injected it into our skulls over and over. They were very excited about women getting the right to vote, the first entry in the reform bill.

"Isn't this grand?" our social studies teacher said. "For you girls, it's essential to understand the importance of this item. Until now, we women were in the same group as mules. We were treated as if we were not part of the population."

I felt pleased at being a girl. Soon, like men, I would be able to cast my vote for our representatives in parliament. However, I could not keep my father's voice out of my head.

"What's the use of voting under a dictatorship regime like this?" he had asked.

"Baba, do you mean we don't have freedom to elect whomever we want?"

Instead of answering me, he hit his forehead out of rage, got up and took out a ballot from his overcoat pocket. He shook it in front of my face. "Look!" Then, he threw it on the floor and stomped on it over and over. "This is how this tyrant rules over us."

"Nima, don't do that!" Maman said. "Remember you must go and drop this in the box tomorrow!"

"Yes!" Baba's angry voice shook me. "This is the one act they trust me to do!"

I noticed that the electoral card was already filled out

with some names.

"This shah," he lowered his voice and spoke with more control, "and the members of SAVAK think we're donkeys; they treat us as such! Today, SAVAK distributed these in my print shop. They wanted us to drop these cards in the box tomorrow."

"Everything is a sham in this country!" Maman said through her teary eyes. "There's no truth anywhere!"

"Deception, deception!" Baba said. "That's all we've got!"

I was puzzled. For old women like Mamani Zahra, grabbing onto Islam with all their strength was the highlight of their lives. They couldn't care less about women obtaining the right to vote. Several times Mamani had told me, "A girl must only read our sacred Koran."

"Mamani, are you happy that soon women can vote?"

She only shrugged and shoved her holy beads to the other side of their thread.

With my mother, Iran, it was different. I could never understand her. Whenever she talked as a teacher, she plastered over her animosity toward the shah and said, "Thanks to our Shahan Shah, he's liberated us and is modernizing the country at the speed of light!" But, when she was safe in the house, I heard different words: "Thank God my son Omid is dead. What's the use of raising a son so that he can be tortured or murdered at the hands of our king's men?"

Her words jolted me. Was Maman happy that her son had died? *Omid* meant "hope"! Did she have any hope for Layla and me?

Every day I listened to my teachers. They all praised our king over and over. My world was in chaos. Were Maman and Baba right? Or were my teachers? I didn't know who to believe!

◻ ◻ ◻

Two days before the referendum for the White Revolution Decree, the old guard opened our class door. We thought he had come to add some charcoals to our furnace. It was a cold, snowy day. But he went to our teacher, whispered something in her ear, and rushed out. Our teacher told us, "Hey, everybody! Pick up your possessions. We must go to the courtyard. We're summoned by our principal."

"What's happening? What's happening?" We sounded like bees released from our beehives.

"I don't know!" our teacher shrugged.

Soon, all the students congregated in the yard with the teachers. We ignored the snowflakes covering us like a blanket.

"I have sad news for all of us," our principal said, standing under the balcony. "We just learned that Prime Minister Mansoor was shot early this morning in front of his house. He's been taken to the hospital. Our school will be closed for three days. Now, let's pray for his speedy recovery."

All of us united in a loud sigh, and then everyone went quiet. The picture of young, handsome Prime Minister Amir Mansoor flashed before my eyes. He looked charismatic behind his desk.

"Is our Shahan Shah all right?" one of the girls broke the silence.

"Of course!" one of our teachers answered.

Then the principal jumped in. "It's very likely we'll hear from Shahan Shah soon!"

"Our crown prince is still young. We can't live without a king!" another girl shouted.

I noticed the girls who wore scarves kept quiet. The religious girls never praised our king. And I breathed no words either. We knew that by the next day our king would select another prime minister. But what would happen if, instead of our prime minister, someone had shot our king? The entire country would be covered under a blanket of chaos. It would be impossible for us to live without our king. We have been ruled by one for over two thousand, five hundred years.

❑ ❑ ❑

Maman arrived home shortly after I did. We were astonished to see Baba in the courtyard, pacing and smoking. He went to her and whispered, "Kamal and his mother are here."

Maman frowned and moved closer to Baba. "Why?"

"For protection!" Baba hissed.

"Oh, my God." She hit her cheek. "Kamal's mother works for the prime minister!"

"Let's go inside!" Baba said to Maman. "They need to stay with us tonight."

We entered the room. Covered in her chador, Mamani Zahra was sitting in the far corner of the room, but Kamal and his mother, Bibi, sat by the door trembling. Her thick, washed-out black chador had enveloped her.

"As far as I know ..." Baba said as he closed the door, drew the curtains, and sat down. After he lit a cigarette, he continued in much lower voice. "Apparently, Mansoor, the servant of His Majesty pushed the representatives to pass the capitulation law ..."

"What's that?" Maman asked.

"It means, for example, that if any Americans living here commit a crime, our police do not have authority to punish them. We have to send them back to America."

Maman shook her head, and Baba took a deep puff. "Then, the leader of the Shiites, Ayatollah Khomeini, in Quom, preached against this dictator—His Majesty!"

"Publicly?!" Maman moved closer to Baba and I pushed myself over to him while listening.

"Baba, what did he say against our king?"

My father remained quiet and puffed on his cigarette. Finally he said, "Khomeini preached, 'Now, in our land, even American dogs have more rights than we do.'"

Maman did nothing to hide the horror from her face. Mamani's *"Allaho Akbar"* filled the room.

"Then, apparently," Baba continued with a controlled voice, "the shah removed Khomeini from his rank and sent him to exile in Iraq." He then asked, "Kamal, did you say your mother witnessed the shooting?"

He nodded while his head was down. His mother looked up and said, "Khanoom!" Her Esfehani twang filled the room, "I saw it all!"

"Did you really?" I rushed and sat by her when I heard Mamani's, *"Allaho Akbar!"* again.

"Then you're an eyewitness," Baba said in disbelief.

She nodded as I heard Kamal says, "The police and SAVAK want to question her!"

"They believe she's one of the culprits!" Baba said and did nothing to cover his mocking smile.

The woman ignored all of us, and turned to Maman. "Khanoom jan," she said, "I saw it all!" She swallowed and looked only at Maman, as if no one else was in the room.

"Lady!" Baba got up. "Get comfortable!" he said when he left the room. My father knew. Bibi was not at ease shrouded in her chador. Following him, Kamal also left the room.

"Bibi," Maman took a breath, "take off your chador!"

She turned to me. "Mitra! Go and bring some tea for khanoom."

I did not want to miss any of their conversation. I rushed to the kitchen. *Thank you Mamani!* She had already prepared the tea. I poured it into our dainty glasses, put them on a tray, and hurried back to the room.

Bibi had dropped her chador. "... today's event! I'll never forget!" Her eyes were watery.

"What did you see?" I asked.

"Khanoom, you know the Prime Minister's house is in Shemiran!" She looked up to Maman Iran.

"Yes, all the rich live there, near His Majesty's palace."

"The bus let me out at the bottom of the hill like it does every day. I walked up the hill to get to his house."

"Then what happened?" I jumped in.

"Mitra, hush! The lady's gone through a trauma!" Maman scolded.

Bibi had a sip of her tea, and then continued, "I had almost reached the door when I saw his stretched car had arrived to take Mr. Mansoor to his office. Every day he comes out of the gate to get into his car at the same time that I arrive." She paused, staring into space, wiping her tears with her black scarf. "Then out of nowhere, I heard the thunder of a motorcycle behind me. It zoomed by me, and I heard two or three bangs. At first, I didn't make anything of it. Allah! Bless his soul ..."

"Allaho masala ala Mohammad va ale Mohammad!" She and Mamani recited the prayers for the dead. Maman stayed quiet.

"But our principal said he was in the hospital!" I cried out.

As if no one heard me, Bibi continued, "On the driveway, I saw him, soaked in his own blood. It was horrifying. Part of his head was smashed—the snow around it was white no more. Red, red, red snow everywhere …" She started to wail, "Yes, my lady! No way to forget this nightmare."

I was aghast and didn't know what to do. In my mind, I repeated what my father had said: *"Killing or even trying to murder a human is absolutely wrong regardless of what wrong the man has done."*

"Lady," I heard Maman's strong voice, "God bless you! Finish your tea."

My mother sounded like she was not sorry for the prime minister, but more concerned about Bibi. After giving it a moment's thought, she asked, "Bibi, did you see the men on the motorcycle?"

She wiped her teary eyes with her chador. "No, my lady! Their faces were covered with masks."

Baba walked back in.

That same day, at dawn, our Shahan Shah had sent a televised message informing us: "Those who defy our modernization are in the minority. They amount to nothing. They are terrorists …"

It was the first time we heard the word *terrorist*. My mind failed to put a picture to this word.

"Actually!" Baba soon interrupted our king's speech, "They call themselves *Fadayan-e-Islam!*"

"Baba, does it mean they're ready to sacrifice themselves for Islam?"

He nodded and said through his teeth, "It's time to rebel against this dictator!"

That night, Kamal and his mother slept on mattresses on the kitchen floor and hid themselves under our blankets. At dawn, they snuck out of the house to catch a bus to their hometown, Esfehan.

Three days later, our dashing prime minister, Amir Mansoor died in the hospital. We heard the whisper of gossip: "The shah's so-called White Revolution was stained by the prime minister's blood."

◻ ◻ ◻

By the following summer, we had forgotten the assassination of the prime minister. The atmosphere had become peaceful. The White Revolution Decree had become law and life went on.

Every afternoon, I looked forward to my daily walk downtown with my father. I loved having him all to myself. Our strolls at dusk usually ended with in an ice cream sandwich for me. I loved to circle my tongue around the hard scoop placed skillfully between the two fragile waffles. The chunks of cream tasted sweet under my teeth. Its saffron color and rosewater smell took me to heaven.

"Nima khan, how are you?" a heavy man with clean-shaven face asked.

On his left arm, he carried a beige cotton jacket that matched his trousers. His short-sleeved shirt hung open displaying part of his hairy chest. It was odd. Baba never went out on the street without his suit and tie, even in the summer. The man shook hands with him.

"Hey, Mozafar!" Baba said affably.

"How are you, Mitra?" The man smiled with recognition.

"Mitra, you remember Mozafar khan!"

He was one of Baba's customers. Gazing at the asphalt, I nodded, and kept on enjoying my ice cream.

"Nima, I'm on my way to Brasserie to meet some friends! Would you like to come?"

The café was famous for its belly dancers.

Baba shook his head without conviction. "No, I don't think so!"

"Why not?"

"My wife's gone to Mashhad with her grandmother, and no one is home to look after Mitra."

"She can come with us. Families often go there!"

I was overwhelmed with excitement and I paid no attention to my ice cream when it fell on the ground. I listened to my father and hoped he would melt under Mozafar's persistence.

At last, Baba agreed to go. I cheered him in my heart.

The entrance door led us to a large courtyard. Full of excitement, I ran inside as if the sound of the flute was wooing me. I realized right away, though, that I had entered the men's world. The tables covered with white cloths were occupied by men of all ages—young and old. There were no other women or children in sight.

"Mozafar, we're over here!" a man with a thick beard, in the far corner, called out.

At his table were six other men, all without jackets, talking and laughing.

I took a chair facing the stage. It used to be a pond, covered with a wooden platform disguised under the rug. Some colorful lights around it served as decoration. I breathed in the breeze of Mount Alborz and waited for the dance.

Smoke filled the air. On every table, there were several bottles of wine and *aragh*, our national drink. This alcoholic beverage looked deceptively like water in clear bottles. It was much cheaper than vodka or whisky imported from abroad.

The man next to Mozafar poured aragh for him and Baba. Everyone raised his glass and said, "Besalamati."

I never dreamed that my father drank aragh like low-class men.

The waiter brought us dinner—mainly lamb shank

cooked in tomato juice and saffron. I was disappointed that there was no fluffy rice on the table. I dared not complain or even show my discontent. I turned to Baba to see if he was happy. He had taken off his glasses and was wiping his forehead with his white handkerchief.

"Mitra, eat your food."

"Baba, where's polo?"

"No rice tonight. Drinking men don't like it," he said under his breath.

"Do they only like meat?"

He nodded.

I started nibbling, and the music's tempo sped up; the Arabic music had begun. I sat straight up in my chair while my eyes searched for a belly dancer. In the blink of an eye, all the lights went off. Only the colorful lights around the stage were on. Standing in the center was a young, tall girl, not much older than me, in a turquoise costume. She moved to the music like a weeping willow in a soft blowing wind. With every beat, she moved her head and her long, jet-black hair whipped the air. She then raised her hands over her head and her silver belly dancing cymbals jingled. I stood up. I was baffled. How in the world was this girl moving her body so fluidly? My attention immediately went to her costume. Only a beaded bra with dangling coins covered her upper body. Her hips were covered with a beaded belt that her belly moved from one side to the other. A long, flowing, sheer skirt with several openings was attached to her wide belt. With each slow beat, she revealed one leg, bare from her thigh to her foot, and the men roared, "Bravo! Such a star! Such a beauty!"

I was struck dumb. On the one hand, I admired her beauty and talent. On the other hand, I felt ashamed at the way she displayed her body. She must not have been religious at all. Her dancing before the intoxicated men could send her right into hell. To my thinking, she was a sinner and there was no remedy for her.

Soon, the rhythms sped up. She kept up with the music and shook her body so fast that my eyes could not follow her. I was in awe. Like a radiant ball, as if she was released from a cannon.

She lighted the entire courtyard. To the sound of music, she came over to each table, and men put some bills in her sequined belt, or in her bra. I was impatiently waiting for her to come to our table so that I could get a closer look at her face to find out if she was pretty. Instead, I heard, "Mitra, let's go!"

My father grabbed my hand, and before I could say a word, I was dragged outside. In my heart, I was happy to escape the heavy smoke and the smell of alcohol. But I was confused. "Baba! What's wrong?"

"I'm sorry I brought you to this place," he said bitterly.

"Why?"

"You're too young to understand now." He stared into my eyes. "In there, the men use that girl for their worldly pleasure and that's wrong!"

"Is dancing a bad thing?"

"This kind of dance uses women to enflame men's lust—yes, that is wrong!" He took his silver cigarette box out of his pocket, and continued, "The poor girl's displaying her body to earn money to feed herself and her family." He lit one. After a puff, he said, "Arabs brought us the Koran and this demeaning dance to force us to forget about the true dance!"

I was baffled.

"Mitra, you know what dance I mean!"

I shook my head.

"The dervishes' dance, or whirling dervishes!"

"Do we call them Sufis, also?"

Baba nodded.

I recalled the first time I encountered a dervish. I was not yet old enough to go to school. At lunch time, when the muezzin on the radio called on everyone to pray, we heard their chanting on the street. One day, Mamani Zahra opened the door to one of them. His appearance scared me. His muddled beard and hair were long, down to his belly. His worn and torn wool garment was white, but spotted all over. He carried a small vessel bowl dangling from a chain in one hand and a wooden stick on the other; he did not look to be breathing. Mamani poured our leftover dinner into his bowl. He murmured, "Allah, bless you." Only then did I know he was alive.

Baba was puffing hard on his cigarette when I asked, "Baba, are you a dervish?"

"I wish." He took another deep puff and grumbled, "This dictator has only one goal: to destroy our heritage."

"Are there still dervishes?"

"There are only a few here and there. They're not allowed to congregate publicly."

My father's words reminded me that I had not heard the dervishes' chanting for a long time. It was as if they had vanished from the earth.

"Baba, how can one become a dervish?"

"A dervish, or Sufi, must cut himself off from the materialistic world. In this life, he has to chant, dance, and seek God. Then, once he dies, his soul can unite with Him."

"Baba, Maman told me once that her mother Shirin witnessed the secret world of dervishes. Was Grandpa Ali a Sufi?"

"No, my child! He respected them and preferred to spend his time with them." Baba puffed furiously on his cigarette. "These days our entertainment is either a cheap version of movies from the West, or to be excited over the movements of young girls."

"What does a Sufi or dervish believe in?"

My father's voice became calmer. "Sa'adi, Hafiz, and Rumi's verses are tapestries of their opposition to our repressive regime. Since the Arab invasion and acceptance of Islam by force of the sword, century after century, these brave men have portrayed their disapproval of this compulsory religion through their magnificent poems."

"In reality, they're fighting for our freedom!" I breathed.

"Very much so!" My father took off his thick glasses. "They could not come out and verbalize their opposition to our conquerors, and so, they hid it in their symbols."

"Instead of fighting and shedding blood," I said, "they took the peaceful way!"

"Westerners call this philosophy 'Mysticism of the East'!"

"Then, what is the love these Sufis talk about?"

"These poets," Baba dropped his cigarette butt on the ground and crushed it as he continued, "they don't mean the physical love of a man for a woman."

"No?" I sighed.

"They talk about the love of a man, or a person, for God."

"Baba, is a Sufi Moslim?"

"Not necessarily! Every Sufi's life is spent praising God. His love of God is the same love as Christ refers to. But, the Sufi's mouth is chained like ours. For him, dying is the only way to get rid of this physical body which he sees as a prison cell." Baba pointed to his chest. "So, after death, a Sufi can become one with the Almighty—Unity with God," he breathed deeply, "to achieve the ultimate freedom."

At that moment, I knew Baba was a dervish at heart,

wasn't afraid of dying. I wondered if it was easy to become a dervish. Not to go to school, not to work, but to go around collecting food, trying not to starve.

"Baba, can I become a dervish?"

"No woman is allowed to go through their strenuous training."

Baba had to be right. I never saw any picture of women whirling dervishes.

When a taxi stopped before us, we got in. On our way home I thought our last two kings from the Pahlavi Dynasty had liberated women. The first one ordered us not to cover our heads, and the second one allowed us to vote, just like men. But neither had liberated us in a spiritual way. I wondered if we were truly liberated.

¤ ¤ ¤

By the end of 1960s, I was fifteen years old and Tehran shimmered among the rest of the capitals in the world. Our Shahan Shah, Mohammad Reza Pahlavi, made a book out of the White Revolution decree. This book was taught at our schools instead of our holy book, the Koran. He was determined to push us toward the modernization. We had to be proud of being Iranians, for our ancestors were Cyrus and Darius the Great. Our twenty-five centuries of history intoxicated us. We were preparing for our largest celebration, which, in two years' time, would show off our rich civilization to the world. Our Shahan Shah and his clans would attend the entire two-week celebration. We, the people, would pay the bills. We had no worries. America fed us its rice and beef, the French clothed us in the latest fashion, and Britain provided our transportation—double-decker buses. In return, we had to give them our black pearls at an astonishing speedy rate.

One morning, when all of us were about to leave for our days, Mamani was still asleep.

"Mitra," Maman said, "Go and wake Mamani up. She hasn't even prayed yet!" I went back to our room. "Mamani, Mamani, get up, get up!" I shook her, but she didn't move. I took her hand in mine. It had no warmth. "Mamani, answer me."

No response—she was like a rock.

I ran out, hearing my heart thumping, and screamed, "Maman, come, come!"

Baba rushed inside and did not let Maman or me enter the room. After a minute, he walked out, closed the door behind him. Maman's wailing jarred me and reminded me of the time Omid died. No more Mamani Zahra for us. She had endured her stormy life with dignity and was gone forever.

¤ ¤ ¤

Not long after Mamani's passing, we moved to one of the Tehran's suburbs in the northeast. This place was far from Shemiran—the wealthy suburb north of our capital where the shah and his kind lived.

"Tehran's swollen," my father said, "we must run away to live in peace." He decided to rescue us from living in a condominium. The houses in our neighborhood were bought-out and bulldozed, just so they could be replaced with apartment buildings and condominiums. People from all over the country were pouring into Tehran with the hope of finding jobs and opportunities for a better life.

Our new house was still one of the smallest in the neighborhood—it was the first one on the block—and had a fairly large backyard, a small willow tree and some rosebushes. A round, small pond in the corner added to its serenity. Baba wanted to cover the ground with grass, but according to Maman Iran there was, "No money to feed the lawn!" Instead, we ended up cementing the yard. We had four rooms—two downstairs with a kitchen, and two upstairs.

My sister Layla and I shared the back room to our family room downstairs. Also, Zaynab, the peasant girl who lived with us (she was a little younger than me) slept on the floor in our room. Her parents had six children and could not afford to feed her or even send her to school. My mother gave her books and notebooks. She taught Zaynab at home whenever she had time. Maman believed that young girls needed to learn reading and writing.

"Mitra joon, a woman who does not have an income cannot be an equal partner with her husband."

"So, if her husband doesn't treat her right, she can get a divorce and live her life!"

She nodded.

Every day, Maman had to commute to the heart of Tehran. She refused to transfer to a school closer to our house. She said, "This is an all-girls school. I would hate to teach here. Boys are smarter and easier to teach." Baba had no choice but to commute. His print shop was busy with printing domestic and translated versions of Western books. Every morning, even in the summer, Baba had to leave the house when the stars were still in the sky. He kept himself awake by puffing his cigarette on the way to the bus stop.

When I was moved to the school near our new house, I befriended Homa, who lived in the house at the dead end street a few blocks away from us. We were in the same grade, but she appeared much older. She was well-developed with full-grown breasts and shapely hips—she wasn't like me, slender as a stick. Her blonde hair and blue eyes fascinated me.

On our way to school, Homa said, "My father, Allah bless his soul, died a few years ago."

"Do you miss him?"

"I barely remember him."

I could not believe any girl could live without her father. I loved Baba so much, even more than Maman. When he was home, he read and spent most of his time in his library. One of the rooms upstairs in our house had to belong to his books. "Why do we need so many books?" Maman protested over and over. "Not only do you spend too much money on them, but now they occupy my room ..."

"But I have an older brother, Javad," Homa told me. "He takes care of me, my mother, and my youngest brother. I have other sisters, too. They're all married and live in the north by the Caspian Sea."

It was too bad that my brother Omid had to die—though, being without a brother is much better than being without a father. *Thank God!* I forced myself to return to my conversation with Homa. "What does your brother do?"

"Javad now works in a textile factory, but he was one of the farmers. My father got some land ..." She was having trouble finishing, overcome by emotion. "When Shahan Shah abolished feudalism ..."

"Homa joon, I'm confused! Why did your family come here? Why didn't you all stay in your village as a landlord and cultivate your own land?"

"My brother had to give our land back to its original landlord. It was one of the second items in the White Revolution Decree. We had to come to Tehran for work." Homa stopped, grabbed my arms, and stared at me with her sky-blue eyes. "Javad always worked under the supervision of his landlord. This man provided us with whatever we needed ..."

"Didn't he go to the government officials to get the necessary tools for plowing?"

"Do you think it's as easy as the shah says? We never could produce enough rice. We never had enough income to feed us."

I released my arms and we continued on our way. When we were far enough from home, Homa instructed me to turn into an alley. After a few steps, she looked around, then took off her chador, folded it, and put it in her bag. She straightened her knee-high uniform and tightened her belt. She then fluffed her blonde hair, stroked her cheeks and pressed very hard on her lips several times. Soon, her rosy cheeks and lips against her milky skin looked as if she was wearing makeup in a subtle way. We girls knew we could not wear makeup until our wedding night.

"Mitra, don't look at me with your angry eyes."

"You don't have to wear your chador?" My hands went to my mouth in shock.

"Wearing chador is a way of life in our village. Here, my mother and Javad force me to cover myself with it. They don't know what I do. This way everyone's happy." A bitter smile crossed her face.

The habit of taking off her chador was not the only thing Homa did. One day, on our way to school, a new Mercedes-Benz pulled up next to us. The driver rolled down the window. "Do you want a ride?" He looked chic in his sleek suit.

With a swift hand motion, I answered, "No! No!" I turned my face away from the car and picked up my pace. My thumping heart was ringing in my head. I had no reason to be so scared—the driver seemed respectable.

Homa grabbed my hand. "Stop, Mitra. Let's get in!"

"I'm not allowed …"

"I know him, don't be scared!"

Homa, without any hesitation, opened the car door and sat beside the driver. When I refused to budge, they drove away.

That day, I did not see Homa at school. All day, I had a hard time sitting still in my seat. As soon as the bell rang, I picked up my bag and left. On my way home, I had to decide whether to go to her house or not. I would have no idea what to say if her mother came to the door and learned Homa missed school that day. I imagined her voice in Rashti twang, "*Khak-e-allam-be-saram*, all the ashes of the world on my head! What did you do to my jewel, Homa?" Or perhaps I would wait until the next day when I'd see her. But the only way I could calm my stirred-up stomach was to go to her house and pretend I was the one who missed school.

After checking on Zaynab and my sister, before Maman or Baba came home, I ran to Homa's house. Thank God, she opened the door.

"Are you all right?" I whispered.

"How was school?" Homa said in a hushed tone.

"Who's there?" Homa's mother shouted from the inside.

"It's Mitra. She didn't make it to school. She wants to know our homework."

Day after day Homa would either cut school or go somewhere after school. She told her family she was with me, in our house, which was far from the truth. She spent too much time with her boyfriend. A religious family had raised a daughter whose life was based on lies. I was bewildered.

"Mitra joon, I really love this guy!" Homa confessed.

"How do you know?"

I had to ask. I had always wished to one day meet a boy

and fall in love with him. But Maman said over and over, "A girl doesn't need the love of a strange man. Men are only after robbing her from …"

"He's rich," Homa said. "He buys me nice clothes and shoes."

A strange man buying stuff for her! That was a no-no in my world. Maman Iran's voice rang in my ears again: "If anyone, especially a man, gives you any gifts, be aware. He'll squeeze double their worth out of you."

"Does your mother know?"

"No, of course not! If she or Javad even dreamed of what I'm doing, only Allah knows what they'd do to me."

¤ ¤ ¤

One day, Homa dropped the bombshell on me.

"I must tell you a secret!" She started crying.

I looked at her pale face and sad blue eyes. "What's the matter?"

"I'm pregnant, and I have to get rid of it!"

"How could you do that?"

"Rahim, my boyfriend, knows a midwife, and he'll pay for it, too. But you have to come with me. I'm scared." Before she let me finish my deep breath, she continued, "We can go early in the morning, as though we're going to school, and come back at the same time in the afternoon. Then I'll tell my mother and Javad that I'm sick. I'll stay home for a few days. No one will ever know."

"Why isn't he marrying you?"

"He can't!"

"Why can't he?"

After a long pause, Homa breathed out, "Mitra, our Allah's law has been changed! Because of our king, men can no longer have more than one wife."

I knew that the shah had changed the polygamy law of Islam. Any man who wanted to get married to more than one wife had to obtain the first wife's consent.

I stared at her in confusion. "Do you mean Rahim is a married man?"

"Yes!"

"So, he can get permission from his wife to marry you!"

Homa shook her head. "She has a rich father, and Rahim works in his factory."

I felt dizzy when I heard Homa's voice again. "We have to do this right away, you know!"

I gasped for air. "When?"

"Tomorrow!"

"So soon!"

"This can't wait! My mother and younger brother have gone to visit my sisters in Rasht. They'll be back the day after tomorrow."

¤ ¤ ¤

All night long, I tossed and turned thinking about Homa and her life. Many questions exploded in my head. I thought Homa was a follower of Islam. She and her mother wore chadors and prayed five times a day; not like my family, who had forgotten what their religion was! How could she turn a deaf ear to Islam and commit such a sin with a man who was not her husband?

My father's voice rang in my ears: "Mitra, don't ever put yourself in a position with a man that allows him to treat you like a dirty handkerchief and throw you away when he is done with you." It was obvious that in this situation Homa was the "dirty handkerchief" and that her boyfriend—unwilling to marry her—was throwing her and the baby away.

Why didn't Rahim want to marry her? And above all, why did I have to be her scapegoat?

At last, my eyelids became heavy, and before I fell asleep, I knew that I had to be there for Homa. She was my doost, friend. I remembered Rumi's poem, "O For A Friend to Mingle [Her] Soul with Mine." She needed my help, and I decided to be there for her regardless of any punishment that I might have to face later on.

◻ ◻ ◻

The next day, everything went according to the plan. Rahim picked us up at the corner near Homa's house, gave her a one-hundred tuman, and drove us to the midwife's house in the heart of Tehran. He waited for us, and brought us back to Homa's house. I helped her lie down on her thin mattress and assured her I would be back to check on her the next morning before going to school.

However, in the middle of the night, the sound of sirens and the smell of smoke awakened the entire neighborhood. When we rushed out, we learned that the house at the dead end had been swallowed by flames and no one survived. At the time, we had no idea what caused the fire. All of my wailing and howling could not bring Homa back to me.

Later on, Javad's picture was in the paper, and Homa's story had been printed. That day, when she and I thought we had fooled everybody, Javad had been following us. Then, at night, when he was consumed by his wrath, he decided to clean his sister's shameful act by engulfing Homa, himself, and their entire house in his self-made blaze. Their mother and younger brother's lives were spared because they were not home.

Through my teary eyes, I saw the largest headline of that day: *"America Landed on Moon! Neil Armstrong Made a Huge Leap for Humankind!"*

But obviously not for women in this land!

13. Rebirth

Los Angeles, California, 1979
Mitra (25)

Air France delivered the *Spirit of Allah*, Ruhollah
Khomeini, to Iranians in Tehran in February 1979, two
weeks after our Shahan Shah, Mohammad Reza Pahlavi,
the last king of our kingdom, left the country. Even though
his departure was under the objective of seeking medical
treatment, we knew he was gone for good.

The news saddened me greatly. I remembered how the
shah had promoted women. For the first time in our history,
he chose a female minister, who had a doctorate degree,
to head our ministry of education. As a result, the doors
of higher education were opened to us not only within
the country but also abroad. However, not very many
girls were allowed to take advantage of the opportunity
to travel to the West and study. Only a handful of the
ones who were from the rich families were educated away
from our country. Their parents could afford to commute
between East and West. When it was announced that
our government would give scholarships to anyone who
wanted to study in the West, my father as my guru called
me in.

"Mitra, why don't you apply for this scholarship and go to America?"

"Do you want me to get away because I don't have many suitors?"

"No! You know what I think about marrying you off."

I nodded. He often reminded me: *"There is always time to get married, but one must obtain knowledge, and it doesn't matter that you're not a boy. You must seek to be independent in life."*

That night, he said in his firm voice, "I want you to go and breathe the air of a free country, America. When you young educated ones come back, you'll be able to make our country like theirs." He smiled.

After passing several English exams, I locked a full scholarship to UCLA and came to the land of free. Not long after that, my sister Layla was also able to secure a scholarship and joined me. We both had the desire to complete our higher education and return to our homeland.

For the first few months after my arrival, I walked everywhere like a zombie trying to find a path from my dormitory to each class. At first, I was astounded that students, males and females, interacted freely with each other. Very few times did I witness a male or female student alone. Soon I realized that American men with their blue eyes, blond hair, and tall stature fancied me. From day one, when I was walking on campus, American guys passing by me would say, "Smile, smile!"

I was baffled. Apparently, everyone *smiled* while walking! Or the guys were overly concerned about my serious and unfriendly face. But I was used to that. In my country, no one acknowledged me as a beautiful girl, except for my sister, Layla.

I was finishing up the last semester of the first year. Every afternoon I went to study at our main library. One day, as soon as I walked in, my eyes seized on a blond haired student sitting all by himself at a table in the corner. For the first time, I heard my thumping heart. He raised his head as if he too heard it pounding. I read an invitation in his ocean-colored eyes.

"May I join you?" I forced the words out of my mouth.

His welcoming smile lighted his face and a hand gesture indicated the chair across the table from him. I sat down and didn't understand my trembling. He put his head down, continued reading, and I opened one of my books trying to slow down my heartbeat.

After a short time, I heard, "Are you new?"

I raised my head and saw his look of admiration for me. "Sort of!" I breathed.

He smiled and turned back to his book.

Not long afterwards, I heard, "I'm John, what's your name?"

"Mitra."

"What?"

"M-i-t-r-a."

"Where are you from?"

"Iran."

"Where?"

"A country in the Middle East ..."

"Oh, you mean Persia?"

I cracked a smile and brought my gaze back to my book. Like an eagle, I felt I was soaring into the sky. At last a guy who was not one of my classmates, and I thought he was handsome, had started talking to me.

My heart nearly burst through my chest when John said, "Would you like to go to the cafeteria for coffee?"

Later that day, John asked me out to dinner for the following Saturday night. In spite of my eager agreement, I contemplated the idea over the next two days. On the one hand, I was pleased that for the first time in my life

I could go out with a lad and discover what it's like to be alone with the one who could make my heart race. My father was right about America. This was a free country. Men and women were allowed to interact with each other without any concern. I witnessed several occasions when my American roommate on campus took a liking to a male student. Without even knowing him, she went right up to him and started a conversation. Truly, men and women were liberated.

On the other hand, I was scared to death to be with a man who I had not known for a long time, and my parents had never met.

At long last, we were seated outside at a café.

"Mitra, you are gorgeous," he said emphatically.

I lowered my head so he could not see the redness in my face.

"I love your long jet black hair and sharp dark eyes!"

I swallowed, not knowing how to respond.

After dinner, we walked to the Santa Monica pier. The ocean breeze was caressing my face. We were holding hands, and I felt as if I had died and gone to heaven. When he attempted to kiss me, I did not let him. He raised my chin.

"Don't you want me to kiss you?"

It felt like my head weighed more than a ton of bricks. No way to move it up or down.

"Never been kissed before ..." I managed to say.

"What? Unbelieveable! Haven't you had a boyfriend?"

I wanted to minimize the seriousness of the matter; that we Iranian women were muffled, not only politically, but also emotionally. That I never dared to tell my open-minded father who had sent his daughter all alone to a foreign land that I held a hidden desire to have a boyfriend, or at least to be able to interact with opposite sex. Then, the picture of my friend, Homa, flashed before my eyes and her horrific fate made me tear up.

"No." I sighed.

"I'm amazed!" John shook his head. He put his hands around my waist, took me into his muscular arms, pressed me to his wide shoulders and whispered in my ear, "Are you a virgin?"

I nodded. "It's understood for us to wait until our wedding night."

"How come you haven't been married by now?" he asked softly.

I wiped away my tears with the back of my hand, ignored the knot in my throat and said, "Because I want to fall in love first before getting married." I gazed into this boy's baby-blue eyes.

"How can you love the person if you don't interact with him?" he countered.

I had no answer for him. However, I knew I could fall in love with this man.

Today, I realized that my dreams were all shattered. John and I remained friends until a year ago when he left for his hometown, Chicago. It was very hard for both of us. He could not act on his emotions and show me how much he loved me. And for me, I was chained down by my tradition, knowing that I had to go back home. I was confused at times. Whenever he kissed me all over, I had to fight hard with myself not to mix my loyalties to my culture with my love for him. Regardless, I dreamt several times that I'd married John. *How unbelieveable that would be! East and West unite and become one!*

"Oh, my God!" Layla slapped her face. "Do you believe this, Mitra?"

My mind was back to our room, watching Khomeini's return to Tehran. We witnessed it on our black and white television set. We had been watching him over the last few months, and we learned that this imam was energizing Iranians toward the opposite gate of modernization. He wanted to turn the clock back to the seventh century, the time of Mohammad, our prophet. This new leader's white beard almost covered his taut face; and his black, bushy eyebrows disguising his mysterious eyes gripped my mind. His white turban was a sign that he held the highest rank a clergyman could hold.

Each day, he had left his house in the suburb of Paris and walked along a snowy path to greet his audience. They were Iranian men accompanied by women covered in scarves, and they had come to catch a glimpse of this holy man. He had appeared out of nowhere proclaiming, "Iranians deserve to reach the gate of heaven."

The sight of him and the spellbound throng made me wonder. Those women had covered their heads to be able to walk behind Khomeini to heaven! For centuries, it was drilled into us that a Moslim woman committed a sinful act by not covering her head. But, on the other hand, Mohammad also said, "Raise your children according to their time!" So it seemed insulting that women in the twentieth century still needed to wear *chador* to get into heaven.

Mamani Zahra's image gleamed before my eyes. If she were alive to see Khomeini arrive in Tehran, she would have been dancing in the streets with the rest of the people. Her voice touched my ear: "We're waiting for our savior, Imam Mehdi. He'll appear to us one day to rescue us from the tyranny of the world!"

Our Savior! Unbelievable! Could it be?! Nay!

Later that night, Layla and I were finally able to get through to our parents on the phone.

"Maman, do you wear chador these days?" I asked.

235

"Yes, of course!" she responded happily.

I could not envision my mother covered up like Mamani Zahra. "Does that mean, when I return after my graduation, I must wear chador too?"

"Mitra joon, we must show our solidarity to our imam."

"Are you forced to do so?"

"No, not at all! We want to express our opposition to the shah, and our solidarity to Imam Khomeini. We women are covering our heads, and men are refraining from wearing ties!" Maman sounded like she was giving a speech. "We don't need Western clothing, or anything else from the West, anyway!"

No need of Western goods! How is that possible? Most everything we have is from the West!

"Are you free now? Can you criticize your imam?" I pressed.

"Mitra joon?" I heard Baba's voice, taking over. "How are you?" His calm words baffled me. "How's everything in Los Angeles?"

In Los Angeles? I had no interest in talking about L.A. I was adamant to hear about our unfathomable revolution! We were used to being ruled by a king, the shadow of Allah, and we had grown accustomed to living like Westerners. And now, here was this old man transporting us back to twelveth centuries ago!

"*Allo*, Mitra are you there?"

"Yes! Yes!" I sighed. "Baba, has your dream of having a free country come—"

"We're fine!" he quickly interjected. "Give the phone to Layla. We have only two minutes."

"Allo? Allo?" Layla looked from the dead receiver to me and frowned. "See, during your conversation, you dipped into your dreams so long! Next time, I'll talk first!" she exclaimed when she banged the receiver on the phone.

I understood Layla's anger. For the last few months, it was almost impossible to connect to our parents by phone. Every day, she and I had to start dialing from sunrise to sunset without any success until today. Our parents had written to us before that it was impossible for them to call us. All the phone lines for calling outside the country had been severed. Those of us who lived in the free world had to try to connect with them.

I sighed. I understood well. Not only was my father's dream smashed, but my dream of returning to a free country was destroyed as well. I could not get Maman's cheery voice out of my head, "... to show our solidarity to our imam." He was not *my* imam.

¤ ¤ ¤

One year after Khomeini's arrival, Pan American Airlines carried me to Rome where Iran-Air then transported me to Tehran. The direct flight from New York to Tehran by Pan Am was abolished. The two countries went from being the best of friends to each other's worst enemies. Our ears and eyes were full of slogans, "*Marg—bar* Shah," Death to the Shah, and "*Marg—bar Amrika.*"

At dusk, when the 747 touched down, I could not prevent my tears from rolling down my cheeks. We, the passengers, were herded into a bus. It transported us to the terminal that looked like a hut in the middle of nowhere. The air smelled icy and unfriendly. We had to stand in line to go through customs, whereas in previous years, we could simply walk through without making any stops. We had been allowed to bring all the Western dresses, shoes, and perfumes our hearts desired.

Inside, through one of the small windows, I saw dusk turning into night. For a moment, I thought my plane had been hijacked and had landed in a different city—we certainly weren't in Tehran's *International* Airport. The building looked stoic. An ominous feeling thickened my heart. Each woman who worked there wore a white scarf knotted behind her head. Black, baggy pants and shapeless dresses hid the curves of their bodies. At least some of the female passengers were dressed like me in tailored skirts, jackets, and fashionable boots.

The line was moving at the speed of a turtle. Finally, I heard, "Khanoom, come forward!" A young man with a dark beard, but without a tie, signaled for me to cross the red line and approach the portable desk in front of him.

"Open your suitcase!" he said in his steely voice and refrained from looking at me.

I gazed at the floor. I noticed him wearing slippers instead of leather shoes. I knew. Since the Islamic regime came to power, most everyone had to pray five times a day. Most workplaces were shut down at noon when the muezzin invited everyone to pray. Men and women wore slippers instead of shoes so they could glide in and out of them at the prayer times.

"Do you travel alone?"

I nodded. He flipped over my passport.

"Did you study in America?"

I nodded again. I had no idea what prevented me from talking. Without any good reason, I felt frightened, like a sheep separated from her flock.

"Do you have any liquor, or alcoholic drinks?" he asked; to my great shock and embarrassment, he tossed all my belongings out of the suitcase.

"Khanoom! Do you …" His voice became louder and harsher.

"No! I—"

He moved to the next table and left me in front of the pile of my garments.

The moment I embraced my mother, Iran, and my father, Nima, I forgot all about the country and its new regime. I immediately noticed Maman was shrouded with a black chador that covered her Western blouse, skirt, and overcoat—the clothes I had sent her from America. Seeing her face without makeup startled me. She never left the house without brightening her sad eyes with eyeliner or mascara. From her face and Baba's, I read the difficulties they endured over the years.

A porter carrying my suitcase followed us outside where we could catch a cab. No one wanted to travel to the opposite side of Tehran so late at night. At last, one of the drivers, after bargaining with my father, agreed to drive us to our house. The streets were empty. It was way past midnight when we arrived home.

As soon as we walked in, my mother took off her chador.

"Maman," I pointed to her chador, "it's hard to carry that burden, isn't it?"

"It's just for outside!" she sighed. "Mitra joon! Go and sit. Korsi's warm."

"Korsi!" I cried out. "You and Baba are still hanging on to this primitive heating system?"

"Dear, do you think now that your father and I are retired we can afford a kerosene heater in every room?"

Korsi referred to a brazier in the middle of a hollow, wooden platform, covered with quilts and blankets large enough to cover our legs when we sat on the mattresses spread out to the four sides. Before I could say anything further, my mother put her head under the quilt to remove the ashes from the balls of fire, to raise the heat for us. When she took out her head with mangled hair, she said, "The prediction is that we'll have a heavy snow fall tonight."

"But this room is pretty large, what do you do to keep your face warm?" I asked.

"Well, when your feet are warm, you won't worry about your face."

She left the room. Baba in his flannel pajamas and I in my nightgown covered with my thick robe sat on each side of the korsi, the way we used to. His seat was the one at the top of the room, mine was on his left, Maman's was on his right, and Layla's place stayed empty.

When he sat down, I saw no box of cigarettes or ashtray. "Baba, don't you smoke anymore?"

He shook his head. "No. I've quit."

"Baba, that's wonderful!"

He took off his glasses, rubbed his eyes, and put them back on.

"Baba, if you're tired, we can go to sleep."

"Not at all! I am waiting to hear about you and Layla in America."

"But, Baba," I responded anxiously, "now that we're safe in our house, and no stranger's listening to our conversation, tell me!" I paused. He stared into my eyes as if he knew what I wanted to ask, but he said nothing. I continued, "How come overnight we lost our two-thousand five-hundred year old kingdom?"

Maman walked in carrying a tray with some sweets and hot tea in clear mugs—there was no sign of the dandy little glasses from the past.

"Baba, how do you like the new regime?"

His dark eyes behind his thick glasses looked droopy and tired. He hit his forehead. "I'm so glad for the ones who died and did not witness our so-called Sacred Revolution!"

"Are we all standing behind Khomeini?"

"Mitra!" Maman wagged her finger at me. "Be respectful to our leader. He's our Imam, Ayatollah Ruhollah Khomeini."

The Spirit of Allah! I had a tough time, however, convincing myself, so I diverted my gaze to the window behind my father and stared at the snowflakes coming down. "Wow! How exciting! It's snowing!"

"Yes, indeed." Baba nodded.

"For fifty years," I felt my blood boiling when I continued, "we were pushed toward the 'gate of modernization'. Today, we're told it was a sinful road!" I was surprised to hear my own anger.

"When a country is built on a façade, and its people live in illusion, that's what its people get!" Baba grumbled.

"Do you remember my kaleidoscope?" I asked.

"I remember you were thrilled with it," Maman uttered.

"Until one day," I smiled, "I got bored with it."

"And you dissected it," Maman said sadly.

"I was so disappointed that I cried all over the cardboard and colorful papers, as though my entire world were in shambles."

Nowadays, I felt the same disappointment, that my cardboard world was in pieces and I had no strength to build it—only to shed tears.

"I really don't understand what you two are talking about." Maman exhaled loudly. She put a sugar cube in her mouth and sipped her tea. "Hurry up! Tea is getting cold."

"Maman I always thought you were a perfect example of a Western woman," I challenged her. "You're a teacher—you're the flag bearer among the rest of the women in our land!"

She shrugged. "Now I really don't think it's a good idea for a woman to work. She ends up working two places: outside to help her husband's income, then inside the house to take care of her children and the household."

I could not control myself anymore. I hit the wooden korsi so hard that I felt the pain in my hand and throughout my body. "But, then you're equal to men, you have your financial freedom! That's what you preached to me over the years. "

I couldn't believe my ears when she replied, "I don't know what that foreign country drilled into your head. I enjoy my days much better since I'm retired!"

"Are you retired now? You haven't worked thirty years yet, have you?" I felt so hot that I withdrew the quilt from my legs and pushed myself out of the korsi.

"Allah, bless our imam! He's ordered every woman who worked during the previous regime to stay at home—"

"What?" I did not let her finish.

Baba could read my wrath and in his soft voice he said, "For example, your mother needed another five or six years to retire. So the regime allowed her to sit at home and get paid every month as if she had worked for thirty years!"

"Is that how it is these days? Men get rid of the women in society and …" I sipped my tea to cool my anger.

"And then the regime only has to control one part of the population," Baba finished my thoughts.

"Which is easier, naturally!" I laughed sarcastically.

I could not believe Maman was happy staying home, playing the part of the housewife. I asked, "What else has changed?!"

"Our imam," Maman started throwing the words out of her mouth without taking a breath, "God bless him, he has opened our eyes. This *Spirit of Allah* wants us to follow the teachings of the Prophet Mohammad. Men should go out and make money and women must stay home and take care of their children. We can't be like the Westerners. The shah destroyed our religion and the unity of our families."

"Now, the men are in control of their wives and children!" I grumbled.

Maman turned a deaf ear to my comment and went on. "The shah promoted the corruption of the West. And let's not forget all the young men he murdered, including my beloved brother, Amir!" She began crying in a loud voice as if she were sitting before her brother's dead body.

I sympathized with her. If anyone did something to my brother or my father, there would be no forgiveness in my heart either. But, how could we ignore the freedom of American men and women, their respect toward each other, and their happiness in life, calling it *corruption*? I closed my mouth while I watched the snow covering our rose bushes and the branches of the tree in our yard. I always thought our king was popular and liked by the majority of people. I had confidence my father could put my confusion at ease when I said over Maman's weeping, "Baba, why did the shah have to kill or torture the men who were in opposition to him? In America, not everybody agrees with their elected president or representatives, yet they express their opposition and nothing happens to them."

"Dear," Baba sighed, "America is a country where everyone has the right to be free and individual freedom is valued. Hopefully, enough of you young ones, educated in the West, will do better than to follow a regime that doesn't understand everyone's right to be free."

I knew. During my friendship with John, he never forced me or talked me into doing something I did not want to do. He did not treat me like a doll merely for his pleasure.

"I realize that you're forbidden to sleep with me, and I respect that," John's warm voice came to my mind. He obeyed my culture and above it all, he denied his pleasure for my sake. Of course, I was not able to verbalize all that. John being my boyfriend was my secret.

When I heard azan I knew it was dawn.

Maman jumped. "I've got to get ready for namaz." She ran outside to perform her ablution.

"Baba, does she pray now?"

He nodded, and his jeering smile covered his face.

"I thought she never believed in praying!"

"That was then, this is now. Your mother, like the majority of people here, has become a faithful Moslim in the blink of an eye."

To see Maman behave as a religious woman rocked my core beliefs. I always considered my family as not a religious one.

"Baba, I could never remember Khomeini. Over there, they said the shah had sent him to exile."

"Our regime always shocked our media. They never told us that Khomeini preached in Quom against the White Revolution, causing the clergymen to revolt."

"What did he have against the shah?"

"His speech was mainly against the abolition of feudalism." Baba shrugged. "That's why some of the landlords stood behind Khomeini, believing he would give their land back to them when he came to power."

"Why did Khomeini go to France then?"

"Because the shah acted hastily. First, Khomeini was exiled to Iraq."

"When did he go to France?"

"It's a rumor that Saddam Hussein, the Iraq president, wanted to get rid of him because of Khomeini's uproar among Shiites over there."

"So, Saddam sent him to Paris?"

While I was trying to accept the reality that Khomeini was our leader, my father's words rang in my ears. "Instead of throwing Khomeini out, the shah should have listened to him as a voice of opposition and tried to negotiate with him. He thought if Khomeini was away, he would be safe. But—"

I looked into my father's eyes, wondering why he paused. He shrugged and said, "Actually, it's a rumor that the Puppet of the West was getting too big for his britches!"

"What do you mean, Baba?"

"Since the CIA brought him back and got rid of Mossadegh."

"Yes, I read about the 1953 coup d'état in the U.S."

"Some say that the shah was building military forces as if there was no tomorrow."

"I heard his confession in one of his interviews. He claimed that we were considered to be one of the most powerful countries in the Middle East!"

Baba nodded. "They even say that he was preparing to bring nuclear power."

"Baba, I watched one of his last interviews with BBC."

He turned to me and asked with enthusiasm, "What did he say? We had no idea!"

"The shah mostly said that with time, our country would be ahead of Britain, and possibly the United States." I switched to quoting him. "Right now, we're equal to Britain and within ten years, we'll be ahead of all the super powers."

"Obviously, His Majesty's masters did not trust him anymore and they brought yet another puppet to rule over us."

An image of the handsome shah flashed before me. It was the day when he had bought two F-14 jet fighters from America, and they were delivering them to us. He wore his military uniform with all his medals hanging off of him, as our leader of all forces; he was there to receive these two state-of-the-art jet fighters. In his speech, he said, "If the super powers do not sell us what we want, we will seek other channels until we find them! We have money! We have power!"

Had the shah, like his father, been kicked off of his throne by the Western world? Or did our people choose the *Spirit of Allah* to rule over us? I understood—we were also the puppets. Our king was the Puppet of the West; my father was a puppet of the regime. My mother and I were the puppets of my father, at least according to the new regime! And my eyelids were getting heavy. I knew it was time for me to go to bed.

◻ ◻ ◻

On Saturday, the first workday of the week, I dressed in my conservative Western clothes and reported to the chairman of the English Department at Tehran University. I felt exuberant for I had fulfilled my wish and my parents' to get a Western education to become a professor, a foothold for starting my new life in Iran.

After keeping me waiting about 30 minutes, Dr. Hajat shouted from his office to his secretary, "Golnaz, tell her to come in!"

I heard the sound of my high heel boots on the bare floor. I wanted to project to my future boss that I would be a determined professor. When I approached his desk, I extended my hand for a firm handshake. I was stunned. He did not shake my hand, nor did he get up from his chair. I felt embarrassed, pulled my hand away, and sat down in front of him. Apparently, the Western world had made me brave. With a stern voice, he muttered, "We were waiting for you. Do you have your doctorate now?" He did not even wait for me to open my mouth. "Without your degree, we can't let you teach!"

I nodded. His face was swathed in a black beard and his suit was missing a tie. "We kept your agreement intact. We continued to adhere to the contract you had with the previous regime."

"Yes, based on it, you provided me with my expenses for my education and in return I am here to teach."

"As I was saying," he threw me a stern look for speaking out of turn, "with the exodus of the educated classes, we're experiencing a shortage of professors. I want you not only to teach here, but also to teach at other universities in Shiraz and Abadan."

No words left my lips.

"You're not married, are you?"

I shook my head.

"No children either?"

"No."

"Once a week I fly to Shiraz to teach at the university. You can come with me to teach over there too."

I felt uneasy. I wiped my sweaty palms with a tissue. However, I gathered all my strength and said, "Dr. Hajat, I'm afraid of flying!"

I did not dare to reveal the secret that I had no desire to fly anywhere with him.

"Scared of flying? Nonsense!" He looked at his watch. "Let's go to the department. I'll show you your office. Your first class starts in a few minutes."

He got up and came out from behind his desk. I noticed the heels of his dusty black shoes were pushed inside, as if he was wearing slippers.

"Do you have my schedule?" I pressed.

"No, not yet! You come here every day. Be here around 8:00, until Golnaz, my secretary, writes up your schedule."

Next, he showed me an office with two desks and said, "Here, this is your office."

"Am I sharing it?"

"Yes. The other woman has her degree from England."

"What about when I want to have a conference with a student?"

He looked at me as if I was speaking in a foreign tongue.

We walked to the classroom. It was an old run-down room with a huge blackboard. It reminded me of the boys' school where my mother taught. Students' chatter filled the room. Most of the women covered their heads and they looked much younger than the men.

"Be quiet, please!" Dr. Hajat ordered.

When no students stopped talking, he turned around, and growled under his breath, "These days, they're ruling!"

He turned to them again and said, "I want to introduce to you your new professor!"

"Dr. Hajat, this means that you won't be our professor anymore?" a student in the back row called out.

He nodded. "Dr. Taheri just received her degree from abroad …"

Abroad rang in my ears. I knew the reason he did not tell them I was educated in the United States. He refrained from provoking even more students while, a few streets away, some of them were holding a few hostages at the American Embassy.

Every day my double-decker bus passed by. All the passengers, like chickens caught in a trap, raised their necks and wiggled in their seats to see if they could catch a glimpse of any hostages. The American flag at the entrance door was ripped off; its gates were shut and instead of two American soldiers guarding that part of their country, they were replaced by a few young, bearded civilian men holding their guns in their hands while sitting on the ground. Most of the times, it was quiet around there, unless we were notified ahead of time that there would be a demonstration in the area. In that case, the bus bypassed the embassy and went through small streets and alleys, reminding me of childhood trips to Quom, where we visited the grave of my father's mother.

We rarely had a class free of interruptions. Sometimes the students didn't even show up for class. Other times, in the middle of a test or a writing assignment, they would mumble something to each other and run out of the classroom. The only words they had for me were, "We're going to demonstrate!" They were unaware of how their actions affected me. At last, one day, when most of them were sitting before me, my desire to find out about our revolution boiled over. Instead of giving them a lecture on symbolism in American literature, I asked, "Aren't we done with our revolution? What are all these demonstrations for?"

"What do you mean, Professor?" one of them asked, speaking in English.

Another yelled out in Farsi, "Why don't you speak Farsi, so we can understand you?"

"Aren't you sitting in an English class?" I pointed out.

"Yes!" the oldest student, with a salt and pepper beard, said in an angry voice. "But, you're an Iranian. You must speak Farsi!"

"I was told to speak English while I'm in the classroom!" I countered.

"Long live Imam Khomeini!" he shouted.

The rest of the students accompanied him shouting three times, "Long live Imam Khomeini!"

I was debating whether or not to leave the classroom

when another male student yelled, "Professor, why don't you cover your head?"

"Do I need to?" I said, meeting his livid gaze.

"Of course!" he erupted. "You're not in America anymore. Now, you live in a Moslim country."

"Yes, Mohsen's correct!" another student shouted.

I remained calm. "Didn't we have a revolution to get rid of the shah, a dictator, in order to have a free country?"

They all looked at me as if I had been dropped from the planet Mars.

"What do you mean, lady?" Mohsen roared as if he had a rifle aimed at me.

"Well," I continued, while pacing and squeezing my hands together, "if we're free now, why do we have to dictate to each other what to do, as long as we're not jeopardizing each other's freedom!"

Mohsen, as if he had everyone's invisible vote to be their spokesperson, said, "In Islam, our Prophet Mohammad, Allah bless his soul, ordered women to cover themselves."

"Why?" I asked.

"Women's hair and bodies are temptations for men—"

I interrupted him in a loud voice. "Where in the Koran does Mohammad say anything about veils for women?"

"Our imam does not address any female reporter without a scarf!"

My face was on fire. I read anger and hate in their huge dark eyes. They were hungry wolves, waiting for me to make a wrong move. I wished I could have screamed at them. *Fools! Why are you fighting to force women to wear veils? Why don't you pressure our new government to guarantee freedom and liberty for each one of us? Wasn't that the reason we all wanted to throw the shah out? We could come together and unite instead of colliding with each other.* But, I knew better. I was no hero and I was afraid for my life. There was no protection for me if some of them decided to attack me. I realized the bitter truth. I could not stand up to them. An invisible muzzle covered my mouth. *One hundred years of ignorance cannot be washed off even with zamzam water.*

¤ ¤ ¤

After a couple of months, one day, as I climbed the stairs to my office, some students ran up to me and said, "Professor, no classes anymore!" My eyes were blinded by the sun. I held my hand over my face to look at them and I saw Dr. Hajat behind them.

"Yes, Dr. Taheri, no more classes!" he confirmed.

"What do you mean?"

"We have to cancel all the classes in higher education … all the classes!" he repeated.

I was not sure if I'd heard him correctly. I asked, "All?"

"Yes! All the universities are shut down indefinitely."

"All?" I repeated in shock.

"You heard me! Our imam ordered all higher education in the entire country to be closed. We do not need their Western education and their *najes*, their unclean system."

He then chuckled. "The English Department is the first one …"

"What will happen to us? No job, no salary!" I gasped.

He tossed up his hands. "It's not that we won't need you ever again. I'm sure after some time we will be reopening …"

"Couldn't we at least wait until the semester's over?" I pleaded.

He shook his head vigorously. "It's the imam's order! I have your phone number. We'll be in touch!" He rushed away and left me drowning in my thoughts. I was appalled. How could a regime play with its people's lives—not only by killing whoever disobeyed, but by preventing the advancement of its young citizens? As if it was not bad enough that they were sending the educated women home, these days they were also enemies of those who had been educated abroad, who had returned with the hope of rebuilding their lives and serving the people.

¤ ¤ ¤

Several months passed. There was no news about reopening the universities. Instead, there was a rumor that the new regime would compel all women to cover their heads in Islamic attire. The new rule added extra fire to my fury.

One late afternoon, when Maman, Baba and I were sitting in the courtyard on a wooden bed covered with a rug, eating grapes and cucumbers, I revealed the burning secret of my heart to them. "I've decided to go back to the U.S."

"Why, Mitra joon?" Maman looked as if she would cry at any moment.

"Here, I have no purpose for living!" I was ready to argue my point; the words jumped out of my mouth like bullets from a gun. "This country doesn't want me. My education is from the West. You perhaps expect me to get married and have children."

"Yes, that's my wish!" Maman smiled through her teary eyes.

I turned to my father and said, "Didn't you wish for me to live in a free country?"

"Yes! Always!"

I read heaps of sorrow in his eyes, but I could not stop myself from saying, "Baba, this regime is forcing me to return to life as Grandma Shirin and Mamani Zahra

252

knew it. I can pretend and jump into the imam's wagon—put on my chador and marry anyone you choose for me. But I don't think this is what you had in mind for me!"

My father kept quiet. His head was down and his shoulders looked droopy, as if he were carrying a heavy load.

"My dear Mitra," Maman expressed, "My deepest desire is to see you sitting on the soozani on your wedding day, like our generations of women."

"Maman, you know that this government has already broken the chain of our family ties."

"Mitra joon! Maybe you're dazzled by the glimmering of America." She was taunting me.

"It has nothing to do with America!" I could hear the sternness in my voice. "Here, I'm forced to obey a regime I don't want any part of! I might as well be dead."

"Where do you plan to go?" Baba asked.

"I'll go back to California. I still have a visa."

Baba gave me a look of sadness. "That visa is null and void. President Carter ordered this a few days ago. It was in the news."

My father had caught me in total surprise. But I did not give up. "I'll go to one of the European countries, and then ask for a visa to the United States."

"Now, you can't do that either!" Baba insisted.

"Why not? We can travel to any European country without a visa!"

"Not so, not anymore!" Maman said.

I was devastated by the thought that I was a prisoner in my own country. But Baba's next words gave me hope: "Perhaps, you can go to Saudi Arabia?"

"Yes, you can go there and get a visa to America," Maman said, nodding her head. "They're our friends now that our country is on the same path as theirs."

"Maman, how is it possible? They're Sunnis and we're Shiite!"

"That's another sham that new regime wants us to believe," Baba grumbled.

"Good, tomorrow I'll go to its embassy to see what they say!"

Maman poured some tea from the samovar. "Mitra joon, drink this. Are you sure you want to leave us here?" Maman insisted again, "It would be great if Baba and I can see our grandchildren."

"Maman, if I stay here, my life will be ruined. Do you know any iranian man who wants to marry a highly educated old maid like me?"

"Besides, you're right, here there is no freedom for you," Baba acknowledged. "I'm sure your mother also agrees with me that we want you to live in a free country rather than being choked by this regime."

"Baba, I think we've gone backward, instead of forward." I grimaced. "Similar to the time when Arabs conquered Persia."

"Mitra, don't insult our sacred regime!" Maman gasped. "Allah would turn His face from you!"

"Maman, He already did!"

"Be grateful to Allah and our imam—"

I had to leave. I could no longer sit quietly as she praised our new dictator. It was impossible for my mind to accept this regime. During the shah's reign, the educated throngs were free as long as they did not criticize him. But these days, we had to follow our leader as if we were his herds.

❋

□ □ □

During the next few weeks, like a bird, I gathered leaves and morsels to make a nest in a place far from my homeland. I found out France, Spain, Italy and others did not grant visas to Iranian citizens. I decided to follow Baba's advice.

One day, at dawn, even before Maman prayed, the three of us took a cab to the Saudi Arabian embassy. We had to enter through the side door. The main door was locked for security purposes. There was a crowd of men in line. I felt uneasy to be the only woman, and one without a scarf or chador. I ignored my churning stomach, and stood at the back of the line waiting for my turn. About nine o'clock, we were guided by a policeman to enter an office. A woman with her head draped in a large white scarf sat behind her desk. She shouted in Farsi, with an Arabic accent, pointing at me. "Hey! You! Come here!" We only use "hey" to address donkeys, not people. Even though I did not like her insulting attitude, I ignored it and approached her desk.

"Why are you here?" she demanded.

"I want to get a visa to Saudi Arabia as a tourist."

"Who is traveling with you?"

"No one," I said calmly.

I wanted to scream that I was going to Saudi Arabia as a bridge to go back to America, where I'd never be addressed like a mule!

"Your husband must come with you!" she stipulated.

"I don't have a husband."

"Take your brother."

"No brother either!"

She rolled her eyes with impatience. "Uncle, father, any male in your family?"

If God had not taken my brother, Omid, from us, or if the previous regime had nurtured my uncle instead of killing him, perhaps today one of them could come with me.

"I have a father. But …" I did not have enough strength to explain.

"Then forget it. You can't go there! A single woman traveling by herself, no way!"

I walked out of there wondering, wasn't I a *human being*? Why couldn't I travel the world alone? I'd lived in a foreign country on my own for several years.

At the German embassy, I was told, "Lady, you don't need a visa to travel there."

"Well, that's wonderful, then …"

"But when you arrive at the airport, if they don't think your business is justified, they'll send you back here."

"Send me back?" I lamented and walked out.

□ □ □

A week later, I learned that Switzerland was the only country giving visas to Iranians. The following day, Maman Iran, Baba Nima, and I left home before dawn again. When we arrived at this embassy, there was a long line shaping behind the door. After hours of waiting, in the early afternoon, my number was called. The representative of the consul, a young man, stood up as soon as I walked in.

"Good day, sir," I said tentatively.

He surprised me with a smile. "I'm pleased you speak English."

After I told him a brief version of my life story, he said, "No problem. How long do you want to stay in Switzerland?"

"Just a few weeks until I can go to America."

As casual as you please, he said, "Come back within two hours and pick up your visa."

When I got up, he also stood up. We shook hands, and

I rushed outside. The air smelled delicious. I could have danced in the street. "I got it! I got it!" I said when Maman and Baba approached me.

"Now you're free to go back to the West and live your life!" Baba said from his heart.

On the one hand I was pleased that I could go to a free country; on the other hand, I felt sad leaving Baba and Maman.

When Swissair informed me I could go to the airport the next day and be on standby for a flight out of Tehran, I purchased my ticket.

"Why are you in such a rush?" Maman asked. Her eyes were wet with her tears, and Baba's face was covered with clouds of sorrow. I swallowed a knot in my throat.

◻ ◻ ◻

At the airport, I noticed many Iranian women in Western dress who were leaving the country. I had to wait until all the reserved seating passengers boarded the plane to see if there were any extra seats. I had no idea how to calm my stormy heart.

"Mitra, what will you do," Baba murmured in my ear, "if in Zurich, they won't let you go to America?"

I looked at his sad face. I did not know how to tell him the secret in my heart. I was determined not to shake hands with the despotic regime as long as I lived. This so-called, *sacred* government discarded me because I had been educated in the West and, more than that, discounted me for being a woman. Instead, I allowed, "I guess I'll be ba—" I swallowed, turned around and noticed that there were only five persons on standby left. They called the first three men who were ahead of me.

"Mitra, it does not look like you can go, so let's go

home!" Maman said, wiping her tears with her chador.

"No, let's wait!" I was determined to sleep at the airport for days until I could get out.

I practically jumped out of my seat when the male ticket agent called me and another female passenger. We approached him and he said, "Listen you two! On my chart, I'm showing the plane is full and getting ready to take off. But, through the radio, I hear they still have two seats available. I can take you two on board, but I can't promise you'll be able to leave. Don't be upset or mad at me if I have to bring you back off the plane. Do you want to try?"

"Yes! Yes!" I thought my heart would burst any moment.

I turned to Maman and Baba and hugged them. "It doesn't sound like I'm going. Maybe I'll see you in a few minutes."

The girl and I ran behind the agent, through the double glass doors, jumped onto his cart with our bags on our laps and rushed toward the plane.

The three of us, the man ahead and two of us behind him, climbed the plane's stairs.

The male ticket agent addressed a uniformed woman standing in the doorway to the plane. "Who said there are two seats available?"

The Swiss stewardess smiled at me and said, "I did! The flight attendants have two seats reserved among the passengers for when the plane lands and takes off. If these two ladies do not mind sitting on our pull-out seats during landing and takeoff, they can have our reserved seats during the flight."

"No, I don't mind!" I screamed, and my traveling companion agreed as well.

The man moved away, and I entered the plane. While buckling up, I wondered if I had tricked my destiny.

I looked out through the small window as the plane gathered strength on the runway, taking me away from my homeland.

□ □ □

A Persian woman had overcome all odds to leave her country behind. She was flying out of an oppressive dictatorship and into a free world. The "Fasten Seatbelts" sign disappeared with a *ding* just as Baba's voice resounded in her ears: "Whatever we do, that is our fate and destiny!"

Glossary

Abadan: city south of Iran; home of first and only Iranian refinery

aberu: dignity

abgoosht: meat, dried beans, peas and water; a dish similar to soup

abi: blue

agha: mister; master; used as a courtesy title instead of the first name

aghd: marriage contract; formal wedding ceremony

Ahriman: spirit of evil in Zoroastrianism

Ahuramazda: spirit of goodness in Zoroastrianism

ajan: police

Akbar: great; male given name

Aladdin: Middle Eastern folk character in the book of *One Thousand and One Nights (The Arabian Nights)*

Alexander the Great: (356-323 BC) king of Macedonians, conquered the Persian Empire, which stretched from the Mediterranean's Sea to India and formed much of what was then considered the civilized world

Ali: Mohammad's son-in-law; Shiites' first imam after the Prophet; male given name

Allah: God in Arabic

Allaho Akbar: "God is great"

Allaho masala ala Mohammad va ale Mohammad: "God bless Mohammad and all of his followers"

allo: hello, on the phone

Amir Kabir: chief minister to Naser Al-Din Shah Qajar

Amrika: America

andarooni: the inside of a house; living quarters for women

aragh: national alcoholic drink made in Iran

Aryan (s): the word, "Arya" means nobles; a group of people who settled about 1500 BC in Iran and the rest of Asia; their race Caucasian and their language Indo-European

Ashhado alla ilaha illallah: "there is no god, but Allah"

Ashhado anna alien valiollah: adhering to Shiites' first imam—Ali; part of Shiites' prayers

Ashura: the day when Shiites commemorate and mourn the death of their third imam, Imam Hossein

Avesta: sacred text of Zoroastrianism

ayatollah: voice of Allah

Ayatollah Ruhollah Khomeini: religious leader and politician; the leader of the 1979 Iranian revolution which saw the overthrow of Mohammad Reza Pahlavi, the shah of Iran

azan: Islamic call to prayer

Azerbaijan: region in northwestern of Iran

aziz: dear; used as grandmother

baatum: baton

baba: father

bagh-e-shah: king's garden

balleh: yes; word of acceptance

bazaar: market; a permanent enclosed merchandising area

besalamati: cheer

besme Allah alrahman alrahim: "in the name of Allah the most beneficent the most merciful"

birooni: living quarters for men

caliph: successor; representative; the title for the ruler of a Sunni's community

Caucasian: people who are light-skinned or of European origin

chador: a fabric covering a female's clothed body from head to ankles

Cyrus the Great: (600—529 BC) aka "father of the Iranian nation"; he founded the Persian Empire about 550 BC

dagh! dagh!: sound of knocking

dahat: village

dallak: washer in a public bath

Darius the Great: (550—486 BC) ruled the Persian empire from 522 BC until his death

Darolfonoon: name of the first male public high school in Tehran

dervishes: beggars who taken a vow of poverty to learn humility; also refers to people who live according to Sufi rules

Descartes: French philosopher, mathematician and writer; lived in 17th century

divan: collection of poems

donbak: national musical instrument, sounds and looks like a drum

doost: friend

dorood bar shoma: Persian word for "hello"

doroshkeh: carriage

Ebrahim: Persian word for Abraham; the Arabic name of the Prophet; male given name

Esmael: Persian word for Ishmael; according to the Koran, the Prophet's ancestor; male given name

Esfehan: city in south of Tehran; capital of Iran in 16th century
Evil eye: malevolent look that many cultures believe able to cause injury or misfortune
Ezrail: angel of death
fadaye-an: devotees
faghir: beggar
Farsi: Indo-European language that uses the Arabic alphabet; the official language of Iran
farangi: foreigner
fatehe: prayer for the dead
Fatemeh: Fatima in Arabic; female given name
Fatima: daughter of Mohammad, the Prophet
Fereshteh: angel; female given name
Firdowsi: (940—1020 AD) a highly revered poet; best known for his literary epic, *Shahnameh*
geleem: a coarse rug much thinner and smaller than an indoor rug
genie: one possessed by an evil spirit
Gertrude Stein: American writer of novels, poetry and plays in 20th century
ghalyan: waterpipe; hookah
ghoul: ogre; giant demon
Gibraltar: a rock famous for giving one a sense of safety; a sure foundation
Golestan: house of flowers; the title of a book by Sa'di
Hafiz: (1325—1389 AD) Persian lyric poet; his work is to be interpreted literally, mystically or both
hajji: male pilgrim to Mecca
hajji-eh: female pilgrim
hakim: doctor
halvah: sweet dish made of flour, saffron, and rose water; typically served at funerals
hammam: public bathhouse

harem: group of Moslim women kept in a palace

Hassan: Mohammad's older grandson; Shiites' 2nd imam; male given name

havoo: women married to the same man

Hegira: Moslim era, dated from the first day of the lunar year in which Mohammad immigrated from Mecca to Medina

Herodotus: Greek historian, lived in 5th century BC

hijab: cover; Islamic clothing for a woman covering her hair; only her face is visible

henna: plant used to color women's hair and nails

hoori: nymph

Hossein: Mohammad's younger grandson; Shiites' 3rd imam; male given name

imam: Shiite leader after the Prophet, Mohammad

Iran: name of the country; female given name

Islam: monotheistic religion articulated by the Koran

Jahan: world; male given name

John Wayne: enduring American film actor, director and producer; well known for his western movies

joon/jan: dear; informal/formal

kaahk: palace

khak-e-allam-be-saret: "all the ashes of the world on your head"

Karbala: city in Iraq where Imam Hossein is buried

Kash(i): city in northwest of Iran famous for its exotic Persian rugs

Kerman(i): city in southern Iran famous for its rugs

khan: sir; in the past, it was a title for landowners, or honorable men

khanoom: lady; madam

khastegari: asking a girl's hand in marriage

kismet: destiny; in Islam, Allah's will

koliy: gypsy

Koran: Moslim's holy book, the original verbal text to be the final revelation of God—The Final Testament

korsi: old-fashioned heating system

La ilaha illa Allah: "there is nothing but Allah/God"

Laily and Majnoon: in the Persian oral literature, two characters equivalent to Shakespeare's Romeo and Juliet

mactab: old-fashioned school where pupils sat on the floor

madresseh: school in Farsi; religious school in Arabic

majlis: parliament

maman: mother

mamani: pretty; used here as grandmother

marg-bar...: "death to ..."

marhaba: "bravo!"

Mashhad: holy city in northeast Iran, where the eighth imam, Imam Reza is buried; famous for its turquoise

Masnavi: collection of Rumi's poetry

Mecca: holy city in Saudi Arabia; Moslims must face this city whenever they pray

minaret: pillar of a mosque; two of them

Mehdi: twelfth imam of Shiites; male given name

mehrieh: amount of gold (or money) groom agrees to pay in case of divorce

mobarakbad: wishing one good luck; wedding music; congratulations

Mohammad: (570—632 AD) prophet of Moslim religion; Persian pronunciation of Muhammad; male given name

Moharram: first month of Islamic lunar calendar

Moliere: French playwright and actor in 17th century

mordeha: dead people

Moslim: adherent of Islam

Mossadegh: (1882—1967 AD) democratically elected Prime Minister of Iran

motreb: old name for a musical band; group of professional dancers and singers

Mount Alborz: mountain range in northern Iran reaching peaks of 5,604 meters

muezzin: person who calls the Moslims to prayer from the minarets

mullah: Moslim preacher

najes: not clean

namaz: Moslim prayers

Naser Al-Din Shah: (1831—1896 AD) one of the most influential Persian kings; reigned for almost fifty years

nay: reed; flute

nazro-niaz: charitable gift upon God's fulfillment of a wish

noghl: small white candy usually served at weddings

noor: light

Nowruz: Persian New Year; celebrated on the first day of spring

Omar Khayyam: (1048—1131 AD) Persian poet, mathematician, philosopher and astronomer

Omid: hope; male given name

Pahlavi Dynasty: reigned constitutional monarchy from 1922—1979

Pari: fairy or angel; female given name

Peacock Throne: famous throne; brought to Iran from India by one of the Persian kings in 1736

Persepolis: ancient capital of Persia

picheh: Moslim veil for women

polo: cooked rice

poshti: fairly large cushion one can lean against

Qajar Dynasty: reigning dynasty in Iran from 1779—1922

Quom: holy city south of Tehran

Ramadan: last month of the lunar calendar; Moslims fast during the entire month

Rasht: city in north of Iran by the Caspian Sea

Reza: Shiites' eighth imam; male given name

Rostam: legendary hero in the book of *Shahnameh*

rozekhani: systematic commemoration of the Shiite martyrs

Rubaiyat: collection of Omar Khayyam's poetry; first translated by Edward Fitzgerald in 1879

ruhollah: spirit of Allah

Rumi: (1207—1273 AD) spiritual poet and thinker who sought enjoinment with the divinity after death

Sadegh Hedayat: (1903—1951 AD) Persian foremost modern writer of fiction and short stories; his writings have been banned or censored at times in Iran

Sa'di: (1184—1283/1291 AD) a Sufi poet; his two famous books, *Boostan* (the Orchid), and *Golestan* (The Rose Garden); reflections upon the lives of ordinary Moslims suffering displacement, plight, agony and conflict

saffron: spice derived from the flower of saffron crocus

sahra: desert

salam: greeting; "hello"

salam'-n-allaykon: old-fashioned formal greeting

salavat: sending prayers for the dead

samovar: vessel used to boil large amounts of water for tea

Sartre: French philosopher, playwright, novelist and political activist of 20th century

SAVAK: organization of Intelligence and National Security established by the Shah; equal to CIA

sayed: a descendant of Mohammad

Scheherazade: a legendary Persian queen and the story teller of *One Thousand and One Nights*

shab-e-motreb-zani: wedding night

shah: king

Shah Abdol Azim: burial site of a saint with a majestic mosque located south of Tehran

Shahan Shah: king of kings

shahi: coin, less than a penny

shahi water: clean water delivered to houses before plumbing system in place

Shahnameh: *The book of Kings* by Firdowsi; completed in the early 11th century

shahre-farangi: stereopticon; children looked through the lenses to see colorful images

shaitan: Satan

shalite: similar to ballet dancer's skirt; tutu

sharbat: sweet cold drink for summer

sheik: title of respect in Arabic; local religious leader

Shiism: branch of the Islamic religion

Shiites: Moslims who accepted Ali as their leader after Mohammad

Shiraz: city south of Iran; used to be the capital for many years

shirazi: individual from Shiraz

Shirin: sweet; female given name

sholezard: rice pudding; prepared only during the month of Moharram

sigheh: unofficial marriage with limited duration

sofreh: piece of cloth spread on the floor upon which food is served

Sohrab: legendary hero in *Shahnameh*; Rostam's son; male given name

soozani: brocaded cloth to sit on

Sophia Loren: international renowned Italian actress

Sufi: person who follows Sufi philosophy; most of the Persian poets were Sufis

Sufism: Eastern philosophy based on love of the Absolute; originated in Persia after the introduction of Islam

Sunnis: Moslims who accepted caliphs as their leaders after Mohammad's death

Taj-al-Saltaneh: crown of the king; the name of one of Naser Al-Din Shah's daughters

tabagh: huge round tray

tafragheh: creating animosity among people

tala: gold

talisman: piece of jewelry used to ward off the evil eye

Tehran: capital of Iran since Qajar Dynasty

Tolstoy: (1828—1910 AD) Russian writer and philosopher

toop-o-toffang: artillery

Tragedy of Karbala: "tragedy of Karbala" (680 AD); on one side Hossein and Shiites, on the other, the forces of Caliph Yazid; slaughtered at this battle the Shiites tribe including Imam Hossein and his entire family

tudeh: name of the Iranian communist party in '50s

tuman: monetary bill equivalent to one dollar

Uncle Tom's Cabin: anti-slavery novel by American author Harriet Beecher Stowe; published 1852

Victor Hugo: French poet, novelist of the Romantic movement; author of *Les Miserables*

Yazid: 2nd caliph and leader of Sunnis

Zamzam: fountain in Karbala believed to give eternal life to whoever drinks from it

Zoroaster: also known as Zarathustra; founder of Zoroastrianism

Zoroastrianism: ancient Persian religion; the first monotheistic religion in the world; founded around 6th century BC in Persia

Questions for Discussion

- What idea seems particularly important in the work? Why?
- What value or values are embodied in the idea?
- In comparison to Western society, which elements and aspects of *Tapasteries of the Heart* are the most fascinating? Explain.
- A major element in the book is the ever changing Middle Eastern society; examine this society and compare it to yours.
- Discuss the ideas about individual growth, marriage, and social convention in the book.
- Is each of the four main female characters a victim of circumstances or a hero? What is Motaref's view? What is yours? Why?
- Which characters in the book change most significantly? To what extent do these characters succeed or fail? How do they try to escape the realities they face?
- Discuss the novel's religious allusion and imagery.
- In Iranian society, what elements would you blame for causing its moving backward?
- Explain the most striking nonrealistic events of the story.

About the Author

Nooshie Motaref grew up in Persia. She studied in four countries –Iran, Germany, Switzerland and United States. She received her master's and doctorate degree in American Literature and Folklore from Florida State University. Her dissertation is a proof of Carl Jung's theory, the "Collective Unconscious," through Persian fairy tales and folktales.

She taught university courses on humanities, literature and critical thinking. In addition, she is certified by the Conflict Resolution Program Act to promote peacemaking efforts worldwide.

In March of 2014, she presented one of her articles, "Women and Islam," at a conference, Women and Education at Oxford University in Oxford, England.

She frequently gives speeches on several subjects related to her birthplace including its culture, traditions and religion. Her purpose is to familiarize Western audiences with the Iranian background and ethnicity of this society.